THE
WORST
KEPT
Secret

Q.B. TYLER

This is a work of fiction. Names, characters, businesses, places, events, and incidents are either the products of the author's imagination and used in a fictitious manner. Any resemblance to actual persons, living or dead, or actual events is purely coincidental.

Content Editing: Kristen Portillo—Your Editing Lounge
Developmental Editing: Becca Mysoor
Cover Design: Emily Witting Designs
Interior Formatting: Stacey Blake—Champagne Book Design
Proofreading: Logan Chisholm

Playlist

I Wish You Roses—Kali Uchis

ICU (Remix)—Coco Jones & Justin Timberlake

Late Night Talking—Harry Styles

Greedy—Tate McRae

That's What I Like—Bruno Mars

Fool For You—Alice Smith

Feels (Ft. Pharrell Williams, Katy Perry & Big Sean)—Calvin Harris

Dirty Thoughts—Chloe Adams

Is This Love—Corinne Bailey Rae

Good For You—Selena Gomez

Pillowtalk—Zayn

For all of you that love a hot dad

(And more specifically a Q.B. daddy)

THE
WORST
KEPT
Secret

Prologue

Avery

THERE'S A SPIKE IN MY HEART RATE THE SECOND THEO Graham enters the room. My skin prickles and although I only notice him out of my periphery as my grandparents stand in front of me going on and on about how proud they are of me for graduating college, he has all of my attention.

Tonight is my graduation party and my parents rented out one of their favorite restaurants for the occasion and invited practically the entire town where I'm from in Pennsylvania to celebrate.

My back straightens as I follow him with my eyes, and suddenly I'm hyper-aware of everything. *How do I look? Is there anything in my teeth? Why are my hands sweaty? Has he noticed me? Fuck, Avery, do not look over there.*

Despite my instincts telling me not to react, I can't help it; my eyes are inexplicably drawn to Theo whenever we share a room. It's been like that for longer than I can remember. He knows how to command attention in any room. He knows how to command *my* attention anywhere.

God, he looks good.

At somewhere over six feet, Theo Graham is still *very* well built after his ten-year career in the NFL even though he now runs a construction company and is no stranger to getting his hands dirty. Warm chocolate brown eyes, a head full of lush dark brown wavy hair that is always styled perfectly, and a light dusting of stubble currently covering his jaw. There have been times he was clean-shaven and also times that he had a full beard so luscious it made me want to run my fingers through it.

Dressed in a linen charcoal gray suit with a black shirt that covers most of the delicious muscles I know are hiding beneath, he's making more than a few women's heads turn as he makes his way through the party.

I'm no stranger to witnessing the attention Theo gets, but it never stopped the sting of jealousy, especially now that I know what his mouth tastes like.

I want to kiss him again.

Two years before he retired from professional football and fresh off a divorce from the mother of his two children, Lucas and Raegan, the three of them moved into the house next door. I was only fifteen when he retired from the NFL, so I wasn't as familiar with the football star version of Theo. I knew the guy who ran four miles every day to stay in shape and worked out in his backyard which I had a perfect view of from my bedroom window. I knew him as the guy who picked Lucas and me up when we ran from a party that the cops busted, and to this day—*to my knowledge*—he'd kept that fact from my parents. I knew the man who helped teach me to drive while he was teaching Lucas because we were always attached at the hip.

Never did I think that he'd eventually be on the list of men I'd go on to kiss in my lifetime. Especially when I'd spent the majority of my ninth-grade year making out with his son. *For practice, not for romance.*

I shiver thinking about that night when Theo had lifted me in the air and pressed me against the wall like I was nothing. Holding me up against him as he pressed his lips to mine. I can still recall that dizzy feeling of his hard body pressed against me and I feel my nipples harden and press against the fabric of my dark green dress at the memory.

I chose this color not only because it's the color of the tassels of my graduation gown but because it brings out the green in my eyes. My eyes typically dance between brown and hazel most of the time, but there are moments when the sun hits them just right when you can see flecks of green.

A fact that Theo had brought up on more than one occasion.

The dress is midi length, but hugs me in all the right places, highlighting my hourglass figure. I'm bronzed from my recent trip to the beach with my friends—our final girls' trip to commemorate the end of college and this chapter of our lives—and I can feel his gaze skating across me, heating the already warmed skin. *You would never know I had any melanin in me with how pale I can get during the winter months.* My hair, initially styled into perfect curls before the East Coast humidity got to it, has fallen into waves. I pull it over one shoulder to showcase my neck, which, if my memory serves me correctly, is Theo's weakness.

I catch his eyes again and he's closer than he was before, like he's making his way through the crowd to get to me.

I mean, it is my graduation party. It would be rude to not speak to the guest of honor.

My grandparents have moved on to mingle, leaving me alone holding a glass of champagne that I want to down before Theo gets to me. I try to meet his gaze again, waiting for him to approach me, and I realize that even though he's not looking at me I can sense that I have his attention.

I haven't seen Theo in almost six months. Six months ago, when we'd made out in his car and I'd sat in his lap and fucked myself with my fingers until I came with the promise of *more.*

It wasn't the first time we'd hooked up, having done so once the previous summer, but it was the furthest we'd ever gone. We hadn't spoken about it after, almost as if we were both pretending it hadn't happened. Me out of humiliation and hurt and him to keep it hidden from the one person he was sure it would hurt the most.

Lucas Graham.
My best friend.
His son.

Chapter
ONE

Avery

Six Months Prior: Winter Break 2022

JUST GOT HOME FROM COLLEGE THIS AFTERNOON AFTER MY most stressful semester of school yet and with a hellish week of finals behind me, I came straight to the bar to meet my friends. Our high school senior class was super close. There weren't any cliques; every friend group just intermixed making us one of the closest graduating classes our school had ever seen. Even four years later, we all go to the same bars when we're home. The same parties. The same restaurants. The running joke is you couldn't see a Riverside High School alumni without seeing at least three more in tow.

Lucas isn't home from NYU yet and his older sister, Raegan moved out and is living with her boyfriend across town, which means Theo has the house to himself tonight. Something I haven't stopped thinking about since Lucas texted me that he won't be home until early next week. The last time I'd been in Theo's house when no one was home was this past summer.

We'd made out for hours, losing track of time until we heard Lucas' car in the driveway and I fled out the backdoor, narrowly missing getting caught.

I'd made out with my best friend's dad.

And I wanted more.

It's several degrees below freezing and still snowing in

Pennsylvania, but we're used to winter precipitation, which means nothing short of two feet of snow is cause for bars to close early. Still, the chill outside whips through the bar and cools the air every time the door opens and shuts.

The second he walks in, I feel the atmosphere shift.

I turned twenty-one this past semester, so I'm not surprised at the look of shock that crosses Theo's face when he spots me. He narrows his gaze darkly before his eyes dart up in confusion, and I think he's trying to recall my birthday to see if I'm even old enough to be here. His gaze finds mine again and then drops to the glass in my hand holding a clear liquid and a lime perched on the side of it.

I tilt my head to the side and give him a cocky smile before turning my back to him to face my friend Aurora hoping that it's enough to entice him to come over. Aurora, who goes by Rory after an ongoing obsession with *Gilmore Girls*, turns towards me with a tiny glass full of amber-colored liquid. She sinks her teeth into her brightly painted red lip. "Fireball!" She looks at something behind me and gives me a wicked smirk. I know why. *Every* girl in our graduating class—Raegan's too for that matter—has a crush on Theo.

Everyone except me, of course. I'm immune to his charms, obviously. Lucas and Raegan are like my honorary siblings which means Theo Graham is like a second dad.

At least, that's what I say when all of my girlfriends gush about how fine he is.

"I'm sorry, are you old enough to be here, young lady?" His words are low and smooth and warm my insides like the shot of Fireball in my hand.

I turn around and meet his gaze, slowly raking my eyes up his body. I scoff and press a hand to my chest, giving him my most shocked and disappointed look. "You've known me for eight years and have been to at least five of my birthday parties and you don't know that I'm twenty-one now?"

He shakes his head and chuckles before looking at Rory who somehow has a third shot of Fireball.

"Aurora." He quirks an eyebrow at her as she holds the tiny glass out for him.

"Mr. Graham! Take a shot with us," Rory says.

"Now, you know it's Theo."

"And *you* know it's Rory," she flirts, batting her long full lashes that are only highlighted by the round frames that sit perched on her nose like a sexy librarian and I can't ignore the pang of jealousy that floats through me. "Your son isn't here yet, so you have to fill in." She rolls her eyes.

"I can't believe you two are old enough to take shots."

"Really? Because we've been taking shots in your basement since we were sixteen," Rory admits with a cheeky smirk and my eyes go wide at my friend's confession.

"Rory!" I squeal and she laughs loudly, tossing her head back before downing her shot without waiting for me or Theo.

"Oh, we aren't old enough to come clean yet? I always assumed he knew. My parents did." She shrugs.

"I had an inkling," Theo says and I wonder if my parents were the only ones who believed that we were all perfect angels whenever I had people over.

Someone calls Rory's name from across the room and she slips away with a wave and a hug to Theo before moving through the bar, leaving us alone.

"Should we take this?" I ask and he shakes his head.

"I'm a little old for Fireball." He sets the glass on the bar behind me and I wish he hadn't because he's close enough for me to smell his sinfully sexy cologne, taking me back to being in his arms and rubbing against him, and *yep, now I'm horny and about to say something bold.*

"Oh? Here I thought you liked indulging in things you might be a little old for?" I raise an eyebrow at him and his eyes widen as he stares me down. His eyes close slowly and when he opens them, they're full of lust and maybe a little irritation at me for bringing up something we have never spoken of out loud.

"You're playing with fire, Avery."

"Am I?" I shrug. I down the shot of the cinnamon flavored

whiskey I've been holding, set the empty glass next to his full one, and reach for his to down before he can protest.

"Avery," his voice is hoarse. "How did you get here?"

"Uber."

"It's starting to snow harder. Do not Uber home. I'll take you when you're ready."

"It's fine."

"It's most certainly not fine. I brought the Jeep, I'll take you home or I'll call your father to come get you. At least I won't be worrying about you riding around in a car that doesn't have all-wheel drive. I'm not joking," he says before looking at the bartender. "Water for her." He points at me. "Drink the whole thing, Avery," he says before turning away from me and disappearing into the crowd.

Sometime later, those two shots of Fireball coupled with the two vodka sodas I had and the week of poor nutrition and lack of sleep have me more than a little intoxicated. I'm not sure how much time has passed or where Theo went, but something tells me he's close by. *Watching.* That thought has me swaying my hips on the dance floor next to Rory who is way drunker than me as she grinds against her on and off high school boyfriend, Justin. *It's winter break, so it's on.*

Another friend of ours is behind me, I think, and while I'm not dancing as obscenely as Rory, I do feel something pushing against my back and hands on my hips. I turn in someone's arms and spot Nate Reynolds, who I'd dated in high school and was absolutely *not* who I expected.

"Nate?" I push his chest gently, putting space between us.

"Avery Summers." He smiles cockily. *That same cocky smile that cost me my virginity and months of heartache.*

I give him a fake smile before rolling my eyes and making a move off the dance floor, hoping it serves as a signal that I am definitely not interested in going on a trip down memory lane or reliving the glory days or whatever the hell Rory and her ex are planning to do tonight.

"You get even more gorgeous every time I see you." His hand runs down my arm and I roll my eyes.

"Please." I chuckle. "Find someone else tonight, babes. It's not going to be me."

"You wound me." He puts a hand across his heart.

I deadpan. "The irony," I say, referring to all the "wounding" he did to me during my senior year of high school. *And freshman year of college.*

I move through the bar, grabbing my coat from the booth where we'd all placed our things, and start moving towards the door, wanting to put as much space as possible between myself and my annoying ex-boyfriend.

"You want me to take you home?" he asks and I scrunch my face.

"No. I came out here to get *away* from you. Read the room." I pull up my phone, contemplating texting my dad to come get me since Theo threatened me with it anyway. But it's almost two in the morning and while he'd do it, he would be irritated as hell that I waited this long to call him if I knew I was going to need a ride.

"Look, I'm sorry about all that shit...but that was years ago."

"Okay?" I chuckle. "I'm not mad at you still, but I'm also not going to hook up with you."

"Who said anything about hooking up?" he says, but that wicked glint in his eyes tells me I nailed what he was thinking despite what he hadn't said.

"Please. I speak fluent fuckboy." I flutter my eyelashes at him and he rolls his eyes before pressing his hands against his mouth and blowing on them. I'm guessing he's regretting following me outside without a coat. *The lengths guys will go to when they* think *there's potential for a hookup.*

"Ave, you ready to go?" I hear Theo's voice from behind us and then he's moving to stand in front of us on the sidewalk.

Nate looks at him and gives him that smile that all the guys give him. They all have Theo on this pedestal and practically worship the ground he walks on. If there wasn't snow on the ground, I wouldn't have been surprised if he dropped to his knees and bowed down to him.

"Theo!"

Theo clears his throat. "Mr. Graham," he corrects Nate. I smile to myself knowing he *hates* being called Mr. Graham, and all of Lucas and Raegan's friends call him Theo. Nate laughs like he's not serious but Theo is less than a fan of Nate; probably because of the weeks he had to listen to me crying in his basement while simultaneously begging Lucas not to beat the shit out of him. He looks at me. "I think I should take you home, it's getting late."

I nod in agreement because I'm ready to be away from Nate and *alone* with Theo. I'm already sending a text to Rory to make sure she has a ride as he ushers me away from Nate and towards his car.

When we're out of earshot, I feel his gaze on the side of my face. "You okay?"

"About Nate?" I snort. "Yeah." He nods and I think he's going to say something but he stops when we get to his truck.

"In you go." He opens the door for me and it's a little high off the ground, so he has to help me up into it, and the mere feeling of his hand helping me is enough to make my skin sizzle. He's around to his side in an instant.

"Wait."

"What?" he asks as he turns on the car.

"I want to make sure Rory has a ride. She hasn't responded yet."

He sits back in his seat and nods. Neither of us says anything and the silence stretches between us. I want to bring up what happened over the summer or something…*anything* that would allow us to have a real conversation about that one interaction that was not like any of the others we've had. Yet suddenly, I feel more sober than I did moments ago. It's as if the palpable tension mounting between us was counteracting my intoxication. What I wouldn't give for a shot of tequila.

"I never thought he was good enough for you," he blurts while staring straight ahead.

"Why?" I ask.

His brown eyes find mine and he lowers his chin with a laugh. "You have to ask? Saw a thousand and one kids like that in my day. In high school, college, while I was in the league." He rubs a hand down his face. "Watched him hit on three other girls before he found you on the dance floor."

While I know he's trying to make a point that Nate Reynolds has, in fact, *not* changed, it still stings that I wasn't his first choice. *Fucker.* My phone vibrates in my hand and I see it's from Rory telling me that Justin hasn't had anything to drink and he's taking her home soon.

"Rory is fine. Justin's taking her home."

He nods and slowly backs out of the parking space. "Now she may not actually be good enough for him."

"Hey," I frown. Rory was one of my favorite people in the world, even if she was a bit of a mess and I wasn't going to let anyone talk shit about her.

"I know Justin was not one of the kids drinking in my basement that Rory so eloquently confessed earlier, and nine times out of ten he was everyone's designated driver. He's a good kid."

It's only about a fifteen-minute drive to our houses so if I have a prayer at round two of our hookups, I needed to turn this conversation towards something infinitely sexier than anything that makes him remember that I was once a *kid* drinking in his basement.

Or maybe that does it for him?

I turn my gaze towards him. "What would you have done if you caught us all those years ago? Caught me one of the times I was sneaking upstairs to the kitchen for more snacks because I always got voted to do the dirty work." I roll my eyes. Evidently, my years of dance and the fact that I was a natural at being light on my feet, made me the one that always had to do all the sneaking around. I even had to go meet the pizza guy once when I was so drunk, I confused the front door with the coat closet and somehow fell into it. *How Theo never woke up that time, I'll never know.*

"I don't know. Probably try to sober you up so your parents wouldn't kill me."

"First of all, they wouldn't kill you."

"Fine, maybe so they wouldn't kill *you*." He corrects.

"That's all you would've done?" I lean across the truck. "You wouldn't have tried to discipline me yourself? Maybe take me over your knee and spank me?"

He turns his head toward me, giving me a look that tells me he's not amused. "I know what you're doing."

"What am I doing?"

"Avery…what happened between us…" He trails off. "I'm sorry. I should have known better."

"Than to what? Kiss the nineteen-year-old girl that lives next door?"

"Than to kiss the nineteen-year-old girl, that is *you*."

"What's the big deal? We're adults."

"There's a very big deal in the form of my son and your best friend." He shakes his head. "Lucas would hate me forever. You're… well, you know how my son feels about you."

"We're friends," I tell him.

"Because you won't marry him." He chuckles.

"Because I don't see him that way," I correct, irritated by his words. "We've talked about it. A lot, Theo. Yes, there were feelings there before, but he's moved on. He doesn't want me."

"Sure, Avery."

"And so, what, I don't get a say in this?"

"And what exactly is *your* 'say?' You want to continue to work your daddy issues out on me?"

Anger flashes in my eyes and in my veins. I feel embarrassed at his words and I snap. "Fuck you." The roads are still somewhat clear at this moment, thankfully, because Theo slams on his breaks.

"Excuse me?"

My eyes flare in shock and maybe a little terror as the realization sets in as to what I said because did I just use the words *fuck* and *you* in that order to Theo Graham?

Like an adult?

Shit!

Well, you can't back down now. "Don't project your issues about this onto me."

"Did you just…swear at me?" His eyes are still wide but I detect some humor in them, like he can't believe I said it and is somewhat impressed that I did.

"If you're waiting for me to apologize, we'll be here all night."

I flash him a smile and he lets out a breath before he begins driving again. He doesn't say anything. "They're not daddy issues," I tell him, still slightly offended for a reason I'm not totally sure, "or maybe they are. What are *your* issues in this situation then?"

He shifts in his seat and leans away from me, leaning against the window. "That you're too gorgeous for your own good and one afternoon after I'd had a few drinks, I stupidly allowed myself to think that you were an option for me." He shakes his head and his eyes flit to mine, dark and maybe a *little* regretful. "I still think about last summer. You and Lucas had just gotten into an argument. I was pissed at him because I heard the way he was talking to you. But you left, and then you came back a few hours later because you could never handle it when you two argued but he'd left for work."

I listen to him recount that afternoon and it's the first time he's allowed me a look inside his head.

"You were just so sad, and I remember thinking the reason he was so angry was because he had feelings for you, and then…fuck. I don't know, somehow, you were in my lap. I don't even know how it happened."

I remember. I was wearing a tiny tank top and he couldn't keep his eyes off my tits so I boldly climbed into his lap to give him a better look.

He continues to drive and then we're moving down the familiar streets towards our neighborhood and I let out a quiet sigh thinking that this night is not going to end the way I'd hoped it would.

"Fuck, Ave, I don't know. All I know is I've felt like the shittiest father for doing that to Lucas."

"Why is he involved in this narrative at all?"

"Because he has feelings for you!" he snaps.

I want to tell him *again* that he doesn't anymore. That yes, a long time ago there were feelings that I hadn't reciprocated but our friendship was able to withstand that bump in the road and now we are fine.

I want to tell him that he's wrong, but something about the way he's so adamant leads me to believe that Theo may be better versed on his son's feelings than I am.

So, I say something else.

"Do you?" I ask and instantly regret it. While I'm sure Theo had his fair share of women before his ex-wife and after they broke up, he left all of that behind him with the NFL, and I don't think I've seen him with a woman in the eight years I've known him. At the very least, he never brought anyone around Raegan and Lucas and by default, me. Him kissing me had to mean something though. *Right?* "You wouldn't just fool around with me for the hell of it, Theo, and don't insult my intelligence by trying to insinuate otherwise."

"I didn't say that," he grits out. "I'm saying, I *can't* have any feelings for you," he emphasizes. "It would destroy my relationship with Lucas and I can't do that." I nod, wishing this conversation was going a completely different way. "Listen, maybe you're right and he doesn't have feelings for you anymore and it wouldn't bother him to see you with someone else. But to see you with *me*? Hell, it might even bother Raegan."

A pang of guilt shoots through me thinking about Lucas' older sister who I wasn't as close with but who was still the closest thing I had to a sister. She'd gone homecoming and prom dress shopping every year we were both in high school with me and my mom not to mention, she was the first person I told when I lost my virginity.

"Isn't Raegan dating a guy damn near your age?"

He groans and lets his head fall back. "Do. Not. Remind. Me."

I giggle. "I just mean maybe she won't care. I assume she's on a bit of thin ice with you right now."

"This guy hasn't known Raegan for a third of her life."

I don't know much about this guy she's seeing, only that he's older and now she's living with him much to Theo's irritation.

"Okay, let me provide another rebuttal."

"Of course," he says, his voice laced with sarcasm.

"Why do we have to tell Lucas or Raegan anything?"

He doesn't say anything and I wonder if that was his hesitation all along. That I'd tell Lucas after rounds of shots. That I tell him everything and a hookup with his dad would be no exception. "Give me a little credit, Theo. I wouldn't tell him."

"Because you know he'd be pissed."

I don't disagree that he wouldn't be thrilled...but I don't respond to that. "Theo, you're a good dad," I tell him. "The best given the circumstances in which you had to parent. Rebecca was never around and...you had to do it all pretty much. I know I don't have to tell you all of this, or the fact that Lucas and Raegan worship the ground you walk on. They would want you to do things that make you happy. You've sacrificed a lot over the years and they're adults now so you don't have to anymore. It doesn't make you a bad father for wanting to have fun."

"Having fun and having fun with *you* are very different things."

He looks at me as we pull into his driveway and park on the side of the house. I'm kind of surprised he didn't pull into mine but I guess he didn't want to risk waking my parents. There are several yards between the houses on our street so there's no chance of anyone seeing us right now from where we're seated in his driveway.

"I don't *want* to want you," he continues. The snow continues to fall around us harder than before and I'm glad we left the bar when we did and Theo brought me home. "I want it to be easy for me to tell you this isn't going to happen and then walk you home." He turns to look at me. "I should walk you home." He says it but makes no effort to get out of the car or even turn it off for that matter. Instead, he puts his hand on my face, letting out a groan that vibrates through my whole body. His hand is large and warm and frames my entire face. Despite the heat still blasting from his vents, I feel goosebumps all over my skin as my sex clenches thinking about him between my legs. His thumb drags over my lips gently and just before he removes it, my tongue darts out to drag over the tip.

"Fuck." He groans and just as I sense him moving towards me, I move towards him, our mouths meeting in the middle with both of his hands on my face. His tongue tastes like mint without a trace of liquor and I wonder if he abstained in case he needed to take me home.

Why else would he have gone out to a bar and not consumed any alcohol?

The thoughts float away as his tongue dances with mine, soft yet firm and rubbing against mine, and instantly I'm transported back to the last time we did this.

I want to be closer, I think, wandering back to the time when he pinned me against the wall and kissed me senseless. His hands under my butt as he ground against me. I grab his coat, pulling him closer to me and his hand finds the back of my neck, tangling in my hair and pulling gently. I gasp as a sexy tingle shoots through me allowing his lips to leave mine and travel down my throat dragging his tongue along the skin.

"Fuck, Avery," he whispers against me and it's just the encouragement I needed to move closer. I push him back and move my way across the console and into his lap. I feel his seat moving backward, and I adjust to the closeness, sliding all the way down so I'm straddling his lap, my covered sex seated directly on top of his dick.

"Touch me," I whisper against him. "*Please.*"

Despite his jeans, I feel his cock twitch beneath me and his chocolate eyes narrow slightly. His hands drop from my shoulders and drag down my frame to my hips, holding me in place as I grind down on him. His eyes drop to where I'm seated before dragging them lazily up my body. "Where?" His voice is low and gruff and I feel it in my clit like a heartbeat. I open my coat and I watch as he trails his eyes over my v-neck sweater. His hands palm my breasts before he drags his thumb over my nipples. Despite my sweater and bra, I still feel the pressure of his thumbs on my sensitive peaks.

His hands move under my sweater, his fingers touching my skin and then he's raising the fabric. He raises his eyebrows in question and I nod, knowing what he wants to do. I slide my arms out of my coat and pull my sweater over my head all within a second leaving me in a white lace pushup bra that's practically see through. "Touch me," I tell him again and he obliges, running his fingers over the cups before his face is submerged in my tits as he takes a deep inhale. I gasp at the feeling of his stubble scraping the skin between my breasts before I feel his tongue between them dragging along the same path up toward my mouth. I reach for his hair, pulling on the luscious strands as I try to guide him back to my mouth even though the feeling of Theo's tongue inches above my nipple is indescribable.

His lips find mine again and I moan as I work my hips along his dick doing the best I can to hit the most delicious spot that might have me coming in his lap. "Does it feel good?" He asks me when he pulls away to pepper kisses along my jaw.

"God, yes," I whisper.

"Are you wet?" He asks and I nod, unable to respond because I feel myself building towards an orgasm. "Show me."

My eyes flutter open, and my head that's been tilted back as he trails kisses up my neck slowly moves down to look at him. "What?"

"Show me how wet you are." I try to move but he holds me in place and looks down between us where I'm seated on top of him. The car is dark but the light on the outside of his garage illuminates the space around us enough for him to be able to see me run my fingers down my body and under the waistband of my leggings.

I slip my fingers beneath it and my panties and drag my index finger through my sex. My mouth drops open and I let out a sigh as it glides through my wetness easily. I whimper and his nostrils flare in response when I feel him pull my hand from between my legs and hold it in front of his face. My index and middle finger are coated with my cum and I watch with fascination as he drags his tongue up both of them.

Oh my God.

He circles his tongue around them, leaving them clean before letting them go. "Make yourself come."

I gasp. "Right now?"

"Right now." He nods. My heart is pounding in time with the pulsing between my legs so it doesn't take much convincing for me to slide my hand back between them. I continue to finger myself while I'm in his lap, my body so desperate for the orgasm. My hand that's not between my legs reaches for his belt in an attempt to tell him what I want, but he grabs it and pulls it away before bringing it to his mouth. "No."

"No?" I stammer out as I flick my clit. "But—"

"Are you close?" He asks and I nod. He pushes my hair away from my face. "I know you are. Come on, beautiful, let me see you."

"Touch me," I beg, wanting him to make me come even though sitting on top of him with my hand between my legs is high on my list of memories I'll use while my hand is between my legs again later.

"But you're doing so well. Rubbing that pretty little clit for me." He licks his lips and I convulse in his arms as I think about him running his tongue through my slit. "I can smell you." He pulls me closer, pressing his lips to my chin while I continue to finger myself. The car is quiet and with it being near three in the morning, the world around us is silent making the sounds of my fingers in my pussy seem ten times louder.

"Theo," I moan. "Please," I beg again, trying my best to entice him into slipping his hand between my legs despite the awkward position we're in. "Fuck me," I moan because I'm at the peak of my orgasm when I have no control over what's going to slip from between my lips. "Fuck me. I want you. Please," I cry out just as I shatter in his arms. I'm vaguely aware that he groans my name but I'm too far gone to recognize any other words he utters. My left hand goes behind his neck, bringing his lips to mine just as my orgasm crashes through me. I taste myself on him and it spurs my orgasm further. I shake in his arms as I continue to rock against my hand and move up and down on his covered dick.

I stop rubbing and pull away from him slowly as I slide my hand out from between my legs. I notice his lips are shiny and I don't know if it's from my lip balm, my tongue, or my pussy and I clench at the sexiness of him being covered in me. I glance behind me towards his house before turning back towards him slowly, staring up at him through my lashes. I reach for the hem of his shirt dragging my fingers along the bottom to clean my fingers. A wicked smirk finds my face as I mark him. "Can I come in?"

Lust flashes in his eyes and he lowers his gaze to stare at my mouth. His eyes flick behind me to his house and then back to me. "Are you sure that's what you want?"

"Yes." I lean down to purr in his ear. "I definitely fucking want." I nibble on his jaw, dragging my teeth along it gently before pressing a kiss to his lips. "Don't you want me?"

"You just fingered yourself in my lap while you dry-humped me, of course I want you. I want to fuck you into the middle of next week." He groans and I giggle as I move off of his lap and back into my seat to get out of the car. I'm reaching for the handle when my phone begins to ring and I frown when I see it's my dad.

"Fuck," I hiss and Theo's eyes immediately dart to my house which still looks dark except for the dim lights that my parents leave on for me when I'm out late.

"Hi, Dad," I answer nonchalantly.

"Avery, where the hell are you and why is it not in this house?" he asks in a tone that's not quite mad but not quite pleased with the fact that I'm out this late. I'm twenty-one years old, so I don't exactly have a curfew but I usually tell them when I'm not coming home and I hadn't done that. I'm preparing to speak the lie that started forming the moment his name flashed across my phone when Theo takes the phone from my hand before I can speak.

"Shawn," he says, "I was down at *The Clover* and figured I'd take her and Rory and some of the other kids home so they didn't have to Uber in the snow." I can't hear what my dad says but Theo chuckles and I cross my arms over my chest angrily at the thought of tonight absolutely not going how I want it to and more importantly where it was headed just moments before. He's off the phone a few seconds later, after telling him I would be home *soon* and I turn to look at him as he hands me my phone. "Don't look at me like that."

"What happened to fucking me into the middle of next week?"

"Ummm, your father called?" He gives me a look. "Kind of lost my hard-on when I remembered you're my friend's daughter which also reminded me that you're my son's best friend." He taps my cell phone screen which is a picture of Lucas and me from earlier this semester in front of The Metropolitan Museum of Art when I visited him in New York.

He points at my phone and when I turn to look at him there's hurt all over his face. "I can't do that to him." His eyes dart away from my phone to my house. "Either of them. They both trust me and… fuck, I don't deserve it."

Chapter

TWO

THEO

Present Day

'VE BEEN DREADING TONIGHT FOR WEEKS. THE SECOND HER father Shawn told me where they were having her graduation party, followed by the invitation that her mother Camille sent over with all of the details, I've felt uneasy. I've been *trying* to avoid all things Avery Summers for what feels like three fucking years and yet she's been able to embed herself into every aspect of my life effortlessly. Her parents still live next door and my son can't go the length of a conversation without bringing her name up so I've been forced to have her name or her face flash through my mind at least once a day and it's driving me fucking crazy.

I tried to tell myself those nights didn't feel as good as they did. That she didn't look as good as she did. That I'm not attracted to the girl that I watched grow into a woman. The woman that my son has or had feelings for—I'm uncertain of where he currently stands. I do believe that if there are feelings, they're not reciprocated on Avery's side. She has always been very clear about where that line was except for their freshman year of high school when I think they spent more time making out than anything else. *According to her, though, that was just for fun or practice or out of boredom, and she's never had feelings for him.*

My eyes find her instantly in a forest green dress that hugs her body like it was custom-tailored for her, and I'm instantly irritated by all the people here because all I want to do is pull her into a corner and run my hands all over her.

Her eyes meet mine despite the dozens of people between us and a sweet smile finds her face. Her parents are pillars in the community, kind and well-liked by almost everyone. Her father is the number one children's dentist across multiple counties and her mother owns *the* bakery in town, *Avery's Café,* named for her daughter with pastries and macarons that are so delicious they make you feel like you are actually in Paris.

Just as quickly as our eyes meet, she turns away, back to an elderly couple that look like older versions of Shawn. I am surprised that I don't see my son or my daughter but I also don't see many of Avery's friends, making me wonder if they are somewhere else reminiscing about their high school days. I start moving towards her to say hello. *Maybe if I just say hi, I can slip out in an hour.* Our eyes lock again as I make my way closer, and the couple moves away. She drains the glass of champagne in her hand and I don't know if I'm disappointed or intrigued by her sudden need for alcohol as I approach her.

"Theo! When did you get here?" I hear when I'm only about ten feet from her. I turn to see Shawn standing with some of his friends and a few men I recognize as Avery's uncles. He waves me over, holding a cigar between his index and middle finger and assumedly a glass of scotch in the other. All dressed in suits without ties, the six men summon me over despite something pulling me towards Avery.

I give them a nod and a smile as I move towards them trying my best to ignore the temptation in the green dress in the form of his daughter. "I just got here," I say, answering his question.

I approach them and he slaps me on the back as the rest of the guys nod their hellos. "Why don't you have a drink?" He waves over a member of the waitstaff walking around with a tray of champagne.

I grab a crystal flute from the tray, contemplating ordering something stronger but decide against it before I know just how many drinks Avery has consumed. She could get me to do just about anything when she's had a few drinks and even more when I've had a few as well. "Can you believe we have kids that are college graduates?" He scratches his jaw and lets out a sarcastic chuckle. "God, when did we get old?" He looks at me and smiles. "Well, I guess you've been old with Raegan having graduated last year." He takes a sip of his drink and I narrow my eyes at him.

"Okay, more importantly, what can you tell us about the Eagles offensive line this year? Because those draft picks have me worried," one of the men speaks up. I've met him a few times when Shawn and Camille had parties, but I don't know him well enough to start talking about anything I know, *which isn't much.*

Talk of football goes on for a considerable amount of time and before I know it, it's been an hour, I've had two glasses of champagne, I switched to a scotch, and I still haven't talked to Avery. I turn my head as our group breaks up after Camille drags Shawn away to talk to someone and I scan the room in search of her. I see her in the corner with Rory and a few other girls I recognize from their high school.

This is good. This is safe. She's not going to try and tempt me in mixed company.

I begin making my way towards them and as I get nearer, I see they all have shot glasses in their hands with a lime wedge in the other. *Oh fuck.*

I watch as Avery licks the salt from her hand and my dick immediately hardens thinking about her tongue licking up my shaft that same way.

I grip the glass in my hand harder as I approach them and all of their eyes light up when they see me.

"Theo!" Rory smiles and I feel like she's gotten older just in the last six months since I've seen her. Her jet-black hair is cut into a short sleek style just above her shoulders with bangs that frame her coal colored eyes. She's worn glasses the entire time I've known her, but I remember Lucas mentioning something about her getting Lasik over spring break.

"Ladies." I nod at all of them, trying my best to keep my eyes off of Avery. "Congratulations." I scan the group of four. "I assume all of you have graduated?"

"One more semester for me." One of the girls blushes as Rory and the other girl I don't recognize nod.

"Thank you and thank you for coming," Avery says.

Now that I'm closer, I can really drink her in. *Christ, has she gotten even more gorgeous?* The last time I saw her was winter break because she jetted off to Cabo with Lucas and a bunch of their friends for spring break this past April so I didn't see her. Seeing her in significantly less clothes than in December has me momentarily speechless as I run my gaze over her.

"Of course, I wouldn't have missed it," I tell her, even if I had been dreading it, I am very proud of her and I wouldn't miss the opportunity to tell her.

I'm trying my best not to openly ogle her in front of her friends, but the alcohol coupled with this green dress that is hugging her in all the right places has given my eyes a mind of their own as they wander over her shamelessly. She's wearing the sexiest pair of open-toe heels and all I can think about is that sharp stiletto digging into my back, piercing me as I finally get the chance to taste her cunt. The dress falls just below her knees but highlights her full hips, her waist, and those full breasts I'd had my mouth over just six months before. Her skin is tanned like she'd been outside for a considerable amount of time and it makes me want to lick her to see if I can taste the sun on her skin. Shawn is black and her mother, Camille, is white, so she always looks sun-kissed, but with her tan and the color of this dress and her dark tresses she looks fucking stunning.

"Is Lucas almost here? He texted that he was running late?" Rory asks, looking up at me and I'm grateful for her question because it instantly stops my dick from getting harder. *Lucas. Fuck. What about Avery Summers had me forgetting all about the reason I shouldn't be looking at her at all?*

"I'm not sure." I shake my head. He'd left this morning to go to the gym before I'd left for work and when I got home, it seemed he'd already left. He was only home for a week or so before he went back to New York to start his new job at an investment firm and it's odd to think about the fact that both of my kids no longer live at home.

Even though Lucas has been away at NYU for the last four years, I felt like he still lived *here* in Pennsylvania with me. The idea of him moving to New York permanently feels like a weight in my chest. "I'm surprised he's not here yet."

"Hey, gorgeous." A tall guy with blonde hair, about the same height I am, infiltrates the circle and wraps an arm around Avery's shoulder bringing her closer to him. "Happy graduation," he tells her as he rests his chin on top of her head for a moment. I don't recognize him as one of their high school friends and a flare of irritation moves through me that I don't know their relationship and then another over the fact that I'm jealous and have no right to be.

"Elijah." She smiles and I notice she doesn't make an effort to move but her eyes find mine. "Theo, this is a friend of mine, Elijah, from school." She tilts her head up to look at him. "This is Lucas' Dad." She points and his eyes light up in recognition.

"Oh damn, of course! Theo Graham, you're my dad's actual God. Do you mind if I get a picture?" he asks, unraveling his arm from Avery and I wonder if they're really just friends, or if he's among the many men that forget about women the second the topic of sports comes up. He moves across the small circle, snapping a selfie, and in that short moment, where he's talking about my last Superbowl game and my final touchdown that won us the game but destroyed my shoulder in the process, I hear my son's voice.

"Fuck, I'm sorry I'm late. They have me onboarding via Zoom all week and the lady from Human Resources was moving so fucking slow." I turn around just in time for Lucas to pull Avery into his arms and press a kiss to her temple. She hugs him back, and when the guy next to me stiffens, I'm even more fucking confused about what's going on.

My son always did clean up nice. He's almost as tall as me and while he's not as built, he is still in great shape from almost fifteen years of soccer, including four years in college. His dark hair is slicked back and he's wearing a black suit with a white shirt beneath it.

He nods at Elijah. "Hey man, good to see you. How've you been?"

"Good," Elijah responds. "Glad you could make it." His tone is cocky, and I think I'm starting to understand what's going on. Elijah wants Avery and he sees Lucas as a threat.

"Glad I could make it?" He chuckles with a smug grin on his face before bringing his hand to Avery's jaw and squeezing it gently to make her lips pucker. "I'm the one Camille called this morning in hysterics that they had all the wrong chairs and needed help transporting the right ones from some warehouse downtown." He lets Avery's jaw go and gives Elijah a pointed look. "Avery's mother," he says condescendingly and I resist the urge to snort.

Avery, who Lucas still has wrapped in his arms, my guess so Elijah doesn't reach for her, pulls away and looks up at him, confused. "She called you?"

"Of course, who else?"

"My dad or my uncles?"

"They were all playing golf." He shrugs as if my son was the obvious next choice for anything regarding Avery.

"Lucas, thank you. My mom was being a nightmare about it this morning when I couldn't care less. She was literally comparing apples to apples." She rolls her eyes and I believe it. Camille Summers is notoriously meticulous especially when it comes to planning parties.

"Literally?" Lucas quips sarcastically and raises an eyebrow at her.

She huffs before smacking his chest. "You know what I mean." And somehow, I've forgotten, or maybe I've made myself forget how Lucas and Avery are around each other. The familiarity and comfort that only years of close friendship can bring. The kind of friendship where from the outside you're not exactly sure if they're together or not, or if there are romantic feelings. I'm not on the outside and there have been times I even forgot. I can remember a few Freudian slips where I'd absentmindedly called Avery his girlfriend while they were growing up.

Which is why it makes my two very inappropriate interactions with her so fucked up and need not repeating.

"Yes, *figuratively*," he corrects and Rory groans.

"Theo, your children are fighting again. Do something." She points between my son and Avery with a chuckle before wrapping her arms around Lucas and hugging him. He returns it and I've noticed that amidst their small back and forth Elijah has disappeared.

"I can't believe you invited that joker," he murmurs to Avery with an eye roll. "Hey, Dad," he says with a hug.

"Son."

"Is Rae coming?" he asks about his sister. "I told her not to bring what's his name. I didn't want you getting pissed off."

"You know his name," I say, referring to my daughter's boyfriend, "and I won't get pissed off," I grumble, even though there's a chance I might. I know it makes me a fucking hypocrite given that I know what the twenty-one year old in front of me tastes like but the thought of my little girl with someone…*my age*. I cringe.

"You sure about that?" Rory jokes as she pops a mini crab cake into her mouth.

"You shouldn't. So, she's dating a guy that's a bit older than her? Who cares? He worships her," Avery argues.

"First of all, a bit?" Lucas interjects. "The guy is Dad's age. And can we not?" He winces.

"So, she likes older men." Avery shrugs and gives me what I want to think is an innocent look aside from the fact that she holds my gaze for an extra second. "Guys our age don't know what they're doing."

"Who are you speaking for?" Lucas balks, annoyed as he gives her a look.

"Guys *his* age don't know what they're doing either," Rory chirps, annoyed and I wonder if there's more to that story. Rory looks over at Avery. "I have to use the ladies room."

"Oh, I'll come," Avery says before looking at us. "Excuse me, gentlemen." She giggles before she's gone, following Rory towards the restroom and leaving me alone with my son.

"So, that pissing match with the guy?" *Whose name I can't remember for the life of me.*

"Elijah? That guy is such a tool. He's been trying to hook up with her since their freshman year of college. Get it through your head dude, she's not interested," he grits out.

I love my son more than anything in the world short of my daughter who I love equally but I want to joke that it sounds like the pot calling the kettle black. I'm not sure where his feelings for Avery are today though, so I leave it alone. *Sort of.*

"Right." I pull my drink to my lips and give him a look over the rim and he glares at me.

"Don't, I was making a point."

"What point was that?"

"Dad, I don't have feelings for Avery anymore. I did, but," his eyes scan the room, as if he's trained to know when she walks into a room because sure enough, she's back and talking to her mom. I know that look. I've had that look. It was the look I gave Lucas' mom, *many many* years ago when she was across the room. The look that there was far too much space between my hands and her body.

"Lucas," I interrupt his staring and his eyes dart back to mine.

"I'm crazy about her, but we're just friends."

"Because that's what *she* wants. Not what you want." I wince.

"I've grown to accept it. I've moved on."

The thought makes my stomach turn and I wonder if now is the time for me to leave. Leave Avery with her friends and my son and away from my eyes and my carnal thoughts. "You drive here?" I ask because I know more than anything that my son hates talking about his feelings for Avery.

"No, I took an Uber. I think a bunch of us are going downtown later." He grabs a glass of champagne. "Thank you." He nods at the waitress with a polite smile and it warms my heart for the millionth time that I raised my kids right.

"Alright, well I might head out soon. Just be careful. Call me if you need me to come get you guys." I know he's twenty-one and lives in New York by himself, but when he's home, I still see him as that sixteen-year-old kid who used to harass me for rides constantly.

"Dad, I'll be fine. I'm probably not going to get too drunk anyway if Avery starts taking shots."

"She already had one before you got here." I chuckle and Lucas' blue eyes, ones that look exactly like his mother's, glare in Avery's direction before turning to me.

A group of guys I recognize from their high school that must have been outside or elsewhere when I got here start making their way over and after exchanging a few pleasantries, I make my way towards the restroom before I make my exit. There are easily two hundred people here; I am sure no one will miss me unless Raegan shows up, but my daughter is notoriously flakey so she may not make an appearance at all.

The bathroom is one floor down from where the party is being held so I'm surprised to see Avery against the wall when I exit the restroom, her legs crossed and a sexy smirk across her lips as she holds a highball glass in her hand with an orange peel floating around the bottom. *Champagne, tequila, and now, whiskey? Fuck.* "Were you going to leave without saying goodbye?" she asks.

"Who said I was leaving?"

"Lucas," she murmurs. "I asked where you ran off to because my father was looking for you."

"Oh. What does he want?"

"Nothing. I couldn't exactly tell him *I* was looking for you." She pushes off the wall and moves closer to me and I take a step back, not wanting her perfume to infiltrate my space.

I nod. "I am probably going to head out."

"Why?"

"I don't want to crowd your space."

She looks up at me and bats her eyelashes at me. "It never bothered you before. I can remember many times you crashed our parties as we got older."

"Ave…" I trail off. "I don't know that it's the best idea for me to be around to watch my son get in a pissing match with every man that breathes in your direction."

She groans and rolls her eyes. "Elijah is a nonissue and Lucas knows that. He just likes fucking with him."

I nod because what can I say? 'I don't *want* to watch my son stare at you with the same stars I'm trying to keep out of my eyes?'

"Please stay?" She says and darts her eyes down the hallway before turning them back to mine. "It's my graduation party."

"I know," I tell her as I reach into my coat pocket and pull out a long envelope that I slide into her hands.

She takes it from me but doesn't open it or even look at it. "Thank you, but that's not what I want."

"Avery...we can't."

"I want to finish what we started last winter break."

"Lucas is home," I tell her because I have no intention of sneaking her in or touching her while my son is in the house or could potentially show up at any time.

"I'm sure you can figure something out." She smiles.

"How are you going to get away from your friends? From Lucas? He's going to want to make sure you get home safely."

"Lucas isn't my dad, Theo. I know how to handle him." She's up against me now looking up at me with the sexiest eyes fueled by alcohol and lust and...*fuuuuuck.* "And then I want you to handle *me.*"

I grit my teeth, trying to hold my breath so I don't smell her. "Anyone could walk down here."

"Say yes," she whispers.

"Why?" I blink at her. "Is this just...why me of all people? Is it because of who I am? Is this just the thrill of someone that should be off limits?" I move and she takes a step back as I tower over her. "What is it about me that has your pussy so wet?"

She whimpers and her cheeks pinken and I wish my words hadn't affected her because she looks so fucking adorably innocent. "I–I've had a crush on you...for a while."

The air leaves my lungs because I wasn't expecting that. I was expecting her to say something equally sexy or about the fact that she's older and can fuck whoever she wants and she wants me.

"What's a while?"

"Since you moved in?" she says weakly and my eyes widen.

"Eight years?"

She nods. "I mean I haven't been saving myself for you or any-thing," she teases and I hate the annoyance that ripples through me at the thought of someone else touching her. "But yeah…" She winces. "I didn't think you'd ever touch me."

"Because I shouldn't touch you."

"But you did and now…I can't stop thinking about it." She shakes her head and takes a step back before taking a sip of her drink. "I should probably get back, but please consider staying or…seeing me later?"

Chapter
THREE

Avery

I HAVE LONG SINCE LEFT MY OWN GRADUATION PARTY IN FAVOR of going downtown with my friends while my parents stayed at the restaurant and entertained theirs. It didn't escape me that Theo stayed longer than I think he planned and opted to leave when we did to head home. He'd mingled with us and my parents all night. It felt almost like a game; how many times could we lock eyes in a room full of people without making it obvious?

A bunch of us are at a club downtown, the time nearing almost one in the morning when I decide now is time to figure out if I'm going to a more private party next. I break away from the group and make my way around the large circular bar in the middle of the club to give myself some space.

Me: Hiiiii

The bubbles indicating that he's typing pop up before disappearing. They pop up again and then disappear again and I giggle at the thought that he doesn't know what to say.

TG: Are you okay?

Me: Yep, I'm fine

TG: You having fun?

Me: Yes!

TG: Good, I'm glad.

Me: Will you come get me?

He doesn't answer right away and I resist the urge to text him again when I sense bouncing in my periphery. I turn to see Rory sipping what I think to be a rum and coke through a straw.

"Who are you texting?"

"No one." I close the message and set my phone to sleep.

"Okay, you're so full of shit," she says through narrowed slits. "But why?"

"Rory…" I've come close to spilling the beans to her a few times. I haven't because sometimes I can't tell if she's just as close to Lucas as she is to me and I worry she might accidentally slip up to him especially if she's drinking. I wish I could tell her, but it's just too risky.

"Are you seeing someone?"

"What? No."

"Someone that lives here?" she pushes.

"Of course not."

"Someone that may have been at your grad party?" She sings and my palms start to sweat.

"Like who?"

She shrugs. "You tell me."

"I am *not* into Elijah, Rory." I deadpan and she rolls her eyes in response.

"Obviously."

My phone buzzes in my hand and I want to look at it but the thought of Rory catching who I'm texting makes me nervous.

"You're hiding something!" She bumps her hip with mine.

"I am not!" I down the drink in my hand. "I have to pee," I tell her. "Do you want to come?"

"No, I'm good," she says and I bolt away from one of my best friends and her very prying eyes. I'm not even through the door of the bathroom before I'm opening his message.

TG: We shouldn't do this.

My head falls back in frustration and an exasperated sigh leaves my lips as I try to figure out what to say. My phone buzzes again and a smile finds my lips at the unexpected words on the screen.

TG: I'm not saying I don't want to.

Me: I want to.

The dots appear and then disappear twice before he replies.

TG: Can you get away easily?

Me: Yes. I'll Irish goodbye!

TG: Your own graduation party? Everyone will notice you're missing, and what if Lucas shows up at your house looking for you later?

Me: I'll figure it out. Lucas won't find out, okay? I know that's what you're worried about.

TG: Aren't you?

The words on the screen make me feel like shit. Should I be more concerned? Does it make me a terrible friend for doing this? Keeping it from him? My reasoning is slightly different from Theo's. It's a secret, a *big* secret I'm keeping from my best friend. But he's not going to find out. *No one is going to know.*

My phone vibrates again.

Lucas: Would you hate me if I left?

I look up in the air. *Thank you!* I mouth, even though I'm sure God isn't really on my side about hooking up with my best friend's father.

Me: Of course not. Everything okay?

Lucas: A few of the guys want to go to Pratt Street.

I snicker, thinking about Pratt Street.

Me: Oh IIII see. Blowing off my grad party for strippers?

Lucas: I've barely seen you! You've been MIA all night. I'll make it up to you. You own me all week, Summers. I swear.

Me: I'm messing with you. Have fun!

Lucas: You want to come?

Me: I'm good lol

Lucas: Oh come on, I'll buy you a lap dance.

Me: Bye Lucas.

Lucas: Where are you anyway?

Me: Bathroom

Lucas: Okay, called the Uber. It'll be here in five. You coming out soon?

Me: Two minutes

I pick up the phone and Theo answers my call on the first ring. "He's not going to find out. He's going somewhere else with his friends."

"You're his best friend. You're not going wherever he's going?" Theo asks and I wince. I don't really want to tell his dad he's going to a strip club but I guess he is twenty-one. More than likely he'll tell him himself.

"His *guy* friends."

"Ah." He chuckles in realization. "Well, when is he leaving?"

"He said he called the Uber and they're leaving in five."

"I can be there shortly after that."

"Are we going to your house?" I ask. "I think that may be risky."

"We aren't," he responds and I hear the sounds of his keys.

"Oh?"

"I got a room." I don't even stop the smile from finding my face. "I'm not saying we're doing anything."

"Sure, Theo." I saw the way he was looking at me in this dress. All it would take is a flick of a wrist to get this dress off and then *game over.*

"I'm serious. If you're drunk…"

"Do I sound drunk?" And the truth is, I'm not. I'm tipsy at best because at my graduation party my mother warned me about getting sloppy around my grandparents and so much of my family. So, I never even got drunk while I was there and when I got here, I was significantly more sober and then I only had one shot of tequila.

"No, but you know how to hide it."

"I'm not. I've been drinking water for a few hours. I wasn't sure if I was going to see you tonight and I wanted to be...aware. I knew *you'd* want me to be aware."

"Hmmm," he says but it comes out more like a growl that I feel throughout my body.

"I'll text you when Lucas is gone."

⁓∾⁓

By the time I get back to my friends, the guys are leaving. Lucas pulls me into a hug, pressing a kiss to my forehead, and tells me we could meet for brunch or whatever I want tomorrow before he leaves.

"You really feel nothing for him?" Rory says as we watch them head outside.

"No..." I scrunch my nose because, honestly, I wish I did some days. I wish I had reciprocated the same feelings he had in high school. Something tells me we'd still be together if I had. It would certainly make my life easier. If he's this way about his best friend, I can only imagine how he'd worship the woman he's with.

"You got that man fucked up."

I gasp, and smack her shoulder. "Rory, I do not!"

She snorts into her glass. "Okay. I'm going home with Justin." She runs a hand through her hair.

"Of course, you are. Why didn't he go with the guys?"

"Because a stripper won't stick his dick in her mouth?" She looks at me incredulously. "Or I suppose she might, but I do it for free." Her red-painted lips form a straight line and she rolls her eyes. "Like an idiot."

I chuckle. "Shut up, you love him."

"I do not!" She mimics me and I raise an eyebrow at her. "Okay, the point is...I'm leaving to go get laid." She leans in to kiss my cheek.

"You good? I assume whoever you're texting is going to come get you." She nods at my phone and I do my best to avoid her prying eyes. "I'm just going home," I tell her as my phone buzzes.

TG: I'm around the side. Wasn't sure if any of your friends would be outside.

Me: Coming

My head darts up and I'm glad Rory is on her phone. "I'm leaving, my Uber is here."

"Text me when you're safe." *And I make a mental note that she doesn't say* 'when you get home.' She kisses my cheek again. "I'm not going to hound you about this right now because I can sense a girl thinking with her pussy from a mile away and I don't want to ruin your *'I'm about to get dick buzz,'* but this conversation is *not* over."

"Fine," I relent because she's right. The buzz has kicked in and nothing in this moment matters more than getting Theo Graham between my legs.

⁓∽⁓

I escape my friends, without having to do a million goodbyes and slide into Theo's Mercedes. He has multiple cars, and I notice he's brought the one that's the most nondescript. The paparazzi rarely catch him doing anything and don't often really even care what he's doing now that he's this far removed from the NFL, but people still recognize him and I'm sure he doesn't want that or worse, to get papped going into a hotel with me.

"Hi," I say with a smile and he smiles back, his eyes drinking me in. He's still in his suit from my graduation party, making me wonder what he's been doing since I left him three hours ago.

"Hi, beautiful," he says and I melt as he pulls out into the street. "Thank you for coming to get me."

"When have I ever not come when you called?" He asks and my heart begins to race.

I raise an eyebrow. "I think this is different."

"Fair." He grunts as he zooms down Main Street.

"Where did you book a room?"

"The Ritz."

"Oh fancy. Are you trying to impress me, Mr. Graham? Am I getting the football star Theo Graham treatment?" He chuckles but I see a bit of a flush moving up his neck. "Oh my gosh, I was kidding!" I move across the console and put my hand on his thigh. "You don't need to try to impress me. You do that by just being you." I tell him as I move my fingers along his thigh and brush against his hardness.

"Avery," he groans.

"Mmmm?" I narrow my eyes and give him a cheeky smirk.

"Don't…"

"Don't what?"

"Tempt me."

We make it to the front of the hotel and despite the late hour, the valet staff are still outside. "Welcome back, sir." A man, probably no older than me, opens the door for him while another opens the door for me.

"Welcome back?" I look up at him.

"I came earlier to check into the room," he says as his hand finds the small of my back.

"I see," I tell him as we make our way through the lobby to the elevator. The second we step into the elevator I feel the tension crackle between us. We are going all the way to the fifteenth floor, so we have a few moments before we make it there.

"You are so fucking beautiful." He drags his eyes down my frame, zeroing in on my feet. "Do your feet hurt?"

I bite my lip because being in four-inch stilettos for eight hours is a lot even on the most experienced of heel wearers. "A little." He moves across the elevator and just as it dings, he lifts me into his arms like I weigh nothing. I gasp, being in his strong arms, and I allow myself to press my face to his neck and take a deep inhale. "You smell good." I continue dragging my nose along his neck and I feel him swallow.

"Avery," he whispers as he walks to the end of the hall where there are double doors to enter meaning it's some sort of suite. He sets me on my feet and backs me against the door. "Front pocket." He grits out. I look up at him questioningly and his lips curl into a smirk. "The key is in my front pocket."

"Oh." I gasp as I reach into the right pocket first, feeling around but not finding the key. I switch to his other pocket and I find it instantly but continue exploring, trying my best to push his slacks closer to his dick to no avail. I pull out the key card and turn around to drag it against the detector when I feel him at my back and his lips resting on my shoulder.

"I couldn't pull my eyes away from you all night."

"I know." I push open the door and pull him inside with me.

"Every time I searched for you, you were already looking at me."

"You are *impossible* not to look at. Believe me, I've been trying," he tells me as he slides his jacket off.

I make it a point to text Rory to let her know that I'm safe. I also respond to a very jumbled text message from my mother asking me if I'm staying out tonight and I tell her yes.

Oh, but she can get drunk. I roll my eyes.

The last text is from Lucas asking me if I'm okay and if I'm home safe to which I also respond yes. *I'll deal with all of that tomorrow.*

Tonight, I just need him.

I close my phone and sit on the couch, noticing how massive the suite is. We're still in the living area but I see the bedroom just off to the right and my skin prickles with anticipation. He sits on the coffee table in front of me and pulls my feet into his lap as he unbuckles the strap around my ankle to remove each shoe. "What started...this crush you have on me?"

I rub my foot against his thigh, dragging it up and down slowly. His hand finds my calf and he moves his rough hands along it. I feel the calluses on his fingers and it reminds me that I don't know what they feel like on my clit or my tits or anywhere intimate. His thumb drags along my ankle and reaches the arch of my foot, pushing his thumbs into the soles and I moan at the feeling.

"Have you seen you? I was thirteen and the most gorgeous man I'd ever seen moved in next door." A ghost of a smile finds his lips.

"And you were nice. Probably the nicest man I've ever met besides someone I'm related to." I cock my head to the side in memory. I've always been bubbly and outgoing and the day they moved in I marched over to their house before they were even done unpacking with a lasagna and a tray of cheesecake brownies my mother made and inserted myself into their lives without even giving them the option.

I pull my foot out of his hands and reach my hand out to pull him to the couch next to me. Within moments I'm in his lap, fueled by the memories of what straddling him feels like. "You're sexy and smart and kind and hardworking and protective...and..." I let out a breath. "On the slightly more fucked up side, you're my best friend's favorite person in the world. He's spent the last seven years trying to be you and while I'm not attracted to *him*, I am attracted to the man he's been trying to *be* ever since he could walk." I bite my bottom lip and I watch his eyes flit to the movement. "And okay, maybe I do have some daddy issues." I let out a breath before I gently brush my lips against his. "You've been such a constant in my life for so long, Theo. But, I don't want him to find out. I don't want the drama, and you're right; he wouldn't like it and he'd be angry at you and hurt by me and I don't want to do that to someone I care about." My tongue flicks out and drags along his bottom lip. "But it doesn't mean I've stopped thinking about what your dick would feel like in my mouth."

His hands drop to my hips where my dress hiked up when I slid into his lap and I grind against him. My panty covered pussy is sitting directly over his slacks covered dick. I begin moving against him, moving up and down and trying my best to make him harder in his pants.

"Fuck," he groans.

"Will you touch me this time?"

"Yes." His voice is hoarse.

"Did you bring condoms?" I raise an eyebrow at him, and I briefly wonder if he really was expecting us to just 'talk.'

He shifts and lets out a sigh. "I didn't."

I frown and pull back slightly. I shift, feeling his hard dick beneath me, and wonder how in the hell he expected us to get out of this hotel room without him being inside me at least once. "Why?"

"I…I am trying to exercise some restraint, Avery. I don't know if we should…go there."

"But you can touch me?" I lean down and let my tongue flick out to trace along his ear. "You can touch my pussy without wanting to put your dick inside it?"

"I'm not ready to go that far with you," he tells me and I pull back, cocking my head to the side.

"Well, I know you're not a virgin."

He narrows his eyes at me. "This is a big thing Avery and I'm not taking it lightly. Explain to me what happens now." He juts his chin up at me. "What happens after tonight?" I blink at him confused. "Are you going to want more?" He grabs my chin. "Because you telling me you've had a crush on me since you were thirteen and then fucking me here tonight is going to affect you more than you think, Avery. Even more than what we've already done." I don't respond because for a moment my brain goes blank after hearing the words *fucking* and *me* fall from his lips. "We are already playing with fire, you and me, because we've been dancing around this for three years." He looks away from me and lets out a sigh before his warm brown eyes reach mine. "And maybe once you let me inside of you, I'm going to lose my fucking mind and want it again. Maybe you only want it once, but…I don't work that way."

I hadn't allowed myself to think about *more* past tonight but the idea that this man may want another night with me sets my skin ablaze. "And if I wanted it more than just once?"

"How do you see that working?"

"Is this about Lucas?"

"This is about me. I could fuck anyone and it not mean anything. But it can't just be sex with you. If it were, I would have fucked you two years ago that first time."

The promise of more lurks beneath his words. "So, you want to date me or something?" I try to ignore the butterflies flapping their wings in my stomach because he does not mean that.

"I can't have that either."

"So, you don't want to fuck me because you think you'll want more than just a night, but you *can't* have more than just a night."

"The most fucked up catch twenty-two, isn't it?"

"Hmmm." I purse my lips. "Then why the room?"

"Because I'm a masochist evidently." He rubs a hand over his eyes before dropping to give me a serious look. "And you asked to see me later."

The thought that I have this much power over him sends a feeling of warmth all over. "What if I asked you to fuck me?"

"Avery."

I bite my bottom lip. "Fine." I stand up off his lap. "I suppose I can respect your boundaries for *now*," I purr. "What can we do?" I ask him innocently and when he doesn't respond, I drop my eyes to his lap. "Can I see your dick?" I cross my arms and raise an eyebrow at him.

"No." He grits out and my mouth falls open.

He can't be serious. "So, you just brought me here to what? Torture me?"

"No. I plan on doing a lot of things to *you*."

"But I can't touch you? Pass. I don't accept," I snap.

He shrugs and leans back against the couch, crossing his leg so his ankle rests across his knee. "Tough, princess."

"You're infuriating. You know what? Two can play that game." I reach behind me and drag my zipper down, letting my dress pool at my feet. I didn't wear a bra, so I'm standing before him completely topless for the first time with the tiniest thong I own covering my pussy. I immediately turn around, showing him my ass, and walk towards the bathroom. "I'm taking a bath," I call over my shoulder.

Chapter
FOUR

THEO

IT ONLY TAKES A SECOND FOR MY DICK TO REACT TO THE HALF-naked woman walking through the suite with the plan to get completely naked. I'm off the couch moments later, trailing slowly behind her, enthralled by the slope of her hips and the way that black string disappears between her ass cheeks. I make my way into the bathroom and lean against the doorjamb, watching as she bends over the massive bathtub to turn on the water and pour in some bubble bath. I make my way towards her and before she stands upright, I reach out to grab her thong. I tug hard, pulling her towards me by the tiny string I can only compare to dental floss.

She gasps and tilts her head up to look at me before dropping her eyes down to where I have the fabric in my fist. My eyes flash to hers devilishly and I pull harder, pulling her against my chest, and I wrap a hand across her stomach, keeping her flush against me as I let the fabric snap against her skin with a satisfying sound. I look down at her body, and saliva pools in my mouth taking in her full plump tits and puckered pink nipples that are pebbling harder under my gaze.

"I assume you don't want to join me?" She lets out a sigh as I drag my fingertips up her sides. She squirms when my fingers graze the sides of her breasts just as I drop my lips to her shoulder.

"I shouldn't," I tell her even as I drag my tongue along the slope. I shouldn't be doing any of this and I was fucking kidding myself for thinking that I was being marginally more respectable for just touching or tasting her and not fucking her. It's all bad. I'm fucked up for all of it.

I'm looking and touching when I shouldn't be doing either.

No. Sticking your dick inside of her is worse, my subconscious tells me.

She spins around and I'm granted a full and longer view of her tits and my eyes drop down immediately, devouring the sexy flesh. She blinks up at me and then slowly, with her eyes still on mine, she lowers her panties to the ground without breaking contact. She tucks her panties into my pocket with a wink and my dick throbs in response as I resist the urge to force her to her knees and push it through those full lips.

She takes a step backward, carefully making her way into the tub, and for the very first time, my eyes drop to the space between her legs. A tiny landing strip covers her slit and I have a moment of realization. I've been wondering what her cunt looked like for years and now I don't have to imagine it anymore. Don't have to guess what her pussy looks like while I fuck my fist because I'll have this image ingrained in my brain for the rest of my life. Avery Summers, naked and standing in a bathtub with a look on her face that's so dangerously sexy, I could almost come in my pants.

She puts her hair up on top of her head before slowly sliding into the water, obscuring her delicious curves from my view and I'm instantly relieved and angered by not being able to see all of her.

I lean against the counter about ten feet from the tub, trying my best to resist getting in with her. I ball my hands into fists as I try to temper the throb in my dick. "Are you happy to be done with school?"

"Small talk? Really?" She smirks before leaning over the side of the tub. I raise an eyebrow at her, as I wait for an answer and she rolls her eyes. "Yes. I'm happy to be home."

Terror and lust course through me making a heady concoction as every part of me is at war over her statement. Avery is planning to take over the business side of her mother's bakery, which means for the foreseeable future, I will be seeing her every day. Thoughts of her spending the summer sunbathing in her backyard after a long day of work or at the bars and restaurants I frequent, tempting me, sounds like my worst nightmare realized.

And also, a fucking dream come true.

She's been home for a week and I already have her at a hotel in town, naked and begging to ride my cock. I can only imagine what will happen when Lucas goes back to New York and I'm left alone with his very sexy and tempting best friend.

Fuck.

"Why didn't you move to New York? I thought that was the plan?"

She sighs as she leans back in the tub and lets her eyes flutter shut. "Did he put you up to this?" She asks, assumedly talking about Lucas.

"No, I'm curious."

"My mom is getting older and her and my dad want to travel for a while before I settle down and start popping out their grandchildren. They want to be here for that so they figure now is the time." She shrugs. "I could have spent a year messing around in New York but my parents have made a lot of sacrifices for me and I wanted to do this."

A smile pulls at my lips hearing her response. "Are you planning to live at home for a while? Or are you getting your own place?"

"Are you offering me a place to live?" She smiles and I want to laugh at her cheeky comment, but I know she's just trying to get a rise out of me and I don't want to encourage her. "If I get my own place, then I could have company over whenever I want." She shrugs. "I go out, meet a nice guy at the bar..." She picks up a handful of bubbles and blows them off her hand before turning off the running water. "If I want him to come home with me, I don't have to worry about anything."

The thought of anyone but me being that "company" in question makes me fucking irrationally irate because I told her no. I told her we couldn't and yet the idea of her with someone else while she's sitting naked in a bathtub in front of me makes my jaw clench. She notices and raises an eyebrow. "Jealous?"

I lick my lips and grip the counter behind me so I don't cross the bathroom and pluck her wet body from the bathtub. "I know what you're doing."

"On the other hand," she snaps her fingers, without acknowledging what I said, "if I live at home, I'll be closer to the hot guy next door I'm trying to fuck." She taps her chin. "I do have a key to his house." She shakes her head. "I'm coming home one night, it's late, maybe I'm a little drunk and I just so happen to go into the wrong house?" She props an arm on the side of the tub and puts a fist under her chin. "What do you think he'd do?"

Her sexy scenario flashes through my mind and I try not to picture her in my bed. *I fail.* "Walk you home."

"Maybe the first time." She giggles before sliding back into the tub.

I press off the counter, slowly rolling the sleeves of my button-down shirt to my forearms as I prepare to slide my hand into the tub and touch her. I've exercised enough restraint and I've fucking had it. I haven't even really kissed her yet and I am ready to lose my fucking mind.

Her eyes light up excitedly as she stares up at me and I drop to one knee. "Avery."

"Theo," she whispers. Her voice is light and airy.

"No one can know about this."

She shakes her head. "I won't tell anyone."

"A part of me hates myself for this," I tell her honestly.

She nods in understanding before she bites her bottom lip. "And the other part?"

"The other part hates myself for denying me this for so long. Denying myself what and who I want."

"It would be a shame. Denying us both."

"I absolutely believe you'd eventually break me down." I blink at her, knowing that it doesn't matter if she was in an apartment across town or in the house next door, somehow, she'd end up in my bed. I reach into the tub and my hand finds her thigh and she lets out a sexy little whimper. I move closer to her, my face a mere inch from hers as I drag my hand inward towards her cunt. Her eyes are hooded and bouncing all over my face from my lips to my eyes and I sense her moving closer.

"Touch me, Theo, please," she whines. "I've wanted this, *you*, for so long. I'm begging you." She holds my gaze as my finger traces her slit and the air leaves her lungs in a gush as she lets her head fall back. "Inside me." She breathes out. "Push...them...inside."

I don't know what's pounding faster, my heart or my erection as I slide my fingers down her slit but I don't push them inside. Instead, I slide my hand out of the water and her eyes fly open. "No."

"What?" she pants.

I stand up and flick away the excess water before starting to unbutton my shirt. "If we're doing this, we're doing it right, which means I want to see and feel everything the first time I touch you." I reach under her arms and pull her out of the tub with ease before setting her on the towel in front of the tub.

Water slides down her body in sexy rivulets making her glisten. I grab a towel from the rack and wrap it around her, drying her off from her shoulders, down to her feet. I drag the towel up her legs and around her ass before dropping the towel because I'm staring at her pussy straight on and it's so fucking pretty. Water clings to her and the bit of hair she has, and before I can stop myself, I've dragged my tongue along the seam to collect the droplets. I don't penetrate her with my tongue but it's enough for her to cry out my name and press her hand to the back of my head. Her legs shake and I grip her ass with both hands to keep her against my face as I run my nose along her pussy, inhaling her scent.

She smells like the bubble bath and soap but I detect that earthy womanly scent lurking beneath it.

"I...I can't keep myself upright while you eat me out, Theo. I... already feel like my legs are about to give out." Her fingers scratch my scalp gently and the feeling of her nails makes my dick even harder.

I stand up and have her in my arms all within a moment as I move quickly through the suite and drop her on the bed before slamming the bedroom door shut behind me with more force than I intended. I slide off my shirt, rip off my belt, and send my pants down my legs leaving me in nothing but my briefs. I opt to leave them on because I'm already leaking precum and there's a naked woman in front of me that I'm not sure I should fuck.

She gets on her knees and begins to crawl to the end of the bed towards me and I take a step back, shaking my head when she reaches for the waistband of my briefs.

"I love your body," she sighs as she drags her gaze all over me lasciviously.

"If you like it now, you should have seen it when I was in the league."

She drags her index finger sexily across her lip. "I wasn't legal when you were in the league."

"You know what I fucking mean, Avery."

"Sure, I should have made a move when I was younger to see the NFL body."

"Don't," I growl. "Lay back."

"Take them off," she responds, not listening to my order.

"No."

"Yes," she sasses, and *fuck* if that doesn't make me harder.

"Don't get smart with me." I narrow my gaze at her.

She huffs in response. "Theo, putting your tongue in my pussy is just as bad as putting your dick in it. Are you really kidding yourself? I don't want this to be just a one-time thing but I'm fully aware that we can't go parading this around all over town. I'm also not going to tell Lucas." She gets up on her knees and drags a finger down her body slowly. "But I do know, that the second I come on your tongue, you're going to want to fuck me. So why are we pretending that I'm not going to get what I want tonight?" She cocks her head to the side. "When it's also what *you* want?" I take a step closer to the bed and she moves closer. "I'm pretty good at sex, Theo." She giggles and *Christ, I want to know why and how and what makes her confident enough to say that.*

"I...I need to go downstairs and get condoms," I tell her and it'll give me a chance to clear my head. *I can't think clearly in this room with her naked body and her scent fucking everywhere.*

She shakes her head vehemently. "You'll change your mind

forty different times between here and the shop downstairs if it's even open this late. I'm on the pill and you can pull out." She shrugs before shooting me a devilish grin. "Or don't." She reaches her hand out and pulls me closer by the band of my underwear and her fingertips graze my dick in the process. "Take them off or do you want me to do it for you?"

This is so fucking wrong. This is Avery. Fuck. Fuck. Fuck.

"Hey, stop freaking out." She's right in front of me now, her hand on my cheek as her eyes scan my face. "It's okay."

"It's not..." I grit out. "But I can't fucking stop it." I press my lips to her palm and gently move her hair out of her face. "I've thought about this moment and you and what it would be like so many times in the last three years that nothing else works to get me off anymore."

She gasps and her mouth falls open. "You think about me when you touch yourself?"

"Exclusively."

"Same," she whispers. "For longer than three years though." I groan, not wanting to think about her touching herself before we'd crossed this line, but a flare of heat moves through me anyway. "Will you show me?" She looks down at my covered dick back to my eyes. "How you touch yourself? So, I know what you like?" Her hazel eyes are filled with lust and I take a step back to lower my briefs.

I tried. *Sort of.*

Tried not to put us in this situation where we'll be forced to lie to everyone in our lives and keep a secret from someone who means the world to me, but I've gone too far. Gone too far past flirting and kissing and rubbing my cock against her with our clothes on. Now I've seen her naked and touched her cunt and I can't turn away from her. Now that I've seen her and touched her and licked her.

I was trying to be a good man, but I'm not a saint.

Her eyes drop to my dick instantly which is standing straight up with a pearl of precum pooling at the tip. She licks her lips and the rest of my resolve fucking snaps.

Chapter

FIVE

Avery

I SEE THE MOMENT HE DECIDES TO SAY *FUCK IT* BECAUSE HE'S on the bed and on top of me in a fucking instant. His lips are on mine and it hits me that this is the first time he's kissed me since we've been in the room and I relish in his lips moving with mine. They're soft and taste faintly of mint, like he brushed his teeth before he picked me up and then his tongue touches mine before exploring my mouth. *I fucking love the way this man kisses.*

He kisses the way I do, like I want to be fucking consumed by the other person. I want to crawl inside Theo Graham's skin and live there. I want to be that close to him and the way he's kissing me makes me think he wouldn't be opposed. And now his dick has dragged against my thigh and is currently rubbing against my sex without pushing inside.

Fuck, this is so hot.

His lips leave mine to find my neck and trail kisses down my body. His dick moves away from the space between my legs as he moves and I whimper at the loss of contact. One hand finds my breast while he pulls away and looks down at the other. His hooded eyes flit up to mine just as he traces the nipple with his tongue. "Oh my God," I moan, my thighs rubbing together as I try to create some friction between them as he flicks my nipple with his tongue before sucking my breast into his mouth. My hands find his silky hair, pulling and simultaneously pushing him harder against me. I wrap my legs around him, locking my ankles behind his back and pressing my cunt into his chest as he continues to swirl his tongue around my nipple. My pussy is wet and tingling and I know the second he even breathes near my clit, I'm going to shatter.

"Theo, please," I moan.

"Please what, beautiful?" He asks as he pulls off of one breast in favor of the other. He switches hands to palm the other breast, rolling my wet nipple between his fingers, squeezing gently and the feeling mixed with him calling me beautiful pushes me closer to the edge. He drags his teeth along the skin before he bites down gently, nibbling on the sensitive flesh.

"God, please fuck me."

"I'm going to. Believe me." His words come out shaky and I wonder if he's nearing his breaking point too. "How do you want me to fuck you?"

"I don't care, just put it in, Theo," I beg. "However you want." My eyes are squeezed shut, my toes are curled tight and I'm clutching the sheets tighter with each kiss down my abdomen. *I am so desperate to fucking come I think I might die.*

"One taste first, I'll be quick," he grunts.

"I'm going to come if you do that," I whimper, not that I hate the thought, but I want him to know it's going to be quick because I am wound the fuck up.

"Oh, please fucking do," he grits out. "This"—he tugs on the hair of my narrow landing strip—"is fucking sexy. Do you always have this?"

"I—I used to be bare," I manage to stammer out.

"Leave it. I was ready to come the second you took off your panties."

"Yes, whatever you want!" I agree, knowing that I'll do anything he says in this moment to keep his hands on me.

"Good girl," he says and goosebumps erupt on my flesh. He spreads the lips of my sex and blows gently on my clit. I clench, and let out a moan. I hear a sharp intake of breath and manage to drop my eyes to look at him just as he drags his tongue through my slit.

"Oh my Godddddd." I moan as his tongue swirls around my

clit before he begins to take long slow strokes up and down my cunt. The sounds that his mouth and my pussy are making are obscene and make me even wetter. "Fuck, Theo. I'm close. Fuck me...with your dick, *please.*"

"Let me taste your orgasm first and then I'll put my dick right here, how does that sound?"

"Yes yes yes." I cry out, because *Christ,* he knows what he's doing. This isn't the first time there's been a mouth between my legs but this is definitely the best it's ever felt. His tongue penetrates my opening and I clench around it before it slides back out and drags upwards towards my clit again. He's pushing harder against me, allowing the bristles of his beard to press against my sex and even pierce my clit which feels different and foreign but sexy as hell. "Oh God, Theo. I'm going to come." My eyes flutter shut as the sensations leading up to what I believe will be a very intense orgasm take over.

"Thank fuck," he says just before he suctions his lips around my clit and I fucking *lose it.* He's holding my thighs down, so I'm unable to close them around his head and it feels so wanton being completely open and exposed to him as my climax washes over me.

"Fuck fuck fuck, Theo. Right there. Oh my God." I cry out as I roll my hips against his mouth and he continues to fuck me with it through my climax. "Ah!" I squeal, and I try to move away from his mouth. "Theo." I grip his hair, pulling him away from my quivering flesh. He growls against me and when his eyes meet mine, they're narrowed into slits. "Don't look at me like that."

"I wasn't done," he bites my thigh gently and I gasp.

"I want to fuck," I tell him before biting down on my bottom lip and I see his nostrils flare sexily. "You said after you tasted me." I reach for him. "Please, I know you're hard."

He moves up my body to hover on top of me and when I look down between us, I see his dick engorged and leaking precum onto my stomach. It's bigger than any I've been with, which is to be expected of someone Theo's size but I'm equal parts excited and nervous about having something that huge inside of me.

"You okay?" he asks, I assume sensing my apprehension.

"I know it'll fit but…" I whisper, before meeting his gaze, "it's so big."

"Yeah baby, it'll fit." He looks down between us and then back up at me. "Are you sure you want to do this? It's not too late to change your mind."

I grab his face, making our eyes lock. "I want it. I want you."

He nods before he drops his face into my neck. "Guide me into you."

I reach for his dick and squeeze gently causing him to hiss in my ear as I drag him through my seam. I slide him back and forth a few times, dragging the tip over my clit and he lets out a sound that sounds like a cross between a chuckle and a groan. "Oh my God, Avery. I'm going to explode, baby."

"Mmmm," I moan, both at the feeling and his pet name that causes a flutter in my stomach. "I like the sound of that." He presses his lips to my temple and then drags it down my face.

"Let me in. Let me in your pretty cunt, right now." I pull him closer and he slides in easily because of how wet I am, even with his size. "*Fuuuuuuck* you're tight." He bites down on my shoulder as he begins to move in and out of me slowly at first. His lips find mine as he grabs my hands and slowly brings them over my head, lacing them as he continues to fuck me and it's even better than I imagined this would be.

"God, Theo. Oh my God, it's so good." I cry out when he pulls away from my mouth in favor of dragging his tongue along my neck and sucking at the skin. A thought briefly floats through my head about having to explain a hickey but Theo spins his hips in a circle and thrusts in deeper, tapping my g-spot and my mind goes blank.

"Avery, fuck me, your pussy feels amazing. I could live inside you."

He lets my hands go and they immediately go to the space behind his neck as I look into his dark eyes. I arch my back and then he's out of me and I whine at the loss of contact. I watch as he gets on his knees and pushes both of my legs back towards my ears. I grab my ankles as he slips two of his fingers in his mouth before dragging them through my slit, rubbing the flesh back and forth and sliding them inside of me, curling them upwards, causing my eyes to roll back and a very loud scream to leave my lips.

"FUCK," I groan.

"You like that?" He growls as he fucks me with his fingers before he slides them out and drops three slaps in rapid succession on my pussy.

"Oh my God! I'm going to come. Put your dick back inside me."

"I stopped because you felt too good. I was going to come and I wanted to prolong it." He lays another slap on my pussy, making my clit throb. "I should put you over my knee for having a body that looks and feels that good." He pauses. "Don't fuck anyone else, Avery," he says through gritted teeth.

"I won't." I cry. "I won't. I don't want to!"

"Good." He grunts. "This pussy is fucking mine now." He slaps it again and I can feel the orgasm starting to form in my toes.

"Yes!" I cry out as he slides his dick inside of me and begins to fuck me mercilessly.

"You're so fucking sexy," he says as he moves my legs to rest over his shoulders. I look down at where we're connected and it's slick from our arousal. He continues to pound into me as he presses his lips to my ankle, dragging his tongue along the skin. "I want you so much, baby."

"Mmmm." I moan. "I'm going to come again."

"Oh yeah? Let me feel you come around my dick. Fucking squeeze me, baby. Milk the cum out of me," he says and my mouth drops open at hearing the polite and kind man I've known for almost nine years saying the dirtiest things to me.

"Oh my God, Theo. Yes!" I cry out as his hand drops to my nipple and tweaks it just as he spins his hips in a circle and his pubic hair drags along my clit. "Fuck!" I cry out as my orgasm washes over me and forces my eyes shut. He doesn't stop thrusting, continuing to fuck me through the most intense orgasm I've ever had as he chases his own. "Fuck, it's too much, Theo."

"You can take it, baby. Take me. You're doing so well."

"Oh God." I cry out and I draw a hand to my mouth and bite down on a finger.

"Tell me how it feels," he says as his thrusts begin to get even more erratic.

"So good." I moan just as he pulls out again and drags his dick through my slit, to rub against my clit. "You're a God, Theo. How do you have more stamina than I do?" I sigh because I know once I have this third orgasm I'm about to have, I'm going to be spent.

He chuckles, "You don't get a woman like you in bed and not give it your fucking all." He grins and my clit pulses at the thought that he just wants to make me feel good.

"Let me be on top," I tell him because I am ready to take control of this ride and make him come. He rolls to his back and I climb on top of him sliding down slowly and when I'm sitting directly on him with his cock buried deep inside of me, he grips my hips.

"When I tell you I'm about to come, you need to get off," he says but the way his eyes slide down my body and his hands tighten around my hips, I'm thinking he definitely does not want to pull out.

I lean down and drag my lips down his chin slowly while I squeeze his dick with my cunt. "I didn't agree to that."

"Avery."

"Yes?" I say as I begin to move up and down on him and I watch as his eyes flutter closed before shooting open.

"Fuck, I shouldn't have let you on top." His tongue darts out to lick his lips as he watches my tits bounce with every thrust and I drag my fingertips up his torso and his six-pack.

The thought that he might come inside me sends a jolt of electricity to my clit and his words push me faster towards *another* orgasm. I lean down and drag my lips over his jaw and then meet his mouth, sliding my tongue between his lips. He groans and his hands grip me harder as he helps me up and down faster with each thrust. His hands wrap around my back as he holds me in place and begins to thrust upward into my wanting pussy.

"Theo, I think I'm going to come again." I drop my face into his neck. "Just like that." I moan into his ear. "Oh my God, you fuck me better than anyone ever has."

"Yeah?" he growls into my ear. "Your pussy is fucking soaking me, baby. It's so tight and hot. How am I supposed to fucking focus on anything ever again other than when's the next time I can fuck you?"

"Whenever you want," I tell him. Half because it's true, half because I'm about to come all over his dick a second time. "Oh fuck, I'm going to come again!" I cry out.

"If you come while I'm inside of you, it's going to set me off. Avery…fuck…I don't want to come inside of you." His voice is low and husky and sets my skin on fire.

"Oh God! Right there, yes!" I cry out as I begin humping him through my climax, slamming down on him harder than I'd done a few moments ago and my orgasm shoots through me like a lightning bolt. I squeeze my eyes shut as I press my forehead to his shoulder.

God, nothing has ever fucking felt like this.

"You're so fucking sexy when you come, Avery. God damn," he whispers in my ear. "So so sexy." I drag my hands up to rest on his cheeks and press my lips to his again and I slide my tongue into his mouth. I don't know how long we stay like this. Our lips pressed against each other as our tongues move at the same pace as his dick inside of me, but at some point, I pull away because I think he's holding back so he won't come. "Please, I want it. *Need* it. Need to know how you feel when you lose it. Show me. Show me and then I'll lick your dick clean." I tell him as I keep riding him.

"Oh fuuuuuuck," he groans as I feel him unleash his load inside of me. "Fuck Avery, fuck fuck fuck!"

"Yesssss," I purr in his ear as his strokes start to slow. I drag my tongue along his ear, down his neck, and back into his mouth.

His dick is still pulsing inside of me and I love the sexy feeling of it as I drop kisses along his shoulder and chest and everywhere I can reach. His eyes eventually open and he rubs his hands up and down my arms and lets out a low grumble that vibrates through my entire body. "You are…" He lets out a breath. "Wow." I move off of him but I don't miss that he reaches for me to bring me closer to him. I look up to find him looking down at me with a concerned expression. "Was all of that okay?"

"Okay? I had three orgasms. Yeah…it was okay." I laugh as I press a kiss to his chest. I sit up and dart my eyes down to his dick, seeing it softer but covered in my arousal. I lick my lips and I hear him instantly.

"No, Avery. Give me a second."

"But…"

"There will be plenty of times for you to suck me off, but let me recover from that."

My eyes immediately meet his. "Plenty of times?"

He's still on his back as he sighs. "I already know I want more."

I'm warm everywhere instantly at the thought of that. "Me too."

He smiles at me and pulls me into his arms, weaving a hand into my hair. "You're so beautiful. I don't know when you became this woman I can't stop looking at but God damn, Avery." His lips find mine and we kiss for a few moments before the sounds of vibrations stop me.

"Someone's phone is ringing," I say and then realize my phone is still in the other room on the table so it must be Theo's. "Who would be calling you at three in the morning?" I say as I turn my gaze to look at the clock on the nightstand. He's up and around the bed, grabbing his pants from the floor, and pulling out his phone.

He sighs. "It's Lucas."

"Don't answer it!" I've never known Theo to stay out all night, especially with having teenagers that were very prone to throwing parties. He didn't trust any of us.

"It might be important."

"He's probably calling you because he got home and you're not there. Hello?" I exclaim.

"Then he's probably worried."

"You didn't leave a note?"

"I—I wasn't thinking clearly. I…I don't know!" He says, clearly exasperated over the fact that he has to take this phone call moments after he was inside of me.

I shake my head at him. "You're going to get us caught! I have to teach you how to cover your tracks better. Well, answer it before he reports you missing." I roll my eyes and get off the bed to get some water. He smacks my ass as I walk by him.

"Smart ass."

Chapter
SIX

THEO

"HEY SON, YOU ALRIGHT?" I ASK AS I WATCH HIS BEST friend's naked ass walk into the living room. *God, I'm going to hell.*

"Daaaaaaaaad," he slurs. "Where the hell are youuuu? I've called you like four times. I even called Raegan, who also did *not* answer! What is wrong with this family? I'm drunk and I'm the one worried about you all. Where are you?"

"I'm out, Son. What's up?"

"Out!? At three in the morning? Oh…*ohhhhhh*. Dad! You got a girlfriend? Shit, am I cramping your style by being here so you felt you couldn't have a sleepover? My bad. I can go stay with one of my buddies. But Dad, I'm twenty-one, I don't care if you want to have your girlfriend over." He laughs.

"No, Lucas, of course not."

"Of course not, to which? Do you have a girlfriend? You should have a girlfriend, Dad. I don't want you to be lonely, especially with me being in New York and Raegan moving in with her old ass boyfriend."

"He's my age, Lucas," I snap.

I'm not thrilled about how much older he is than Raegan but can we reign in the cracks on his age?

"Whatttttteevvvverrrrr. So, you not coming home?"

"I'll be home in the morning."

"Okay, wrap it up! I don't want a little sibling."

Avery appears with two bottles of water in one hand and her phone in the other and my eyes go to her stomach on instinct and I have to fight the intrusive thoughts of her round with my child. *Fuck.*

She gives me a thumbs up in question and I nod. "Right. I'll see you tomorrow."

"Later," he says without another word before hanging up.

"Well, he's drunk."

"After a night on Pratt Street, no. You think?" She laughs as she holds out a bottle for me before climbing back on the bed and just the visual of her on it makes me want to fuck her again.

"I am going to look like shit in the morning, I don't have any of my skincare stuff." She runs a hand over her face. "Please remember me like this," she says waving a hand across her face, "and not the troll I will look like in the morning for not taking my makeup off?"

"Oh," I say as I reach into the bag I brought from home. "I brought some things from Raegan's bathroom that she left there. I don't know that you use the same products, but I know there's at least makeup wipes and some face wash and lotion in there and I brought an extra toothbrush for you."

She looks at the bag in my hands and then up at me before getting off the bed, still naked and glistening with sweat and maybe a bit of my cum. She looks down at it again but still doesn't say anything, she just blinks up at me curiously, so I continue. "I knew I was picking you up and you obviously wouldn't have anything. I brought you some of her clothes too, in case you didn't want to go home in your dress. Something nondescript so it wouldn't be too obvious whose it was."

"Theo...wow, that was so nice." She presses her hand to my chest and reaches up on her tiptoes to reach my lips but she's still a little short so I lean down to meet her. "Thank you, this is perfect." She takes the bag from my hands but I don't let go.

"For the record, you could never look like a troll. You always look beautiful." I tell her because I have seen her hungover, having forgotten to take her makeup off, and a few nights she probably spent with her head in the toilet, but she's always been a beautiful girl. In the last few years, she's gone from beautiful to gorgeous and stunning, and leaving mascara on for one night won't change that. She gives me a shy smile before retreating to the bathroom.

After about ten minutes, we are both back in bed, her head resting on my chest and her leg threaded through mine. Part of me wants her again, to fuck her in this bed because who knows when we'll have another chance. *Especially not this week with Lucas home.*

"So, we probably can't see each other this week?" she asks.

"I'm sure we'll see each other."

"You know what I mean."

"I don't know. Probably not."

"When he goes back to New York?"

"It'll be easier for sure, though, you think you can get away with sneaking over to my house without your parents seeing you?"

She looks up at me. "Maybe I need my own place." She laughs and I smile back at her.

"Would certainly make it easier."

What am I doing? This is exactly what I was trying to avoid. Getting so wrapped up in this that it's becoming more of a priority than how Lucas will feel about it. I should tell her that we can't do this again. I'm staring at the ceiling, my mind and heart racing at the thought that I'm in the beginning stages of fucking up my entire relationship with my son when Avery's breasts come into view and I realize she's on top of me.

"I can hear you thinking. Relax. Everything's fine. No one is going to find out."

Maybe she's right. There may be some feelings on both sides, but we both know it can't go further than a physical relationship. So, it's just sex. Great sex with a woman I've known since she was thirteen who is now twenty-one and fucking sexy as hell and takes my dick better than anyone ever has. Lucas won't find out and one day we won't be doing this and we will have gotten away with it and everything will be fine.

"Do you want to have sex again?" Her words cut through my

thoughts and when my dick hardens beneath her, she giggles. "I'll take that as a yes."

"Fuck yes."

⁓

I'm woken up the next morning by Avery on the phone. "Dad, I'm fine. I stayed at a friend's house." She sighs and when I turn over, I see her lying on her back with her hand over her eyes. "I talked to Mom last night. She was very drunk though but I told her I was staying out. No, I probably won't be home for brunch. Oh no, I don't care, you guys have fun. Yes, I know, dinner tonight. Okay, I'll ask him if he wants to come. Mmmmhm, okay. Bye, Dad." She puts her phone on the nightstand and turns towards me, her eyes lighting up when she sees I'm awake. "Hey," she says with a sleepy smile.

"Good morning."

"Sorry, did I wake you?"

"It's okay, I'm usually up around now anyway." I look at the clock behind her that reads just after eight.

"Yeah, but we went to bed two hours ago." She chuckles as I pull her against me and drop my lips to her forehead and then her nose and then her lush mouth. She whimpers against my mouth and my cock twitches in response.

"Was your dad upset?" I ask, trying to make sure everything is fine before I try to fuck her again.

"No, I guess Mom passed out last night before she could tell him that I was staying out and he panicked when I wasn't home."

"Should we head back?"

"Yeah, because you can drive me." She snorts. "I'll take an Uber, and you should wait an hour or so before leaving."

"An Uber? Avery…" I groan because what kind of gentleman spends a night with a woman and then sends her home in an Uber. *The kind that shouldn't have spent the night with said woman in the first place!*

"What other choice do we have? I could call Rory to pick

me up but that would incite a thousand questions and you said I couldn't tell anyone."

It might be nice to have someone who knows in case we ever need an alibi but...Rory? "Can you trust Rory?"

"Not to blab to Lucas? I don't know. She's a chatty drunk. That's why I haven't told her anything about you."

"Nothing?"

She shakes her head. "She's loyal to me but she loves Lucas too and she might feel caught in the middle and if they're ever together without me and drinking and...I don't know. She went to school in Connecticut so she went to New York a lot to party so they hung out even more without me. I was worried she might slip up one night."

"That's fair, and I suppose you Ubering is the only way this works."

She nods and looks up at me. "I had fun. Thank you for my graduation present."

"This was *not* your graduation present," I correct her.

"Says you. This was the best thing I could have gotten. Multiple orgasms from the man I've been obsessed with for years? I can promise you a lot of girls would trade most of their graduation presents for that."

"All that being said, there's a check in the envelope I gave you." I roll my eyes. "So, don't lose it."

"I don't know if I feel comfortable taking a check now. Feels a little...transactional." She taps her chin as her lips form a straight line.

I scoff and rub my forehead. "For the love of God, Avery, it's not payment for the sex it's a gift because you graduated college."

"Still. We've had sex now."

"Yes, we have and we are going to have sex again. You're still keeping the check."

"Fine." She smiles before climbing on top of me. "You're fun to rile up."

"Can you not?"

"No." She smiles and leans down to brush her lips against mine. "Because you like it."

⁓

Avery's been gone for about an hour and I'm packing up to leave when I get a text from her.

> **Avery: I'm home and showered without a ton of questions from anyone so all good. I'm going to take a nap. I'll probably see you later?**
>
> **Me: Good and I'm sure. Looking forward to it.**
>
> **Avery: *heart eye emoji***

After checking out, I call Lucas wondering if he's hungry and wants to go get breakfast. Breakfast is our favorite meal of the day—Raegan's too—and there were so many Sundays that we went out for it. *Many times, with Avery in tow.* She's an only child and in the beginning, I think she was lonely so she was always around, and then when Lucas started developing feelings for her, he dragged her with him everywhere he went.

"What?" he groans through the phone and I chuckle because when Lucas is hungover, he is fucking useless.

"How you feeling, champ?"

"Like shit. We did way too many shots. Why are you calling me?"

This little fucker. "Want to run that by me again?"

"I mean why don't you just come in my room?" He explains.

"I'm not home yet," I tell him and I wonder if he even remembers our conversation.

"Oh, where are you?" he asks with a yawn. "I vaguely remember this. You have a girlfriend?"

"I don't have a girlfriend."

"You only answered one of my questions."

"Because it is the only one I'm answering. I was out, that's all you need to know. Do I call you in New York asking where you are?"

"Scuse me."

"So, I assume you're too hungover to get food?"

"Hmmmm." He groans. "Maybe when you get here, I'll feel differently. We don't have *Hazy Mornings* in New York and I could go for some bacon and a bloody Mary."

"Aren't you hungover?"

"Aren't you familiar with hair of the dog?"

"Okay." I chuckle.

"I'm going to call Ave to see if she wants to come."

The words that she's taking a nap are almost out of my mouth before I stop them. *Fuck, I am not good at this and it's going to get us caught if I'm not careful.* "Sure. I'm going to call your sister. Did she even show up last night?"

"No, she ended up texting Avery that she wasn't feeling well. She thinks she has the flu."

"Oh, I'll call her. See you in a bit."

Raegan doesn't answer when I call her and I narrow my eyes at my phone. *Sick or not, she better get back to me in a timely manner or I'm showing up at her house.*

Twenty minutes later, I'm pulling into my driveway and my eyes immediately flit to the house next door with the delusional hope that I'll see Avery even though I know she's asleep in her bedroom.

When I make my way into the house, I hear movement in the kitchen and the smell of coffee wafts around me. I walk into the kitchen and see Lucas scrolling through his phone in nothing but his boxers. "There he is," he says when he sees me. "And you have an overnight bag? So, it was a premeditated sleepover." He lowers his gaze to the bag slung over my shoulder. "So, is my new stepmom coming to brunch?"

Panic courses through me at his words thinking about being with Avery in a way that would technically make her Lucas' stepmom. *If he didn't kill me for sleeping with her, that thought might send him over the edge.*

I cock my head to the side. "Lucas, it's not like that."

"Not like what? I've never known you to just go sluttin' around." He chuckles. "Even when you were in the league."

"I'm not *sluttin' around*," I glower at him. "And you've been gone on and off for four years. Did you think I was just sitting in the house twiddling my thumbs?" I tell him because if I don't give him something, he won't let this go. "I am a long way off from making anyone your stepmother, so let it go. When there's something for you to know, you'll know it."

I don't wait for his response before making my way through the foyer and up the stairs to my bedroom. I drop my bag in my massive walk-in closet that my clothes don't even account for half of before making my way towards my bed. I drop to it, realizing how tired I am before turning to my side and imagining Avery next to me. I wouldn't be surprised if she was in this very bed with me next week and the thought sends a jolt to my dick. I don't know how long I'm lying there, but I must have drifted off to sleep because when my phone vibrates, I feel slightly groggy and it hits me how little sleep I've gotten in the past thirty-six hours. I open my phone and smile at the name on my screen.

Avery: What's this I hear about you having a girlfriend? Should I be concerned?

I glare at my door, towards my son who evidently can't keep anything to himself.

Me: No.

Avery: Okay, grumpy. Maybe you need a nap too.

Me: What did he say?

Avery: That you didn't come home and he's happy that you met someone. But you're being secretive as hell about it.

Me: Well, I can't exactly tell him that I was out all night fucking you senseless in a hotel room now, can I?

Avery: Don't get smart with me

I can't stop the smile from finding my face.

Me: I think that's my line.

Avery: Are you flirting with me, Mr. Graham?

She hasn't called me that in years, and seeing her call me that now has me thickening in my shorts.

Me: Yes.

A FaceTime request comes through instantly and my eyes widen. My house isn't small by any means, and Lucas' room is at the end of the hall, but I'm not about to accept a FaceTime call from Avery while he's in the house.

But you could lower the volume.

I'm off my bed and moving into my bathroom, grabbing my AirPods out of my pocket before turning on the fan and closing the door behind me.

"Yes?" I ask her before putting one in my ear. "You think this is a good idea? What if I was with Lucas?"

She purses her lips into a frown. "First of all, Lucas went for a run," she puts her index finger up followed by her middle finger. "Secondly, change my name in your phone, Theo."

I hate that I hadn't thought of that on my own. "Fine." I look at the corner of the screen for the first time, realizing I was asleep for about thirty minutes. "What are you doing?" I ask her, noticing she's still lying in her bed. She props her pillow under her chin and gives me a smile. Her hair is pulled back, giving me a look at her gorgeous makeup-free face.

"Nothing. Just wanted to make sure you weren't freaking out." She props her phone up on her nightstand and pulls her shirt off over her head revealing her naked tits and I wish I could climb through the phone and suck her nipples. "Do you want to come over?" She winks and I sink my teeth into my bottom lip to prevent myself from telling her I'll be right there.

"You and I both know I can't." *Why the fuck is she my neighbor?*

"My parents aren't home." She teases. "And won't be home for a while." She licks her lips and runs her hands over her breasts, tweaking her nipples.

I grit my teeth. *I can't believe I'm sleeping with someone who can actually use that as a way to entice me to see her.* "Avery."

"I'm kidding." She teases as she lets go of her nipples. "Well, they're really not home, but I know you can't come over right now. Lucas mentioned something about brunch." She's lying back down, her naked tits covered, but I know they're there. Naked. *God, let me see them again.* "I told him I'd think about it. But…can you handle that?"

"Me?"

"Yes, can you handle being so close to me after last night?"

"Can you?"

"Of course," she answers. "I've hidden my feelings for you for years."

"This is different."

"True, but I'll be fine. I wanted to make sure it was okay with you before I said yes. He's already coming to dinner with my family tonight so I don't really *need* to go to brunch with you guys."

I can't stop the curious look that finds my face and I briefly remember her talking to her father this morning and her saying *"I'll ask him."* Lucas going to dinner with her family or Avery coming to dinner with us is not anything new, but it's the first time I feel a spike of jealousy at the ease with which Lucas fits into her life.

"You know you're welcome to come," she tells me, probably reading my face.

I shake my head. "No. And of course, come to brunch. It'll be fine."

⸺⸺

It was absolutely not fucking fine.

Avery is wearing a very short and flowy sundress that highlights her tits and her waist and her toned legs that even while in flat sandals has me picturing them wrapped around my waist. Her dark hair, held back by a pair of sunglasses falls around her in waves that make her look like she's just been fucked, causing very vivid memories of last night to start playing through my mind on a loop. She's sitting in the back behind Lucas because of course I'm fucking driving all of us because I'm a masochist and I can't avoid being around her even when I should. Her perfume is overwhelming my senses, transporting me back to last night when she was writhing beneath me and begging me to touch her, kiss her, fuck her. I roll my window down, desperate for a break from the pheromones that are currently playing with my dick.

"Thanks for letting me tag along," she says leaning forward between us. "Where's Rae?" She asks, as there is usually a fourth person in tow whenever we go out for brunch.

"She's not feeling well," I tell her. I finally got her on the phone where she told me she really does believe she has the flu. Despite my discomfort over her boyfriend's age, I know he cares about her, so I'm sure he's taking care of her, but a part of me still wants to go over there and make sure she's fine.

"She said she hasn't been able to keep anything down. Hopefully she's not pregnant," Lucas jokes and I jerk my head to look at him.

"What!?"

"I mean… isn't that like sex 101? Girl feels like shit in the morning because she's knocked up?"

"No more talking," I say, holding up a finger towards Lucas.

"I mean it's not like she's a teenager. She's twenty-three, if she were pregnant, would it be the end of the world?" Avery leans forward between our seats and looks up at me.

"No more talking for you either," I tell her and she rolls her eyes before sitting back in her seat. I rub my forehead trying to will the headache away that just that one sentence caused.

No one says anything for a minute, and I wonder if they're heeding my warnings or if they really just don't want to poke the bear. "It wouldn't be the worst thing," I say. "It would just catch me off guard and she hasn't been with this guy all that long. I hardly know him and…" I trail off because I don't know what to say. In the last few years, as he's grown into adulthood, Lucas has become the one person I trusted more than anyone in the world, so I know he knows what I'm saying. But, Avery being in the backseat has my thoughts jumbled and confused and I worry I'm coming off like an asshole.

"I get it, Dad," Lucas says.

"Yeah, same," Avery chirps from the back and when I turn my head over my shoulder, she gives me a small smile.

⁓

We've been seated at a table for twenty minutes, long enough for Lucas and Avery to order Bloody Marys and for me to order a coffee while we engage in mindless small talk as we decide what to eat. After deciding—and it's no shock to anyone that Lucas is getting the chicken and waffles—he excuses himself to go to the bathroom leaving me alone with Avery and the overwhelming need to lower the tiny straps off her shoulders to reveal her perky breasts.

On instinct, my eyes immediately drop to her chest, ogling all of the flesh on display that I'd been trying to avoid while in my son's company. I'm seated directly across from her, while Lucas sat to her right, so I have the perfect view of her.

"Are you looking at my tits?" She asks with a cheeky smirk. Her eyes float to where Lucas disappeared before darting her eyes back to mine.

"Yes," I tell her as I hold the coffee cup over my mouth and take a healthy sip. "Did you wear that dress just to torment me?"

"No." She shakes her head as she swirls her straw around her drink before pulling it to her mouth. "But I thought you'd like it."

Watching those full lips wrapped around something has me picturing them wrapped around my dick and I clear my throat as I do my best to discreetly adjust myself. I lean back in my chair and stare her down as I run the tip of my index finger around the rim of my mug. "I do. I'd like it even better on the floor next to my bed."

Her mouth drops open and her eyes dance mischievously. "I don't want to wait a week to touch you again."

My nostrils flare, because *fuck I don't either,* but someone had to remain level-headed and sneaking around is one thing, but sneaking around while sharing a house with Lucas is crazy. My eyes dart toward the restroom before I can reply and I'm glad I did because Lucas is only a few yards from the table.

"Hey, what'd I miss?" Lucas asks as he drops to his seat.

I shake my head still trying to calm the erection that is rising at the thought of touching Avery. "Nothing." She shrugs and takes another long sip of her Bloody Mary before setting it back on the table.

"I can't believe you're going to live here," Lucas starts, "and not in New York." He leans back in his chair, his arm still firmly resting on the back of Avery's. "You sure there's nothing I can do to convince you to move to the city?"

"You would need to convince my mother to expand the franchise." She giggles.

"Fuck, I'm going to miss you."

"It's no different than us going to different colleges," Avery challenges with her eyebrows pulled together.

"That was different."

"How so?" She counters and my eyes float to his, wondering why he's choosing to have this conversation now and while I'm here.

He shrugs. "I don't know. This is real life now, and I always pictured us living in the same state. Meeting up for drinks after a long day of work. How we were in high school but…adults."

She gives him a smile that seems somewhat placating and I suddenly feel guilty and ashamed all over again because I can read between the lines. Is he thinking that living in the same city would allow her to develop feelings for him? Was he hoping to create a bunch of little platonic moments that could lead to something real and intimate?

"I'll visit," Avery says as she puts a hand over his. He looks down at her hand and gives her a curt nod and a smile. If I know my son as well as I think I do, it's one hundred percent fake.

Halfway through brunch, which includes two drinks and a shot of Jameson for both of them, I feel my phone vibrating in my pocket. Avery had gotten up to go to the bathroom and Lucas is scrolling mindlessly on his phone. When I open it, my eyes immediately look up and flit around the room, making sure that my son's attention is not on me. He's still looking down when I open the message from Avery. I hadn't changed her name yet because I didn't know what to change it to, so it's just her phone number which I worry is just as bad because I wouldn't be surprised if Lucas has it memorized. I hold my phone under the table, turning the brightness on my phone down as paranoia takes over, and open her text.

> **Unknown Number: So, I was thinking**
>
> **Me: About?**
>
> **Unknown Number: That I don't know what your dick tastes like**
>
> **Me: AVERY**
>
> **Unknown Number: What?**
>
> **Me: I'm not doing this with you here**
>
> **Unknown Number: Let's fix that next time. Preferably while I sit on your face.**

My eyes widen at her words and my dick jerks in my pants. I cough in an attempt to stifle a groan just as the girl responsible slides into the seat across from me like she hadn't just told me she wants to sixty-nine as if it were the most casual thing in the world.

A hint of a smile finds her face before she turns back to Lucas. "Do you want to take another shot before we go?"

"Obviously," Lucas says as he raises his hand towards the waitress.

"Haven't you guys had enough?" I ask them, the question I really want to be asking lurks beneath which is '*Avery, haven't you had enough if you're sexting me at a table with Lucas?*'

Lucas chuckles and shakes his head. "Dad, you can head back, we can Uber home in a bit."

"Yeah, Theo. Don't worry so much. Everything is *fine*." She blinks her eyes several times at me and gives me a smile. I can't tell if it's flirtier than usual and I don't know what the fuck I want to do in this moment: stay here and watch the two of them drink too much and risk her continuing to entice me with her sexy messages or leave. But leaving means I don't get to be around the woman who is slowly getting under my skin and I don't like that option either even if she is driving me crazy. I pull the glass of water to my lips and take a long sip, trying to temper the envy I feel over my son dismissing me so he can be alone with the girl that spent last night riding my dick.

This is Avery.

Your son's best friend.

You cannot be jealous.

You are not allowed to be jealous.

"Right, well I'll just get the check and be out of your way." I smile at both of them and see a flash of disappointment cross Avery's face. I hate how much that thought pleases me. *That she wants me to stay.*

"Are you sure?" She asks.

"He'll be fine. I'm sure he can go hang out with his new lady."

A wicked smirk crosses her face and I do my best to warn her with my eyes not to pull at this thread but she looks at Lucas before turning back to me. "That's right. Lucas seems to think you met someone?"

"I'm not talking about this with either of you," I grit out and Lucas chuckles.

"Testy." He shrugs.

I'm relieved neither of them push it and I'm even more relieved when my phone begins to ring but that relief is immediately replaced with annoyance when I see who it is.

My ex-wife and the very irritating mother of my children.

"Rebecca."

Lucas' eyes immediately flash to mine in panic before he looks down at his own phone, assumedly to see if she'd called him first before she tried me. He draws a line over his throat. *I'm not here,* he mouths and I nod, like I haven't done this dance with both of my children and their mother for the better part of a decade. It comes with being the favorite parent. *I love and hate that title.* Love that they know they can always come to me and that I'm always in their corner. But I hate that they don't feel those same feelings for the woman who brought them into the world. Raegan had come around a little more as she got older, but Lucas has been my shadow since birth. His relationship with his mother was more difficult to repair after she essentially abandoned them to travel around the world with the man she cheated on me with.

By no fault of my own, my children have always been aware of the circumstances around the demise of our marriage and definitely chose sides. *Not that Rebecca gave them much of a choice by choosing to dick ride that asshole that never paid any interest in her children.*

It shocks all three of us that they're still together all these years later but birds of a feather, so they say.

"Do you have any idea what your daughter has done?" She shrieks and I pull my ear away from the phone before turning the volume down.

I sigh and pinch the bridge of my nose. "What's wrong?" I'm calm because there's no way if Raegan was really in trouble, she'd call Rebecca before she called me. More than likely they're just in an argument and Rebecca is calling me to complain, which is odd behavior even for her because she knows I'd never take her side over my daughter's.

Lucas and Avery share a look before leaning forward in almost perfect sync like they can hear through the phone.

"SHE'S GETTING MARRIED! And I haven't even met this guy! You had ONE job, Theo. Talk her out of dating this old guy. YOU said we had to let her make her own decisions and now look at this mess."

"WHAT?" I snap into the phone because fuck the fact that she's getting married; I'll deal with my irritation over that in a second. *She told her mother before she told me? And this asshole didn't even ask me?* "How do you know? She told you that?" I ask.

"What what?" Lucas is mouthing out loud at me. "Told who what?" he whisper shouts.

"Hold on, Rebecca, Lucas will not shut up," I growl at him.

"Oh, let me talk to my baby!" She squeals and I should have known the mere mention of Lucas would turn her attitude around.

"You can talk to him in a second," I grit out, shooting Lucas a smug grin and he lets out a groan before scrubbing a hand over his face. "Did Raegan tell you this?" I ask her.

"No. Laura told me so you know there's got to be some truth to this." Laura is the mother of Natasha, Raegan's best friend, so unfortunately, I do believe this is probably accurate information. *Fuck.*

"So, they're engaged officially?" Lucas' mouth drops open and Avery's eyes widen, having put together what Rebecca just told me. Avery points to her left ring finger and I nod at her and shrug because I'm still a little unsure about the truth.

"Well, not officially, I guess. Laura said Natasha said there's a ring," Rebecca says and I let out a breath thinking about my sweet little girl with some guy twice her age that I barely know. "They've only been together six months. This is a mistake!" Rebecca wails. "You need to fix this, Theo."

"ME? I'm sorry, have you met your daughter? Headstrong as hell and stubborn?"

"She listens to you, Theo." She sighs. "Look I'm still in Italy, but I can come home if—"

"No, don't come home in a panic. It would just set everything off. Let me see what the hell is going on before you get all hysterical."

"Fine. Call me back," she says without another word and I roll my eyes at my ex-wife's inability to ever say goodbye before hanging up. *That shit used to piss me off.*

It still does.

I set the phone down and look at both of them. "So evidently, Natasha told Laura there's a ring."

"What the hell? They've been together for like five minutes. We've met him twice. How? We should go over there." Lucas points back and forth between us.

"Worst idea," Avery interjects and my eyes find hers. "You two going over there guns blazing over what very well may be a rumor is the worst idea! And it's going to make an already sensitive situation more precarious. She knows how you guys feel about Wes."

"We use his name?" Lucas blinks at her like she just used the name of his sworn enemy.

"Sure." She shrugs. "She posts him on Instagram with his name. I know you weren't raised in a barn; have some manners for your future brother-in-law." She gives him a smile, blinking her eyes several times.

I groan and point at Avery. "You are not helping."

"Wait for her to come to you." She looks at me with those bright hazel eyes that had me on my knees last night. "When has she not? Are you worried she's going to elope? She wouldn't do that."

"Wes," Lucas interrupts before I can respond, "should at very least come talk to Dad. Want to talk about not having manners?"

"And maybe he will! All the two gossiping Gabbys have come up with is that there's a ring. That can mean so many things."

I feel out of control at the moment. Last night. Being here with Avery. Talking to my ex-wife—which always makes me feel a little uneasy afterwards. And now my daughter potentially making the biggest mistake of her life. I flex my hands before balling them into fists while looking at Lucas.

"I'm going to head out. You good with getting home?" I say, not looking at Avery because I don't want her to think this is about her.

"Yeah of course, but you want us to come?"

"No, you guys stay." I sign the check and stand before either of them can protest.

"Dad, if you're going over there, I want to come."

"I'm not. I just…need some air," I say without another word.

SEVEN

Avery

M Y EYES FOLLOW THEO OUT OF THE RESTAURANT and I wish I was going with him. I wish I could hold his hand and tell him to breathe and that everything will be fine. I wish I could sit on his lap and kiss him and rub the stress off of him.

But if I'm being honest, I'm not sure if it will be or if I'm even the right person to help for that matter. I don't know if his agitation is about Raegan potentially being engaged to someone he barely knows or the fact that he's twice her age, thereby making his feelings a little more complicated and maybe even a touch hypocritical given that he spent last night sleeping with his son's best friend who happens to be half his age. It's probably a little of both which is likely why he wanted to get away from me.

"Damn," Lucas shakes his head. "You want to go sit at the bar?"

I nod, knowing that under any circumstance other than what happened last night, my only concern would be Lucas and talking it out with him with shots of tequila and fried foods. We find two empty bar stools and Lucas orders us two shots before I'm even in the seat.

"Remember we have dinner with my parents tonight."

"Right." He looks at his watch. "In six hours?"

"I'm just saying," I tell him, hearing his underlying meaning that we will definitely not be drunk by then.

I want to text Theo, but sitting directly next to Lucas is not the time to do it.

"I have to pee. I'll be right back," I tell him as I hop off the stool and make my way into the ladies' room. I push into a stall and have my phone to my ear before I've even locked it behind me.

"I assume you're by yourself."

"You assume correctly." I expect him to say something else and when he doesn't, I speak up. "Do you want to tell me what you're thinking?"

"Not really."

"Can you tell me where you're going?"

"Home."

"Okay."

I can hear the distance in his voice and I don't know what to say now that won't come off clingy so I decide just to end the conversation. "Alright, well…I'll see you."

"Wait," he says. I don't respond but I don't hang up either. "I want to see you tonight."

My stomach flips in response. *Okay, this is good.* "I know it's a stupid idea but…I just…I need you again."

I bite my bottom lip and I squeeze my thighs together because *SAME.* "Okay." I try my best not to let him know that I am squealing on the inside at this man wanting another night with me.

"I don't know how."

"I'll figure it out," I tell him because I know I have the most obstacles in this situation due to my plans to go out to dinner with my parents *and* Lucas. "But, I should go."

"Mmmhm. Don't drink too much."

"Okay, Daddy," I sass and I wonder how he'll take the nickname.

"Fuck," I hear him whisper into the phone. "Avery, you're going to fucking pay for that."

"Promise?"

"Talk soon." He grunts into the phone. "And be safe."

_____⟋∾⟍_____

"Fuck it, I'm calling her," Lucas says as we are walking out of the restaurant. It's an hour later, and we each had another shot and two more drinks, so while we aren't drunk, we are teetering on the edge and I do not think calling Raegan and exploding all over her is a good idea.

"No! Don't." I put my hand over his phone.

"How could she keep something like this from me? From me!?" He shakes his head. "It would be like *you* keeping something from me." Guilt gnaws in my gut at his words. "I'm always on her side about everything. Yeah, I give her a hard time about her new boyfriend but if she's marrying this guy, I need to know what the fuck is going on." He begins pacing and I realize he's definitely not calling our Uber, so I open my app up to request one. My fingers itch to text Theo in case he has to do damage control if Lucas drunkenly explodes all over her but I decide against it for now.

"Rae!" My eyes dart to his and I realize he's on speakerphone. *Relax!* I mouth at him.

"What?" She snaps, annoyed. I remember she's supposed to be sick but she doesn't sound all that sick?

"Ummm… how are you? I heard you weren't feeling well."

"Oh better. It might have just been a little bug."

"Oh good, you're not pregnant, are you?" He chuckles and I smack his arm and shake my head at him.

She snorts. "What do you want, asshole?"

"Oh, well…what else is new?"

"Nothing…?"

"You sure?"

"God, Luke, what are you getting at?"

"Okay, don't shoot the messenger, but Dad already knows and so does Mom, so I guess I'll just come out with it because they're both freaked the fuck out. Natasha's mom outed you about your boyfriend having a ring to propose. Is that true? Or has Laura been mixing Xanax with vodka again?"

"Oh my God, I'm going to kill Nat. Mom *and* Dad know?"

"Yeah, Mom called Dad in hysterics while we were at brunch."

"Thank God I bailed on *that*."

He narrows his eyes. "Are you even sick?"

"No."

"Why are you avoiding us?"

I cock my head to the side and look at the phone because I'm even interested in the answer to that question.

"I just have some stuff going on."

"What stuff? Why are you being so fucking secretive?"

"You aren't entitled to know every little thing about my life, Lucas."

"Well excuse the fuck out of me for caring about my big sister."

Calm down! I mouth at him and he shakes his head. "We're fucking worried about you. We don't know anything about this guy and—"

"Wes is amazing. He's not like holding me hostage if that's what you're thinking."

"I wasn't." He grunts. "There can be other ways that he's not good for you that don't fall under the umbrella of him breaking the goddamn law, Raegan."

"I just mean...he loves me."

"Of course, he does! You're a catch, but can't he find a girl his own age? And there's already a ring in the mix? What's the rush?"

I wince, thinking about what he'd say about his father and me, my relationship with him aside. *Would he say the same thing?*

"Lucas, this isn't your life. I get you have concerns, but this isn't your decision."

"So, this is it? You're just marrying this guy?"

"He hasn't asked! I should have known that Natasha couldn't keep this from Laura even after I begged her not to say anything. He knows he has to ask Dad."

"Is this what you want though?"

"Yes. Lucas, I love him. I know it's fast but...when you know, you just *know*. He's just so kind-hearted and amazing and loves the hell out of me. He's the most amazing guy I've ever met."

Lucas pinches the bridge of his nose and lets out an exasperated breath. "Yeah, because you're twenty-three and haven't met anyone yet!"

She huffs. "You're annoying me and I may be inclined to take this narrative from Dad, but you are not him so back off."

"Rae—"

"Bye, Lucas," she says before she hangs up.

"Well, that could have gone over better," Lucas grumbles.

"It could have been worse?" I offer. "And hey, at least we know now that he's going to ask your Dad for permission!" I say trying to diffuse his irritation.

"That's bullshit, he has a ring, and she knows about it. For all intents and purposes, they're engaged." He shrugs. "If my Dad says no, he's still going to ask her and she's still going to say yes."

"She may not."

"You heard her, she loves him. And my Dad can't deny Raegan anything. He's not going to refuse this guy the opportunity to ask her even if he wants to."

"I mean would it be the worst thing in the world for her to marry him? You guys don't even know him, but *she* does? What I do know is that the harder you push, the harder she's going to push back, and it's going to drive a wedge between you guys."

The ride home is quiet and I can tell Lucas is agitated, because he barely says anything to me. By the time we get back to our houses, I'm heading towards mine when he nods towards his house.

"You want to come in?"

"Do you want me to come in?" I pull my sunglasses from the top of my head and slide them in front of my eyes.

"Of course. I'm not mad at you, Avery."

"Well, it would be silly if you were." I cross my arms over my chest.

"For a long time, it was just me and Rae…when our parents were going through all that shit. We only had each other and no one else in the world gets it because we are the only products of two people that have spent half our lives arguing."

I wince because I do remember the beginning of their divorce when the three of them moved in next door and it was ugly. *Especially when Theo not only got custody of their children but refused to pay alimony. Plus, he had a prenuptial agreement. Needless to say, Rebecca was pissed.*

But her boyfriend at the time whom she was living with and *whom she did cheat on Theo with*, allegedly made a fuck ton of money, so I suppose I understood Theo's refusal to pay alimony when she was already getting a hefty settlement for bearing two of his children.

"I get it." I run a hand down his arm. "But I'm going to go to my house for a bit. Let you and your dad talk in private. I'll be over in a little?"

"You know you can hear anything we talk about. I trust you just as much as I trust my dad and Rae." He tucks a hair behind my ear and it's one of those gestures that sends off the alarm bells that maybe he does still have feelings for me. Like when he kisses my forehead when he's drunk or wraps his arms around me and drops his nose into my neck. Those gestures make me feel like he's inching us past the line of just friends towards something more. It makes me feel like shit.

He trusts me.

And I'm fucking his Dad.

I wince, not wanting to have this internal monologue right now. "I know, but I want to talk to my mom about dinner."

"Alright, well just come over when you're ready." He taps my nose and nods towards my house.

I roll my eyes at him wanting to make sure I get inside safely at three in the afternoon on a Saturday in the safest neighborhood in the most boring town in all of Pennsylvania. As soon as I'm through my front door, I immediately hear my parents on the back patio with my uncles and aunts, probably still celebrating from last night. My parents aren't big partiers, but when they do, they go big, and I suppose their only daughter graduating with honors from an

Ivy League college gave them carte blanche to go big all weekend. *I don't even blame them.*

I slip upstairs not wanting to engage with them and make it to my bedroom which is on the fourth floor. There is only my room and a bathroom up here but it means my room is massive and I can also see into the next backyard despite the fact that the house is several yards away.

I see Theo sitting on the patio sipping something out of a tumbler and I wonder how much time I have before Lucas makes his way out there. I grab my phone from my purse and send him a text.

Me: You look so lonely out there.

He pulls his phone from his pocket and looks at it.

TG: You here?

Me: In my bedroom.

He turns his head slightly towards my house, up to where he knows my room is, and nods before turning back to his phone.

TG: What are you doing?

Me: Wanted to give you and Lucas some time to rile each other up over Raegan without my interfering. I felt like you guys didn't want my opinion

TG: It's not that.

Me: He called Raegan.

TG: Shit, what did he say?

Me: Not the worst conversation but it ended with her hanging up on him. I'll let him give you the details.

I watch him drain the contents of his glass and his head falls back.

Me: You look so tense.

TG: I fucking am.

Me: Is there anything I can do?

TG: Plenty you can do. But you can't right now.

Me: Can you go to your room?

TG: Let me talk to Lucas. Give me a bit.

Twenty minutes later, my phone vibrates.

TG: Tell me something good.

I frown not knowing what he means, and I start to ask him to explain but I see the bubbles indicating that he's typing.

TG: Not sexual. Something good about you. Something that makes you happy.

I tap my chin, wondering what I should tell him when I think of the email my advisor sent me just a few days ago after I had already graduated.

Me: Pitt invited me to give a lecture next semester. I'm not going to teach a class or anything. It's just a seminar on social media and the impact it has on businesses.

TG: That's amazing, Avery. Wow. You're incredible.

My heart skips a beat. I hadn't told anyone yet, because I didn't think it was a huge deal even though I'm freaking out about it. It makes me happy that he's as excited for me as I am.

Me: I'm excited.

TG: You should be. I'm glad everyone sees how talented and special you are.

Me: *heart eye emoji*

Me: Your turn.

TG: At the moment, I can only think of one thing.

Me: Which is?

TG: You

I can't stop the squeal from leaving me, and I press my fingers to my lips.

Me: The thought of seeing you again tonight makes me happy as well.

TG: Yes, how are you going to make that happen anyway?

Me: Just make sure you're out of the house when we get home and I'll fake a headache or something so Lucas won't want to hang out and then I'll come meet you.

TG: Alright. Looking forward to being alone with you. I don't even mean just for sex. I just feel like I breathe easier around you.

I don't reply right away because I don't know what to say, and before I know it, minutes have gone by and I haven't said anything. I'm trying to calm the rapid beat of my heart over his words.

TG: Shit. That was way too much. Ignore me. Probably shouldn't have had that third whiskey.

Me: No! No. Sorry, I was trying to figure out what to say that wasn't a thousand heart eye emojis.

TG: I'll take your heart eyes.

Chapter
EIGHT

Avery

D INNER WAS EXACTLY WHAT I EXPECTED. A LOT OF MY parents gushing over how proud they are of me. All the stories about me as a child and how they knew I was destined for greatness and my uncles asking me to help guide my teenage cousins in the right direction. That's the downside of being the oldest cousin; I have to help all the younger ones, even *the ones that don't want to be helped.*

"Lucas, I think I'm going to call it a night," I tell him as I point toward my house.

My parents decided to go do karaoke with my aunts and uncles leaving me with a very empty house that I would love to invite Theo over to. That is, if it weren't for the guy in front of me who would find that extremely odd.

"You sure? You okay?" he asks, reaching out to touch my cheek.

"Yeah, I think just all the drinking we did today and having a glass of champagne when we toasted and then wine at dinner is all getting to me.

"Okay. Well, I'll see you tomorrow."

"Of course, hey!" I call out to him as he walks away. "We never talked about it but what did your dad have to say about you talking to Rae?"

"Oh…he says we need to give her some space and let her come to us at this point. Evidently, he talked to her also, and while she wasn't as angry as she was with me, she was short with him and he didn't like it. I don't think their conversation ended particularly pleasant."

"I think that's best for now. Maybe the ring isn't for months down the line."

"I guess." He shrugs and gives me a smile. "Catch you later, Summers."

Moments later, when I'm in the house, I prop my phone up on the credenza in the foyer and FaceTime Theo. He answers instantly and the smile on his face takes my breath away.

"Hi, beautiful."

"Hi." I smile back at him.

"Where are you?"

"Foyer, my parents went to karaoke." I giggle and he chuckles in response.

"You didn't want to go with them?"

"No, I wanted to see you."

"Did Lucas go home?"

"I think so. He always makes sure I'm in the house first."

"As he should." He presses his head back against the headrest and rubs his forehead. "I hate talking about him after what I've done. What we're doing."

"You didn't *do* anything. We...*wanted* this," I tell him.

"It's not that simple and I hate the war I feel within myself when it comes to you. I can't turn this feeling off, and I fucking need to."

"Is it bad that I'm glad you can't?"

He lets out what sounds like a sigh of defeat. "No."

I smile and press my teeth into my bottom lip. "Where are you?"

"The business park on Wilshire."

"I can't walk there." I frown, realizing that he's a few miles away.

"Obviously." He chuckles. "Just walk around the corner and I'll pick you up."

I twist my mouth as I mull over that idea. "What if someone sees us and realizes it's us?"

"Do you have a better idea?"

"The elementary school?" I offer.

"That's at least a seven-minute walk and it's dark. No, Avery. Unless you're going to risk taking your car. And wait I don't think I want you doing that—how much did you have to drink?"

"Just a glass of wine and a glass of champagne."

"And everything else you drank today. No driving, Avery."

"I sobered up after brunch!"

He lowers his gaze at me. "You heard me."

The space between my legs throbs at the forcefulness of his tone. "Okay, you're really limiting the options here, and I really want to suck your dick. Can you stop making this so difficult?"

His eyes widen before letting out what I can only surmise to be a horny chuckle. "God, you're going to be the death of me. And I was the one who said just meet me around the corner."

"We have nosy neighbors."

"Well, I don't know what to tell you, kid. It's ten-thirty at night and I'm not going to have you traipsing around without a care in the world."

"Maybe you should just come over," I say, kicking my heels off. "Good one."

"Seriously, you could come in through my side door that's not facing your house." I pull the clip out of my hair that was holding it back and let it fall around my shoulders. I watch his eyes trace the movements before he shakes his head.

"Avery, you don't want to get in my car for fear of someone seeing you, but you want me to sneak into your house?"

"Don't you want to see me?" I ask, giving him my most innocent expression. I blink my eyes at him several times. "Or I suppose I'll just have to spend the night with the other Theo Graham." I sigh and his eyes darken.

"Excuse me?"

"My vibrator I've named after you, of course." I run my hands through my hair. "He's gotten *a lot* of action over the years."

"Fuck me, Avery." He groans as he lets his eyes close.

"I AM TRYING TO!" I stomp and he chuckles again.

"You're being a brat, Ave."

I run my index finger between my cleavage. "Is it working?"

"No."

"Oh? So, you're not contemplating how to get in my house and into my bedroom?"

I grab my phone and make my way up the stairs to my room. Once I close the door, I set the phone on my nightstand and pull off my dress leaving me topless in a pair of panties and I hear a whispered "*Fuck.*"

"Do you want to watch me use it?"

I reach for the bag under my bed when I hear a pained, "*Wait,*" leave his lips.

I sit up and stare at the camera. He shakes his head. "Please don't. If you bring out a vibrator that you've named after me, I will lose my fucking mind." He gives me a stern look. "We thought we were going to have to wait a week until Lucas left and now, we can't even go a day?"

"I thought you wanted this too…"

"I do, which is why I said *we*, but not with all these risks. If your parents were out of town, I'd consider it, but they could show up at any minute."

"We both know they'll close the bar down."

"And this could be the one time they don't. Something happens. Maybe someone gets too drunk and needs to come back. There are too many wild cards in play right now and—" His eyes narrow and I notice he pauses the FaceTime.

"What?"

"Lucas texted me. He's going out."

"Oh?" My clit throbs instantly like it knows it's about to get some attention.

"Said you're not feeling well, so he's meeting some of his friends to have a few beers." he says as his face comes back into view.

"Okay, then can I come over?"

"Yes." I can't stop the smile that crosses my face. "But we're going out. I can't risk him coming home while you're in my bed. At least this way, you're not walking outside by yourself. I'll wait for him to leave and then I'll come back."

We're off the phone moments later and I'm sliding on a short, black t-shirt dress that is perfect for car sex. I slide off my panties, deciding to forego them completely, and slide on a pair of sneakers. Ten minutes later, I'm in Theo's Jeep, the same one from last winter break. I assume he chose this one because it's got the most space. He backs out of his driveway and we are out of our neighborhood in minutes, making me breathe a little easier. He pulls into an abandoned parking lot and lets out a sigh before turning to look at me. Neither of us have said anything since we got in the car but the tension crackles between us.

"It hasn't even been twenty-four hours since I touched you."

I look away from his eyes because I don't know how to respond to that and turn towards the back of his truck. "Did you bring the truck so it'll be easier for me to sit on your face?"

He groans as he scrubs his jaw and looks up towards the sky which we can see through his open sunroof. "How do you make that sound so innocent?"

I turn back to him and move my hands across the console to reach for his belt. "You're so tense."

"Do you blame me?" He grabs my hands and brings them to his lips, kissing each of the fingertips one by one.

"No. You've had an…interesting day."

"To say the least." He sighs. "And to think it started off pretty great." He holds my hands in his, not letting them go and I wish he'd let me touch him because I know how to relieve some of the tension he's feeling. "My daughter hates me and my son would too if he knew where I am and what I'm doing right now," he says finally.

I wince.

"Raegan doesn't hate you," I whisper. I'm not sure I can refute the second part of his statement but I do know Raegan doesn't have a hateful bone in her body and if she did, it would not be towards her father.

"Fine, but she's certainly pissed."

"Maybe." I shrug. "But by tomorrow she will want to talk and work it out."

"Yeah," he murmurs.

I stare at Theo, who's still staring straight ahead, not looking at me and I wonder if all of this is worth it. I care about Theo and if this is going to torment him, I don't want to be the reason for his internal struggles. "Theo...we don't have to do this. If it's too much...you and me?" I let out a breath and pull my eyes away from him to look out the front window. "We can just stop. I don't want to add to everything you've got going on. I—" My words are halted by his hand behind my neck and then his lips on mine. I would have imagined it would be aggressive but it's soft and sensual. His lips move against mine so slowly, dragging my bottom lip between his teeth and nibbling gently before he slides his tongue to swipe along mine.

He pulls back slowly and his lips are shiny and wet and I lick mine, tasting him on me. "It's not too much." His voice washes over me and goosebumps erupt on my flesh as a low pulsing begins between my legs. "It's no one's business what goes on between you and me."

I don't want to go back and forth about it or ask for any more reassurances. *This isn't a relationship. It's supposed to be fun and sexy and if I can serve as a distraction, then I'll be that too.* I unbuckle my seatbelt and reach over the console again, grateful that he also decided to wear clothes suitable for car sex. I grab his dick through his sweatpants before pulling him out with ease and he lifts his hips so I can push his pants to his ankles. I run my hand up the long and thick length of him before dragging my thumb over the tip causing him to suck in a breath through his teeth. "No underwear?"

"Seemed a little pointless," he says as he lifts his hips again, pushing his dick harder into my hand.

"In gray sweatpants? You're kind of slutty, huh?" I scrunch my nose before leaning over the console and dragging my nose down his cheek. "I like it," I whisper.

"Shit." He groans as I lower myself and let my tongue ghost over the tip of his cock. I'm very aware that my bare ass is in the air as I lean over the console and my short dress is barely covering *it*.

I grin to myself, wondering how long it takes for him to realize that. I wrap one hand around the base of his dick and slide my mouth down as far as I can go. I knew he was big and I find myself struggling to take his full length. I swallow, trying to open up my throat to push him further but I choke slightly, letting saliva slide down his dick to my hand.

"Don't force it, baby."

I pull back to look at him, my skin humming at him calling me baby again. "I want to." I bite my lip. "I want to get your whole dick in my mouth." I move forward so that I'm an inch from his face. "I can be kind of slutty too." Lust flashes in his eyes and his nostrils flare as I press two of my fingers to his mouth, before sliding them in. He runs his tongue over them, sucking them hard before I remove them and move them down my body and between my legs.

"You going to touch your pretty pussy while you suck me off?"

I nod. "Sorry in advance if I get your seats wet." I quirk an eyebrow at him and he lets out a breath.

"I don't give a fuck. Put your mouth back on it, baby." I settle my face back in his lap, placing a hand between his spread legs to hold myself steady while I'm still fingering myself. I'm still completely covered, but his hand is now on my back, stroking me gently and I know it's only a matter of time before he lifts it. "Jesus Christ, Avery. Oh my Go-oddd." He moans as he pulses in my mouth as I push myself further down on his dick with each suck. "Give me your fingers, I want to taste you." Heat flashes up my spine as I pull them from my wet cunt and into his view. It only takes a second to feel his lips wrapped around them. He groans around them as I continue fucking him with my mouth.

I slide my fingers from his mouth after he's done running his tongue all over them and licking them clean to wrap my hand around his dick to move in tandem with my mouth.

"God dammit," he lets out a breath and I wish I could look up and see him at this moment but the angle makes it impossible. *Next time,* I promise myself.

Cool air hits my skin and a growl so low and throaty rings in my ears like a promise. "You don't have panties on." He sputters like he's trying to hold off his orgasm.

"Uh uh," I say through a mouthful of his cock.

"Fuck. You should have led with that." He grabs my hair and yanks me off his dick, not hard enough to hurt, but enough that I feel a prickle at my roots that travels all the way down to my clit.

When I sit back on my heels, he's already moving his seat back and I move across the console to settle into his lap, pulling off my dress and the lacy bralette I'd worn beneath it. I haven't slid down on him yet, sitting on his thighs, his dick standing proud between us slick with my spit.

"Your mouth." He grunts as he drags his thumb across my bottom lip. "Jesus." He presses his lips to mine just as he lifts me up and slides me onto him. He pulls back to drag his lips down my neck. "I'll come in it next time."

"Please," I beg.

"I just couldn't wait."

"Oh God!" I cry out, as I take the full length of him. My pussy is still tingling from my earlier assault so I know it won't take long for me to come.

"Yeah?"

I begin moving faster up and down on him, knowing that both of our orgasms aren't far out of reach. His lips find one of my nipples, and I throw my head back as he sucks my entire breast into his mouth before moving to the other. "Yes!" I whimper when I feel him bare his teeth.

"You going to come on my dick?" I moan in response as I feel my orgasm looming. "Use your words." He lifts me, effectively removing himself from me and I cry out at the loss of contact.

"Yes, yes I'm close, put it back in! Please!" I beg just as he drags the tip of his dick through my slit. He taps it against my clit soft at first before smacking it harder and harder and rubbing against it. The sounds are slick and sexy and I want them to play on a loop in the back of my mind like an endless soundtrack.

"Come the fuck all over me, Avery. I want to smell your pussy on me for the rest of the night." He lets me fall back down and onto his dick and I begin fucking him harder, pushing us towards our climaxes. I rub my clit against his pelvis with every down thrust and just like that I'm at the peak of my orgasm. "Oh God, yes. Theo, I'm coming! Right there!"

"Fuck yes. Your pussy. Jesus." He grits out and maybe some variations of my name but I'm too far gone, my orgasm dragging me under like a tidal wave. I don't have a coherent thought in my head as this man has fucked them all out of me. All I can feel is him wedged between my legs and his lips on my neck. I'm still moving up and down on him when I feel his hands tighten on my hips. "I fucking love your pussy," he moans in my ear and if I hadn't already come all over him, I would have again. "You're so wet. Fuck, you're soaking me." He groans and then I know the moment he comes long and hard inside of me, with my name on his lips.

I press my lips to his, swallowing his groans. I press my hands to his chest and I can feel his heart pounding beneath my palms. He wraps his arms around me, holding me to his chest as we both come down from our powerful orgasms. "I think I got your shirt wet," I whisper as I trail kisses along his jaw. I rub my finger along the hem of his t-shirt and he chuckles.

"I don't care."

"I wish I could come home with you." I bite his jaw gently. The high of the orgasm hasn't quite worn off and I find myself feeling clingier than I did an hour ago. I want to go home with him and shower with him and then snuggle with him in his bed.

"Me too."

I've been in his bedroom a few times, in totally innocent situations and I'm eager for the first time I get to sit on his bed for reasons other than with Raegan the few times we helped him choose what to wear on a date.

Date.

I cringe thinking about him with another woman. *Would he date someone else while we are doing this?*

We aren't dating.

We're just…fuck whatever we're doing.

"I'm still inside you. Why the face?" he says and I realize that I'd pulled back and stared off into space. His hands reach up to cup my face and his thumbs drag over the apples of my cheeks.

"I…I didn't think this through," I whisper. "Not wearing panties."

"Yeah…I…." He chuckles. "I even brought condoms." He narrows his eyes at me. "But that's not the reason for the face. Talk to me. What's wrong?"

I hate that he can see through me. *Is it because he's still inside me?* I immediately pull off of him hoping that it breaks whatever mind-reading capability he suddenly has but he holds me in place, disallowing me to move off his lap. I look down and see the mixture of our fucking slowly dripping out of me and onto his lap. I watch in fascination as he cups my pussy, running his hand through my slit to capture what's slipping. "Do you want it?"

I nod and he slides his fingers into my mouth allowing me to taste us. *Fuck.* I hold his hand at my mouth as I lick it clean before letting him slide out from between my lips.

"Did I do something?" His face is worried and I hate that I've ruined this moment.

"No!" I shake my head. "It's silly and…we aren't together so I can't be…" I look around the car, trying to figure out how to phrase it without coming off like a jealous, clingy girlfriend.

"Avery." He says my name like a command and it works because my eyes meet his instantly. "Who said we aren't together?"

"I—you?" I offer weakly.

He narrows his eyes into slits. "When?"

"Last night…"

"I agreed that we couldn't go shouting all over town that we are doing this, but I also said do not fuck anyone else." I had forgotten that little fact but that still could have been something he said in the heat of the moment. A moment of possession where a man will say anything before the post-orgasm clarity. "I wouldn't ask you not to do something and not expect you to hold me to the same. I'm not fucking anyone else. I don't want anyone else. We *are* together. I take this very seriously, Avery."

I smile, letting his sexy sweet words wash over me.

"And next week when I have an empty house, I expect you to figure out how you're going to get out of your house and into my bed because I want you there." He rubs his hands over my nipples before placing a kiss between them. "Just because this can't be anything more than sex does not mean it doesn't mean something."

Chapter

NINE

THEO

S HE'S BACK IN HER SEAT AND I'M GLAD I HAD THE foresight to bring another shirt that I hand to her. She pats herself dry as best she can before holding the shirt to her chest. "I'll take this home to wash it, but...don't expect it back." She smirks and I smile at her, my inner caveman wanting to beat his chest with pride at the thought of her wearing my clothes. She slides on her bra and her dress and I pull up my sweatpants, my dick happy but also disappointed that this tryst is over.

I just came five minutes ago and it wasn't enough.

I still want more.

Ten minutes later, I watch as Avery makes her way into her house. I don't see a lot of lights on, so it seems like her family may still be out. She turns and waves before she heads in and I find myself irritated all over again that I'm in this situation with her. If she were any other woman on the planet, short of my ex-wife, I could walk her into my house right now without any questions or prying from Lucas. I make my way inside and hear people talking. I immediately slide my jacket on, grateful I'd brought it, and also that I decided to wear a black t-shirt because the bottom of it is definitely wet from Avery's cunt.

"Dad!" Lucas calls from the living room and when I walk in, I see him and two of his friends watching the highlights from tonight's 76ers playoff game. They both wave before turning back to the television. "Where you been?"

"Gym," I tell him, already having the lie ready in case he was home.

He nods because it wasn't unheard of for me to work out late. "You want to have a beer with us? Did you watch the game while you were there? It was fucking insane."

"Maybe in a bit, let me shower first. And no, I was going to catch the highlights. I saw they won though."

"Fucking crushed them." He cheers as he takes a sip and I head up the stairs to my bedroom feeling my phone vibrate before I even reach the top of the stairs.

I know without looking who would be texting me at midnight and I smile when I see the nickname I've chosen on my screen.

> **Heart Eyes: Between last night, this morning and tonight, I am very sore.**
>
> **Me: Then I'm doing my job.**
>
> **Heart Eyes: Yes, you are.**
>
> **Me: I'm about to shower and then Lucas is home, so I might hang out with him for a bit. If I don't answer, that's why.**
>
> **Heart Eyes: Shower, huh? Me too. Shame we aren't doing it together.**
>
> **Me: I'll think about you while I'm in there.**
>
> **Heart Eyes: *heart eye emoji***

Sometime later, I make my way downstairs to see Lucas sprawled out on the couch scrolling through his phone. I see his friends have left and I drop to my lounger in the corner. "So, you ready for your new job?"

He doesn't look away from his phone and I realize he's scrolling through pictures from Avery's graduation party. I turn my attention away from his phone because I don't need to be reminded of how sinfully sexy Avery looked in that green dress.

"Yeah, I guess."

"You don't sound as excited as you were when they offered it to you." I can still hear him shouting into the phone when they called with his offer. I went into the NFL right after college, so my situation was different but I still know that a hefty six-figure salary right after graduation from undergrad isn't the norm, and I was so happy for him. He'd worked his ass off in college and he deserved this.

But I know my son, and I can hear the '*but*' lurking beneath that '*yeah, I guess.*'

"The plan was for Avery to move to New York. We were always going to live there after we graduated. *She* changed the plan."

I would have poured myself a drink if I knew this was what we were going to be talking about. "Okay well, sometimes things change. You guys made that plan, what, four years ago, after high school?"

He turns to look at me. "We talked about it after sophomore year too and junior year."

"Okay, well again, things change." I cross my arms. "Camille is tired and she and Shawn want to travel and she's been handling a lot herself for years. The café is going to be Avery's at some point, so she wants to get involved now. Don't tell me you're giving her a hard time." I'm at war with myself because I would be saying this if it were about anyone, but I'll admit the fact that it's about Avery has me feeling a bit more aggressive about it. *But really, he's holding her to a promise they made at eighteen after graduation and too many shots of tequila?*

"I haven't said anything to her, Dad." His eyes shoot to mine and I can see they're filled with annoyance. "I'm talking to *you* about it. Excuse me for being disappointed that she's not moving to New York like I thought. Rory is bummed too for the record."

"Rory is moving there?" I ask because I hadn't been aware that it had been a group decision.

"Yeah, but she wants to work in fashion, so New York was the obvious next step."

I contemplate my next question, wondering if I want to live under the veil of ignorance regarding his feelings for Avery to help ease my guilt.

Fuck it. "Son—"

Careful. My subconscious warns. *Once he says it, you can't un-hear it.*

"I don't want to hear it about Avery," he interrupts. "We're friends, that's it." He stands up and the fact that he's trying to shut down this conversation by leaving the room speaks volumes. *Avoidance.*

"You're okay with that?" I ask as I follow him towards the kitchen.

He tosses his beer bottle in the recycling bin. "I made peace with it a long time ago."

"So you've said, but you don't act like it."

He leans against the counter with his arms crossed defensively. "How should I act? She's my best friend."

"I just mean…you don't treat her like she's your best friend. You treat her like your girlfriend. You always have."

"Dammit." He sighs. "You don't get it, Dad. That's just how we are."

The denial is so loud, but for my own selfish reasons, I don't push it. Maybe he really is just trying to get over her and being in different cities will definitely help. He'll meet someone in New York and forget about Avery.

Distance can absolutely make the heart grow yonder *not* fonder, after all.

I try to ignore my conscience arguing with the rationalizations I'm making because regardless of his feelings for her, sleeping with your son's best friend is definitely a terrible fucking idea.

⁓

Over the next few days, I spend more time with Lucas and see little of Avery unless she's with him. I haven't so much as touched her since that night in my car on Sunday and I feel like I'm fucking losing it. We have exchanged a few sexy texts back and forth but we haven't even FaceTimed or talked on the phone because the timing just hasn't lined up to allow us to do either.

I'm sitting on my patio, having some coffee and going through emails, enjoying a quiet morning while Lucas is at the gym. I took a few days off from work to spend time with him before he moved to New York and for the most part, I haven't been needed at work.

I lean back in my chair and stare into the massive pool that sits behind my house just as I hear my front door close and, "Dad?" being called through the house.

My head snaps towards the source of the sound just in time to see Raegan sliding the screen door open and stepping outside. Her dark hair is pulled into a sleek bun behind her head and she's wearing what looks like a men's t-shirt as a dress and sneakers, which surprises me because I don't think I've ever seen her not in some sort of heel unless she's going to the gym. For a moment, I'm rendered speechless at how much she looks like her mother. I stand and hold my hands out to her.

"Rae." She rushes into my arms like she's been wanting to do it for days.

"I'm sorry, I snapped at you on the phone!" She cries into my shirt and I press my lips to her forehead, holding her tighter.

"Why are you crying? Water under the bridge. What's going on, huh? Here, sit down." I pull a chair out for her and she sits diagonal from me. "Are you hungry? Want something to drink?"

"No." She shakes her head and puts her bag on the table, a *Louis Vuitton* tote I bought her for her birthday a few years ago that she *had* to have or she'd die. *Her words.*

She pulls a bottle of water out of her bag and takes a long sip. "Dad." She scrunches her nose and I notice that all of her freckles are out which means she's been out in the sun lately. "Lucas isn't here, is he?"

"No, he's at the gym. Just us here."

"Good, he'll just…" She shakes her head. "Dad, I want you to know that first and foremost, I'm excited. I…I know you're not going to be at first, but I think once you get to know Wes and realize this is for real, you'll breathe easier."

Anxiety bubbles inside of me. *She got married or she's pregnant. Fuck. Fuck. FUCK.*

Okay, deep breaths.

"Just give it to me straight."

She nods. "Okay." She lets out a breath. "I'm pregnant."

I blink several times at her and flex my hands just as many times, trying to get a hold of all of the mixed feelings coursing through me.

At least, she's graduated from high school and college! She has a stable job and a health plan. She's an adult.

Yeah, who got pregnant by the first guy—

First guy? Yeah okay, Theo.

What if he doesn't treat her right? She barely knows him! Then she'll be connected to him forever. With a baby!

But a baby! You love babies. And this one you won't be responsible for. You get to give this one back to its parents when it cries!

"Dad?" She breaks the back and forth inside my head, sliding her hand on top of mine and gives it a gentle squeeze. "You okay? Are you in shock?"

"I—no." I let out a breath. "I'm good. Just…caught off guard. I think?" I rub my forehead. "Honey, was this…planned? I just—"

"No! No. I mean, we weren't trying for this…" She winces. "But we weren't really trying all that hard to not—" She looks up in the air.

I put my hands up. "Ah ah ah. No." I point at her. "I don't need the uhh…details."

"Dad, you're not going to get all weird about it like when you tried to give me the sex talk?"

"I wasn't weird," I defend.

"Uh…well…you see…when a man and woman love each other very much," she imitates me and clears her throat, "ask your mother."

"Well, you clearly did not take my advice!" I say, standing up.

"How do you figure?" She stands up and lifts her chin, trying to appear tall but I'm still at least a foot taller than her.

"You love this guy?!"

"Yes!"

"Oh, really?" I ask, quirking an eyebrow at her.

"Yes! Dad…I know it seems like we haven't been together that long, but we've known each other for a while." *Well, that makes me feel slightly better.* "And we were exploring things for a while before we made it official." She blushes. *That does not.*

"Raegan Marie, please spare me." I glare at her.

"Sorry." She sits back down and looks up at me and the tears in her blue eyes gut me. "I need you to be on board with this. Mom is going to freak the fu–hell out and you know I can't handle her without help. Lucas is going to handle it whatever way you do. I need you on my side."

I sit down and lean forward to grab her hand in mine. "I am *always* on your side, Rae." Her shoulders sag like she's had the weight of the world on her shoulders and hearing my words removes some of it. "Is that the reason for the ring? Honey, I am not concerned about you being pregnant and not married—if that's what this is about? I mean yes, I would prefer—"

"Dad…" She interrupts and she gives me a small smile. "Wes and I have been talking about getting married since before I got pregnant." She bites her bottom lip, even as her lips tick upwards. "I am so crazy about him, Dad. And I know, it's uncomfortable with him being your age, and I wish I could make that less weird for you."

"I'll get over it, I guess." I cock my head to the side, my mind going back to a time, what feels like a hundred years ago when she looked up at me with those bright blue eyes and asked me to pick her up and put her on my shoulders.

"We really tried to stay away from each other especially with it being against the code of ethics and—"

I'm vaguely aware she's still talking but my ears perk up at that. "Wait wait wait, Rae, back the hell up. Code of ethics? You work for him?!" I stand up again because now I've got a fuck ton of different questions.

She blanches. "So, this is going to be the hard sell." She nods. "I knew there was going to be one."

"Don't be cute, Rae. Explain."

"Okay, so…yes, he's my boss *technically.*"

"Oh my God, Raegan. That's what all this is? You know how this looks? He got his subordinate pregnant, and to prevent himself from getting fired, he's talked you into selling some bullshit fairytale? I know you're smarter than this!"

"WHAT?" I hear from the kitchen and then Lucas is coming through the screen door as Avery lingers in the doorjamb. *Good fucking grief. I don't need this right now.*

"I'm so sorry, I can go." Avery starts to shut the screen.

"No wait!" Raegan says to Avery who looks like a deer in the headlights at what to do and I know Raegan is thinking that Lucas and I won't fly off the handle if she sticks around. Avery stands in the doorway as Lucas comes to stand next to me, his arms crossed.

"Dad, Luke, I know you guys are just trying to protect me," Raegan starts, "but that's not what's happening here. I told you, we were already together before we got pregnant. We've been together for months. We've gone to human resources. I was saying in the beginning we did have to hide it, but now they know. Everyone knows. They can't fire Wes. He owns the company."

"He reports to someone, a board of trustees or whatever and they can absolutely force him out for misconduct," I tell her.

"At least the guy's got money," Lucas says as he looks at me with a shrug.

I shut my eyes as irritation at both of them flares through me. "I'm sorry, did you two forget how you were raised? Since when do Rae or you, might I add, need anyone else for money? You both have always done a very good job at asking me for it."

Avery snickers from the corner and Lucas looks at her with a playful glare and she shrugs.

"It's not about the money, and Dad, I haven't asked you for money in probably a year," Raegan argues.

"Honey, you moved out six months ago and in with your boyfriend." I lower my gaze. "I'll give you a thousand dollars right now if you can tell me how much Wes pays for rent or a mortgage."

Raegan stands and puts her hands on her hips. "I know, but I am not going to tell you."

Lucas chuckles. "Unbelievable."

"Oh, I'm sorry, and Dad shelled out how much money for your apartment in New York?" Raegan snaps.

"Yeah, while I was in school! He paid for your college housing too, Rae. I'm taking over the mortgage for it *now*."

"Look," I interrupt, before they continue with this back and forth, "we are getting off topic. You are both spoiled as hell. That is not the point. I am happy that I've been able to do whatever I can for you and will always do that."

"Yeah, the point is you got knocked up by your sugar daddy!" Lucas says and though I hear the joking in his tone, it's too much.

"Lucas," I grit out and Raegan's eyes well up with tears.

"That is not what happened." She stamps her foot. "This is why I wanted to talk to Dad alone about this. You're such a dick, Lucas." She grabs her bag, trying to sniffle back her tears.

"Rae—" I start, following her, hating my part in making her upset.

She turns around. "Bye Dad. I'll call you later." She gives me a quick hug before turning towards Avery. "See you, Ave." She presses her cheek to Avery's and makes a kissing noise before she turns around and looks at me and then Lucas with a sneer. "Maybe if you weren't such an asshole, you'd actually have a shot with her."

Lucas gives her his middle finger but I can see the anger in his eyes and I sigh because both of my children have gone way too fucking far and I know just where to unleash my annoyance as I follow Raegan into the house.

"Too far." I grit out, closing the glass door behind us to give us a bit of privacy and leaving Lucas and Avery outside to deal with the awkwardness of Raegan's comment.

"Oh please," she says. "We're still pretending that he doesn't follow her around like a freaking puppy begging for affection?" She opens up the refrigerator and grabs a sparkling water. "We're all too old for it."

"You need to apologize."

"For what!" She whines. "He started it. Wes is not my Sugar Daddy."

"I'm going to make him apologize too." I cross my arms. "And the difference is, you believe there's truth to what you said. He was just making a jab at his age. I don't think Lucas really thinks he's your… that." I cringe, not wanting to say it out loud.

"Fine." She sighs. "I'm still leaving though. I'm tired."

"How are you feeling by the way? How far along are you?"

"Eight weeks and pretty great actually. Some morning…and afternoon sickness. That's why I bailed on Avery's grad party."

"You've been to the doctor?"

"Yep, twice. I go in again at eleven weeks."

"I remember." I nod with a smile. "I'm going to be a grandfather?"

"Unless Mom has been lying about paternity all these years." She gives me a smug grin and I roll my eyes before I pull her in for a hug.

"I spit you and Lucas out; I wouldn't even believe a paternity test that said otherwise. You look too much like me. Now, go apologize to your brother." I press a kiss to her forehead.

"Whatever." She grumbles before she slides the door open. "Sorry, asshole!" She calls out, and Lucas, who's seated on one of the pool chairs with Avery lying out next to him, waves before flipping her off again.

She closes the sliding door. "Happy?"

"You think he still loves her?" I ask her, ignoring her sarcasm. Raegan has always been perceptive and picked up on everything. She had a nasty habit of eavesdropping on conversations as a kid, which is how she found out about her mother's affair.

"Lucas? Yeah, Dad. I think he's still crazy about her."

"He says he doesn't have feelings for her anymore."

"And you believe him?"

"He's twenty-one, if he tells me something, what reason would I have not to believe him? Furthermore, what reason would he have to lie to me about it?"

She takes a sip of her water and shrugs. "Embarrassed that he lives in the friend zone? Especially when his dad is *The* Theo Graham? You can't swing a stick without hitting a woman who would sell her husband for a chance to go out with you." I try hard not to laugh but I can't help the smile that pulls at my lips.

"Not true. And it's definitely not like that anymore. Maybe when I was playing or a few years after I retired."

"Sure Dad, women are only interested because you were in the NFL. Not the nice house, or the piles of money, or the six-pack." She rolls her eyes. "Whatever, the longer you stay single the more I get in the will, so you won't hear me complaining." She stands on her tiptoes and plants a kiss on my cheek.

"Ha—Ha. Thanks. Just for that, I'm giving more to Lucas." I laugh at her dark humor because I know without a doubt between my two children, when it's my time to go, Raegan will be the one who won't be able to handle it.

She's out the door and I make my way outside to see Lucas on his back and Avery on her stomach on two side by side loungers. I make my way over to them and it's the first time I really allow myself to look at Avery in her red two-piece gym gear that clings to her curves so fucking deliciously. The shorts are molded to her ass and if Lucas wasn't here, my hands would be on her cheeks squeezing them.

"Don't call Wes that, Lucas," I tell him.

"What? We were all thinking it!" He raises his hands.

"I wasn't," Avery interjects as she turns over and looks at him before up at me.

"Whatever. I can tell you who is also definitely going to think that." I groan thinking about who he's referring to. "Yeah, how do you think your ex-wife is going to feel about this?" Lucas chuckles.

"You know she hates when you call her that."

"No, *she* hates when I call her Rebecca. *You* hate when I call her your ex-wife because you don't like to be reminded that you married her and knocked her up twice." Avery laughs and Lucas meets my murderous gaze. "What? Look, you brought her into *my* life, not the other way around. I didn't ask to be brought into the dysfunction." He stands up and holds his hands out. "Happy to be here though." He slaps my back and walks toward the house. "Ave! Want a drink!"

"Whatever you're having!"

"Tequila it is!"

"Tequila!?" She whines.

"I'm only home for two more days!" He calls back and my cock jerks in response at the thought of having Avery to myself. I begin cracking my knuckles to try and divert my attention from the situation in my pants when he closes the door.

I look down at her. "Hi."

"Hi," she whispers. She's still got her sunglasses on so I can't see her eyes. "How ya doing?"

"Been better." I breathe out.

She nods. "You kept your cool. Did you yell before we got here?"

"No...I don't think so. I blacked out for a second, I think."

She nods again. "How do you feel about it?"

"Am I allowed an opinion?"

"Of course you are. You're her dad. Besides, it's just me here."

I sit on the chair next to her and rest my forearms on my knees. "I'm happy if she's happy. I only hope she's just not so enamored with the idea of all of this and then she wakes up in a few years once the novelty has worn off and she's wildly unhappy with this guy. Yeah, she can leave him but she's still forced to deal with him because they have a baby together." I scrub at my jaw. "It's tough, not getting along while having to co-parent."

It's not something I've discussed with Raegan or Lucas, nor do I think I ever will, but Rebecca getting pregnant with Raegan is why we got married. That's not to say I didn't love her at the time, but it certainly pushed us down the aisle sooner than I had wanted to. We didn't have a huge wedding; we eloped in Fiji and everyone thinks it was impulsive and romantic when in reality it was a response to a positive pregnancy test and wanting to do the right thing.

We had her and then Lucas a year and a half later and the next time I blinked, Raegan was five and Lucas was three. It was like I'd been in a sleepless fog for five years and I was just realizing how Rebecca and I just didn't fit.

Eight years and an affair later, I'd had enough.

She peeks past me before returning her gaze to me and leaning forward, putting her hand on top of mine. "I get it," she whispers. "I mean, I don't really get it because my parents are super in love but...I can imagine it's tough." She pulls her sunglasses off and meets my gaze and *God her eyes*...I could get lost in them. She's barely wearing any makeup, but she's got on a few coats of mascara, elongating her lashes and I drag my gaze down past her nose to her full bare lips that still have a pink hue.

Visions of pushing my dick through them come flooding back and I lean back adjusting myself as discreetly as possible but Avery smiles baring her teeth. "I'm going to go shower. I'm still kind of sweaty from the gym. Tell Lucas I'll be back, okay?"

I nod and without even looking at me, she stands and drags her fingertips up my arm gently as she walks by me.

And now, I'm hard as a rock.

Chapter

TEN

Avery

I SHOWERED AND CHANGED INTO A SHORT OFF THE SHOULDER black gingham print dress that's both casual and sexy and I'm hoping Theo has hung around long enough to see me in it. I'm moving down the stairs when I hear my mom call for me and I see her in the kitchen pulling a cake out of the oven wearing an *Avery's Café* t-shirt and shorts underneath an apron. Her dark curly hair is pulled back into a tight bun like she always does when she's cooking if she's not wearing the cute chef's hat my dad got her.

"Taste this," she says, holding a spoon with light green icing.

"Mint?" I ask her, because she's always trying to revamp how she prepares mint chocolate desserts.

"Mmmhm, I swear this batch tastes like toothpaste." I lick the spoon and scrunch my nose.

"Definitely Colgate-y." I giggle. "That batch you made over Thanksgiving break last year was perfection." *Truly, I've had dreams about how good those mint chocolate brownies tasted.*

"Your father has not stopped talking about that damn batch and I went rogue and I can't remember what I did." She puts a hand over her forehead and squeezes her eyes shut like she's trying to remember how many grains of salt were in the pinch that went into the batch.

"I mean, Mom, your mint chocolate is already amazing, like everything else you bake, why do you let this get to you?"

"Because it's different every time I bake it! I need consistency. Hello!?" She huffs. "So, you're coming to the café with me tomorrow?"

"Yep."

"Even if you're hungover." She raises an eyebrow and looks behind me out the back door that is a shortcut to Lucas' house.

"Yes, I'll be there."

"Fine. Be careful coming home." I move towards the door when she stops me. "By the way, did I see Raegan's car over there? Is she home?"

"She came by, but she was in and out."

"Mmmm, I hear she's seeing someone."

"Oh?" I ask, wondering what exactly she knows.

"Yes, an older fellow." She nods at me with her eyebrows moving up and down.

"How do you know?"

"Macey told me when we were at tennis!" I roll my eyes at Macey Hudson, the town gossip. "She said she saw them at the grocery store, shopping, looking pretty cozy." She points a finger at me. *They grocery shop together? Oh, that's so fucking cute.* "I did hear he is quite handsome though. I wonder how Theo feels about it."

I shrug. "Maybe he doesn't care."

"Oh please, a girl dates a man old enough to be her father, trust me her actual father cares." She giggles. "Please don't do it to me. Your father will be insufferable."

I chuckle despite the blast of guilt I feel.

We aren't dating, totally different.

Not getting married.

Not having a baby.

My dad will never have to deal with it. Nor will my mother.

"You don't have to worry about that."

She puts a spoon to her lips. "I hope not. Oh God, I could brush my teeth with this!" she cries before tossing it in the bowl. "Oh! Take these." She hands me a batch of pumpkin snickerdoodles.

"Pumpkin in May?" My eyes widen in excitement as I take a cookie off the plate and take a bite. *God, my mom can bake.* "And why would I give these to them!" Pumpkin anything is my favorite, but

THE WORST KEPT *Secret* 111

she doesn't usually start making anything until August in preparation for fall so I'm shocked to see them this early.

"You just graduated college and they're your favorite and Lucas' favorite." She points behind her. "There's still a batch here."

I side eye her. "Alright then. Don't let Dad eat them all!" I tell her as I re-lay the cellophane.

I'm out the door after a few moments and pushing through the gate on the side of his house that Theo installed when Lucas and I were back and forth constantly between houses. It leads to the backyard, and when I get there Lucas and Theo are sitting at the table, each with a margarita.

"What did Camille send!?" Lucas asks the second he sees what's in my hands.

"Pumpkin snickerdoodles."

"In May!?" Lucas' eyes widen.

"That's what I said. Apparently, it's because we graduated."

"Give it up," Lucas says holding his hands out.

"Keep them away from me," Theo says. "Every time your mom sends a batch of something, I end up five pounds heavier."

"Who said I was sharing?" Lucas jokes as he lifts the plastic.

"Margaritas and pumpkin cookies, we're kind of mixing vibes here."

"Who cares?" Lucas says through a mouthful.

"Where's mine?" I frown as I stare at the two glasses on the table.

"I made them and you're not a guest here, you know how to pour your own drink," Lucas says as he points towards the door.

"My son, the perfect host." Theo chuckles. "I'll get it for you." He smiles before heading inside.

It takes everything in me not to follow him with my eyes and shoot him my flirtiest *thank you.* "Thanks, Theo!" I cheer without even looking at him. *God, Lucas I love you but can you go away?! What I wouldn't give for him to have something to do so I could have just a few moments alone with Theo.*

A thought floats through my head, and I almost squeal with glee when I realize how this plan will work. It's Thursday, it's two o'clock, and half our friends just graduated college.

"So, what should we do? Should we have some people over? You know? For old times' sake?" I wink.

—⁂—

An hour and a trip to the liquor and grocery stores later, we are expecting a number of people to swing by and hang out. Partly to say goodbye to Lucas before he leaves for New York on Saturday—*he had a graduation party two weeks before me,* so it would serve as more of a goodbye party—and partly because we are twenty-one and we never need a reason to party.

"Alright, I'm going to go shower, because I didn't after we got back from the gym, I'll be back." Lucas knocks my shoulder gently with his fist before he makes his way up the stairs. Theo graciously offered to help us clean up even though the Graham house is rarely not spotless, so he's still in the kitchen with me. The second we hear Lucas hit the top step our eyes meet.

"Tell me you're wearing panties underneath that." His voice is low and seductive as he nods at my short dress.

"Why don't you touch me and find out."

His eyes float upwards as he takes a step closer and when he hears the sound of water he lets out a breath. "Thank fuck." He grabs my hips and lifts me onto the counter with ease before stepping between my legs and within seconds his hand is between them, dragging his finger over my covered slit.

I wrap my arms around him and press my lips to his, kissing him for the first time in almost a week and I melt into his arms. Based on his height, his dick lines up perfectly with my center and he presses it into me. "Fuck me please, Theo." I moan.

"That's what you want, angel? We don't have time for everything." He licks along the seam of my mouth. "I want to eat your pussy."

"You can later, give me your dick." I undo his jeans and push them and his briefs down as his mouth kisses down my neck. I stroke him a few times before he swats my hand out of the way.

"I've been ready since I saw you in your gym outfit. Are you?" He pushes my wet panties to the side and his fingers glide inside.

"Fuck." I moan. "Yes."

"I've got to get you close because we don't have a lot of time."

"I'm close, Theo." I whimper as he flicks my clit with the tip of his finger and gasp at the pleasure coursing through me. He grabs his dick and drags it over my clit and pushes inside me with one thrust before clamping a hand over my mouth just as a choked cry escapes.

"You need to be quiet." I nod. "Good girl," he whispers low in my ear and a delicious shiver moves through me as I clench around his cock. He rears back and pushes in again and my eyes roll back in my head momentarily at how good it feels. "Fuck." He grits out and his hand is still on my mouth so I narrow my eyes in question. "I don't have a condom."

I grab his hand, removing it from my mouth. "I don't care."

"We need to start caring, Avery," he says, but I notice he doesn't make an effort to stop.

"Next time," I whisper as I lock my legs behind him and push him back into me. "Fuck me, please. I've missed you."

"You have no idea. I've fucking missed you so much. Missed *this*." He continues to fuck me, while trying not to make noise. I'm acutely aware that we are facing his backyard and anyone could walk back there and see us. Or anyone could walk in the front door, because who of Lucas and my close friends rings the doorbell? But I don't care. I want him and this and my orgasm and his orgasm filling me up and nothing can stop it. I still hear the sounds of running water, so we're still safe. I just have to hope no one shows up super early.

I lean my head back and he licks up my neck before nuzzling his lips there. "You're so fucking perfect, Avery."

"So are you," I whisper. *His dick certainly is.* I've had sex with three other people and his is the only one that finds this particular spot that feels fucking indescribable. Every time he taps it, I have to bite my lip to stop myself from promising I'll do whatever he wants for the rest of our lives if he'll just keep doing that forever.

Right on schedule. He pushes in harder and circles his hips just as his hand drops between us and I feel friction against my clit. "Remember, quiet, angel," he murmurs in my ear. *I thought I was!* I wrap an arm around his neck and push my face into it, taking a deep inhale, smelling his raw manly scent mixed with the cologne he wears. I push my lips to the skin, letting my tongue dart out.

"Baby, I need you to come," he says. "I'm getting close and I... fuck, I don't know how long we've been doing this. Time stops while I'm inside you."

"Mmmm. But it feels good."

"I know and we can do it again later if you come now."

I feel drunk as my orgasm approaches. Drunk on him. On this feeling. On us.

I pull back and look at him through hooded eyes as he slows his strokes and I can feel every ridge of his cock as he moves in and out. "You promise?" I bite my bottom lip.

"Of course. Whatever you want. I'll give you whatever you want." He pants against my lips. "Please just...come on my dick right fucking now." I hear the rush in his voice, like he can't wait another second to feel it.

"Mmmm, say something nasty." I raise an eyebrow at him and he lowers his gaze, his eyes dark.

"We don't have time for what happens to you when I say something nasty, Avery."

"Please," I purr.

"Fuck." He groans as I feel him start to lose control. "If you come now, later tonight, after all of your friends are tipsy, you're going to not too drunkenly stumble into my bedroom and I'm going to put my tongue in your cunt. Understand? I don't care what you have to do, Avery. Do not leave this house tonight without coming in my mouth first, got it?"

"Oh God!"

"That's it. Come on baby, I got you. Come for me."

"Theo," I whisper against him and then I come, fucking hard. I don't know how long I'm spasming when I feel him quietly groan against my neck. He jerks a few times and I clench in response causing him to chuckle as he slowly slides out of me.

I move off the counter and rearrange my panties, staring at him as he tucks his wet dick back into his briefs and pulls his jeans up.

"Don't look at me like that, we don't have time for it to go in your mouth." He laughs and I let my bottom lip jut out before giving him a smile.

"I'm going to freshen up."

He runs a hand through his hair. "Yeah, I'm going to do the same." He pushes my hair back and runs a finger down my neck. "I tried to be careful of my stubble." He rubs a thumb down the slope of my neck. "I just love kissing your neck." He lowers his eyes to my lips and then down the rest of my body. "Hell, I love every part of you." He grabs my chin and presses a kiss on my lips. "I meant what I said." He cups me between my legs and squeezes gently. "I better kiss these lips at some point tonight."

Several hours later, *inviting a few friends over for drinks* has turned into half my high school graduating class showing up like the ragers people threw when someone's parents went out of town. Only this time we are older, and smarter, and have IDs stating we are old enough to drink in case the cops happen to stop by. Lucas has never thrown a huge party here, but he definitely had friends over a few times when we knew Theo was working late, and the setup feels so nostalgic. The long folding table outside that is set up for beer pong or flip cup, the slew of red cups on the island that we use for drinking games, the low hum of music playing from the speakers, and the chatter of all of our friends cutting loose after a long day.

"This was *such* a good idea," Rory says just as she downs a shot of tequila. "I've barely been out since your grad party and it's been a long week." She rolls her eyes. "I put in my two weeks at the store and they are making me work what feels like every minute of it." She groans. Rory has worked at Sephora at the mall all through college and is leaving to move to New York after getting a job at Dior in their corporate office, *otherwise known as her dream job.*

"Well, you are their favorite employee. It's going to be hard to replace you," I tell her as I sip my margarita.

My eyes pan the room, looking for Theo and I spot him in the corner talking to some of the guys that played football in high school and one who played in college and I assume he's giving advice about going pro. His eyes aren't on me, so I take the time to ogle him for a moment until Rory smacks my arm.

"Speaking of which, you little tart." I snap my eyes to her, worried that I'd been caught staring at our friend's dad when she raises her eyebrows up and down. "What happened after your grad party? Who did you meet up with?"

"What are you talking about?" I ask, knowing the best way to get out of this is to deny and talk her in circles until she gives up.

"Don't do that. You had the 'I am getting dick tonight' look in your eyes and I said I would let it go but that we would circle back." She taps her red solo cup to mine. "This is me circling back. So, spill."

"Rory, nothing. There is no one. I went home."

"Bullshit." She stamps her foot. "I am your best friend. Regardless of what Lucas thinks! Tell me," she whines and I realize she's starting to get tipsy, which means this will be easier than I thought. "Oh God, was it Nate? Please tell me you're not going back for another round with your loser ex. I love you and I will always support you but not with him."

"No." I make a face. "Definitely not. I don't even think he's home yet. I think he's still in Boston," I say thinking about what I remember from mindlessly scrolling social media.

"Oh well, whatever." She puts her hands under her chin as best as she can with a cup in her hand. "Please!"

"There's nothing to tell!"

"DICE GAME!" I hear shouted from the center of the room

and I see our friend Lexie, holding her hand up as she bounces on the balls of her feet. "Come on, for old time's sake!"

I groan, remembering all the trouble that used to come from these fucking dice. She shouts outside to the people at the beer pong table, one of whom is Lucas, and tells them to come in and a few do while some stay outside. "Come on, you're playing," Lexie says, grabbing my hand and pulling me around the island.

"I am not taking my shirt off," I tell her with a glare.

She rolls her eyes before tucking a long chestnut strand behind her ear. "I don't know why, you have great tits. I'd never wear tops." There's a group of seven of us around the island including Lucas and I breathe a sigh of relief when I realize Theo isn't over here though I don't know if it's worse if he's watching.

"Oh my Gosh, Theo you have to play with us!" Rory cheers from next to me and I swear my fucking eye twitches.

"Rory, really?" I say, so only she can hear me.

"What! We'll keep the game PG today, right guys?" She looks around the circle and I can already see a number of the guys are not on board with that.

"I did not agree to that." Lexie furrows her brows before looking at me. "You want PG and she's not taking her top off?" She points at me. "Who are you and what have you done with my friends? You get one college degree and suddenly you're too old for our favorite game?" Lexie puts a hand over her forehead dramatically. "I am disappointed in both of you." She points at us before turning towards Theo. "Come join!" She claps. "Does everyone remember the rules?"

"Maybe I'll sit this one out. See where it goes first before I decide to join." Theo chuckles but still hangs close by...I guess to watch?

This is going to be a shitshow.

I briefly meet his gaze and I'm happy that Rory is on her phone, probably texting Justin if I had to guess. "Okay, well, I'll give you a brief rundown and also a refresher for everyone else. So, you pick a person, ask them truth or dare and then choose a number. If the person rolling the dice rolls that number then you get to ask them the question or dare them to do something, whichever they choose. We usually only do dares but for the sake of keeping things"—she shoots me and Rory a look—"more PG because no one wants to take their clothes off anymore"—she rolls her eyes—"we'll offer truths."

"Excuse me," I say holding a finger up. "I would like to add here"—I look at Theo—"Theo, we have never taken our clothes off. There may have been a time when we may have *flashed* something, but the clothes always stayed on." I glare at Lexie. "Can you not make us sound like we were a bunch of horny degenerates?" I chuckle.

"Hmph." She shoots her nose in the air jokingly. "Well, who wants to start?"

We go a few rounds that are mostly dares for people to take a shot, chug a beer, a light kiss between friends, and a few truths asking what really happened during our senior week. I've been mostly avoided, having been one of the people dared to take a shot, but for the most part, it's been a pretty mild game and now people are starting to lose interest. *Thankfully.*

"I'll go." Lucas chuckles and I groan because I know that means he's going to pick me. We used to have a system in place. We'd choose each other so others that were wild cards wouldn't target us too much. We had an approved list of truths and dares that were acceptable and we rarely veered from it. *Let's just hope he remembers it.*

"Rory," he points and I'm surprised at that, "truth or dare."

"Truth!"

"Lame." Lexie coughs into her drink and I laugh.

"Okay, if I roll a seven," he smiles at the easiest number to roll, "you have to tell us what happened with you and our physics teacher after graduation."

Her mouth drops open and so does mine because even I don't know the details of that. "Lucas!" She says and I think she may actually be a little irritated because while there was a rumor, for one of her closest friends to bring it up would lead most people to believe that something really did happen.

He holds his hands up. "Listen, I waited four whole years for this moment. And you were eighteen! It's not like it was illegal, come on!"

I chuckle. "Avery!" Rory smacks my arm and I can't stop the smile on my face because I really want to know too.

"What! What do you want me to do!?" I point at him. "I didn't tell him to ask that!" I can't stop giggling as I start to feel my drinks a little and she glares at me. "Okay, Lucas, this is not the conversation for mixed company." Another laugh breaks free even though I'm trying my best to be serious. "She doesn't have to answer."

"The hell she doesn't!" Lexie cheers and leans forward. "I knew it by the way! How big was it?" She holds her hands apart and moves them back and forth to guess the length. "Tell me when."

"You guys suck." Rory snaps. "We made out, that's it. Get your minds out of the gutter."

"She's lying!" Lexie cheers as she points at her. "Oh, this is good." She nods at Rory. "I know. I know." She mouths, fanning herself. "He was so hot."

"I hate all of you." She snatches the dice and looks at me. "And you, giggles." She glares at me. "Truth or Dare!"

I let out a breath, not knowing which the safer option is. *Truth, always truth.* "Truth." Her eyes narrow at me and for a second my stomach drops. *No no no do not ask.* "Rory," I warn, hoping she can figure out what I'm trying to tell her with my eyes.

DO NOT GO THERE.

"If I roll a seven, you have to tell us who you snuck off with after your grad party." She winks and scrunches her nose and my eyes immediately go to Lucas who's staring at me with a furrowed brow.

"Wait what?" Lucas asks and I am trying my best not to make eye contact with Theo.

"Seven!" Rory cheers before looking at me with a grin. *I am going to kill you,* I tell her with my eyes.

"You said you went home?" Lucas says and Rory's smile fades instantly before she turns to me.

"Wait, it wasn't Lucas?" She whispers to me behind her hand and when I glare at her she blanches.

"Who?" Lucas chuckles. He looks around the room, probably thinking it's someone from high school before turning back to me.

"First of all, I didn't sneak off with anyone. I did go home and this game is dumb."

"Hey! Don't blame the game," Lexie says as she takes a sip of the wine in front of her. I finally meet Theo's eyes and they give away nothing. Most of the people standing in the circle don't give a shit about my answer, but the damage is done and now Lucas suspects I not only lied to him but that I'm hiding something. "I have to go to the bathroom," I say without another word before walking out of the kitchen just as I feel my phone vibrate.

Rory: SHIT! I am so sorry. I figured it was Lucas!

Avery: I could kill you! Why would I hide that from you?

Rory: I don't know. Because you've been friends forever and you're finally getting together! And maybe you weren't ready to tell people yet? It would be huge!!

Avery: So, you were going to out us during a drinking game!? You're the worst!!!

Rory: I know ugh, I'm sorry!! Don't hate me. That really was why I asked. But, look no one cares.

Avery: Lucas cares, Rory!

Rory: So!? He's not the boss of you or your man.

Avery: I told him I went home that night so he thinks I lied

Rory: Did you?

Avery: Yes, okay! I did meet up with someone. You don't know him, he's from Pitt. We used to hook up sometimes. That's it.

Keep things vague, I tell myself. *No names, no descriptions, he could be anyone. No face, no case!*

Rory: How could you not tell me this!?

Avery: Because it meant nothing! Do I know about all of your hookups!

Rory: Uh, yes?

Avery: Well…sorry.

Rory: What's his name? Is he cute? Pics!!

A knock on the bathroom door startles me and when I open the door, I see Lucas in the hallway. I came upstairs to use the bathroom to get away from everyone and also to hide for a minute.

"Hey."

"Hey," I say, turning off the light and stepping into the hallway.

"You good?" He asks as he leans against the wall.

"Yeah, of course. That game is just super invasive. I never liked it," I lie, because I used to love it.

He hears the lie, and more importantly, knows *why* I'm lying now. "Are you seeing someone?" He asks.

"I—ummm…" *Think and think quick.* "It's not serious."

He scratches his jaw and looks at me contemplatively, like he's not sure what to ask me next. "So, you did meet up with someone that night?"

"Well—"

He crosses his arms in front of his chest. "You lied to me? Why?"

"I didn't want you to worry about me and you tend to ask a lot of questions." I bite my bottom lip nervously.

He chuckles. "Because I care about you, obviously. Who is it?"

"Does it matter?"

"Sort of?"

"Why?"

"I don't know, Avery. Maybe I want to know who my best friend is dating!?"

"We aren't dating. It's a guy from school and it was casual. He was leaving to go back home. That's it. It's over."

He narrows his gaze at me and then finally shrugs. "You could have just told me that."

"Could I have?"

"What does that mean?"

I sigh, the unspoken words hanging between us.

Because I don't want to hurt you?

─◦◦◦─

Hours later, it's nearing midnight and most of the party has cleared out. *Including Lucas,* who decided to leave with a bunch of people to go downtown. He didn't even press it when I said I had to be up early tomorrow so I shouldn't go out and I wonder if it's because of the revelation from earlier. The air between us shifted in that two-minute conversation and I wonder if this is a turning point in our friendship. Theo had long since gone upstairs, after the Truth or Dare game, and hadn't returned. Although, now everyone is gone and as I start to clean up *because that had always been my job when Lucas was too busy puking or passed out,* I hear someone coming down the stairs. I smile because we are finally alone and more importantly, I may finally get to fuck Theo in his bed.

He moves through the kitchen, his hands in his shorts pockets, and stares at me as I throw away the last of the red cups. When I start wiping down the counters with Lysol wipes, he speaks up. "You don't have to do that."

I cock my head to the side. "Two things. One, you'd be pissed if you woke up tomorrow and the kitchen was a mess, and two, who do you think always cleaned up after Lucas had people over?"

"I figured." He moves closer to me and pulls a bottle of whiskey from the cart in the corner. "Have one with me?" He asks.

Even though I'm still a little tipsy, I nod and he pours some in each glass. "Did he give you a hard time?"

I shake my head before tossing the wipe in the trash and washing my hands, wanting to be done cleaning for now. "No. I told him it was a random guy from college."

He nods. "Rory doesn't know?"

"No, she knows I left that night. But I never told her who with.

Evidently, she thought I left with Lucas and she was trying to have some drunken dramatic reveal that we are actually together. I'm quite mad at her right now." I'm only half joking because while I am mad, I know it won't be for long.

"Fair." He chuckles as he moves closer to me and pulls me into his chest. "Interesting little game." He pulls his hand out of his pocket and reveals two dice. He moves them around his hand, before giving me a sexy smirk. "I would imagine it's more fun in...smaller parties."

Chapter
ELEVEN

THEO

W E'RE IN MY ROOM AFTER WE'VE FINISHED CLEANING up the kitchen. I also set the alarm in case Lucas comes back before I expect him and it gives us at least a little bit of time for Avery and any of her discarded clothes to be moved out of sight in case Lucas wants to pop his head inside to say good night. My heart fucking stopped earlier hearing Rory's question, but Avery handled it well. Effortlessly cool and not at all like she was also panicking. I'm sitting on the edge of my bed with Avery in my lap straddling me as she moves around far too much.

I brought the bottle of whiskey upstairs with us and we each had another drink and now Avery is practically attached to me. "I'm horny," she moans in my ear before biting down gently on it.

"Good," I tell her. "So am I. It'll make the game more fun."

"Touch me, please," she says, reaching between us for my belt when I grab her hand.

"Get on the bed," I command and she does, getting into a kneeling position with her legs slightly spread. I take a sip of the whiskey and hold the dice in my hand. "Truth or dare."

"Dare," she whispers.

"Oh." I smile cockily. "Someone's brave all of a sudden." I roll the dice around in my hand. "If I roll a six, you have to take off your dress." I throw them on the bed and they bounce before landing in front of her and sure enough, it lands on a two and a four. Her eyes move from the dice to me. "I should probably tell you, my dad taught me to play Craps when I was about seven years old, so I'm pretty good with a pair of dice."

"Oh." She smirks. "Lucky me." She gets off the bed slowly slides the dress down her body leaving her topless, clad only in a pair of panties. I rub my dick, desperate to relieve the ache when I see her starting to remove her panties.

"Just the dress," I grunt. "Leave them."

She moves around the bed until she's standing right in front of me. "Fine." She raises an eyebrow conspiratorially. "Can I have a sip?"

"Since you asked nicely." I hand her the glass and snatch the dice off the bed to hand them to her.

"Truth or dare?" She asks.

"Truth."

"Scared?" she asks before taking a long sip of the whiskey.

"No." I shake my head.

"If I roll an eight, you have to tell me about the first time you thought about me while you touched your dick."

I let out a breath, knowing she was going to ask me something along these lines and I nod towards the bed, telling her to roll. She does and of course, *an eight.*

"First of all, how old was I?"

I scoff. "You are a horny little degenerate." I repeat her words from earlier. "You were eighteen."

"Like the stroke of midnight on my birthday, eighteen? Or like eighteen and nine months."

I cock my head to the side. "You want to hear the story?" She giggles and nods her head. "It was the summer after your freshman year of college and there was a bunch of you in the backyard at the pool and…you were wearing this black bathing suit that…God, it should have been illegal. It showed entirely too much of your ass. But I didn't notice." I shake my head remembering the moment she went from Avery Summers, the girl that lived next door, to the smokeshow who had me fucking my hand every night. "There were some guys in the kitchen"—I roll my eyes at the memory—"getting ice for their *non-alcoholic drinks* of course, and one of them mentioned you and they started talking about how hot you looked and some other not so respectful things. Things they wanted to do to you…whatever. I heard it. Reamed them out for it and told them to get out of my house." I take another breath. "And then when I looked outside, it was like I was seeing you in a whole different light. Maybe it was their words still ringing in my head, I don't know. I never noticed your breasts or your ass before and now it was…very hard to miss them. I went to my bathroom and fucked my hand for an hour."

"Oh my God," she whispers and presses against me, running her fingers up my chest. "Take this off."

"You didn't dare me."

"I don't care."

I oblige because I'm getting warm and I love her eyes on me and the way she ogles my body. I pull my shirt over my head and she presses her lips to my chest. "That is so hot. Will you fuck me now?"

"Why the rush?" I smile. "It's my roll." I grab the dice. "Truth or dare?"

"Dare."

"If I roll a seven, I get to drink this whiskey…off of your body." I run my tongue over my bottom lip.

Her eyes dart from my mouth to the bed waiting for my roll and when it lands on seven, she smiles wickedly. "Should I lay on the floor?"

"Of course not, get on the bed." I gesture for her to lie down.

"What if you spill whiskey on it?"

"I won't."

"Have you ever done this before?" She lies on her back, her tits still on display and I realize I haven't even touched them. I give her a look and I don't mistake the envious look that flashes before she shuts her eyes.

I lean over her, dragging my tongue around one of her dusty rose nipples and her eyes pop open just as I close my lips around it, sucking it hard. "Don't be jealous," I tell her as I move to the other, kissing and licking it before hollowing my cheeks and letting her go with a loud, wet pop.

"I'm not."

I snort. "Okay, angel. You ready?"

She nods and I tip the bottle just enough for it to pour into her belly button. I get on the bed and kneel between her legs, and slowly move my hands up her smooth thighs until they meet the apex.

"Theo. Don't tease me, I'm trying to hold still."

"Hmmmm." I moan as I press my nose to her panty-covered sex. I inhale her, smelling and feeling how wet she is against the tip of my nose.

"God!" She whimpers as I drag my tongue over the satin covering her pussy. She shakes but still manages to keep the whiskey in her belly button. I hover my lips around the area before my tongue darts out and I lap at the alcohol slowly, swirling my tongue around her skin before sucking it all into my mouth. Once I clean all the traces of alcohol from her skin, I drag my tongue up her torso between her breasts and into her mouth, wanting a taste of her tongue.

"Best shot of whiskey I ever had," I grunt against her lips before moving off her and helping her to her feet.

"Truth or dare," she says and I can tell she's getting antsy because her eyes are glued to my groin and she's rubbing her thighs together.

"Dare."

"If I roll a seven, I want you to get naked." She starts to roll before she stops. "And I'm going to get naked."

"Okay." I chuckle because I'm not going to argue with that.

She starts to roll again but she stops. "And then we sixty-nine." She smiles.

"I don't think you're playing right? I think you get one, I gave you the second…"

"Are you complaining?" She drags a finger down my body and cups me through my pants. "What happened to wanting to put your mouth on my pussy before I left here tonight?"

"Oh, believe me, that's happening."

"This is fun and all but I just…want to get the party started already."

I nod. "Okay so you roll a seven and you sit on my face while you suck my cock."

She bites her bottom lip and lets out a breath before shooting them on the bed and letting out the sexiest *fuck yes*, when it lands on seven. I barely have a second to register the number before her hands are on my belt and I realize she'd already pulled her panties off.

"Fuck me, Avery."

"Yes, yes *please*, let's do that."

"I want to put my mouth on you first," I grunt as I slide off my jeans and briefs leaving me naked. I get on the bed, my dick hard and leaking and dying to get inside of her as I lay on my back. She drags her eyes all over me and shakes her head.

"God, you're so hot." She kneels on the bed and I reach for her, pulling her to my chest and pressing a kiss to her lips.

"You somehow grew into the most gorgeous woman I've ever laid eyes on." She narrows her eyes like she doesn't believe me and when she starts to pull away, I grab her by her jaw, squeezing it gently. "Tell me you believe me."

"Sure, Theo. You were a football star for a decade and met models and movie stars and women all over the world but the girl next door is the most gorgeous? You've already got me in bed," she teases and shoots me a look. "I don't need all that."

I squeeze harder and sit up slightly. "You calling me a liar?" I raise an eyebrow at her. "Because I won't let you come if that's the case."

Her mouth drops open. "That's not fair. I dared you and I won."

"Fuck the dare." I tell her. "You were sitting on my face regardless. Now I'll ask you again," I say as I drag my finger over her nipples that pebble under my touch. "Are you calling me a liar?"

She shivers and shakes her head. "No."

"So you believe me when I say that while yes, I've met tons of women throughout my life, nobody has turned my head like you have. *You* are, by far, the most gorgeous." She nods and if I'm not mistaken, I see her eyes glisten slightly. "Now be a good girl, and put your pussy on my face."

Her eyes widen and she gives me the sexiest smile before she turns around to straddle my face and I don't waste a second before reaching up and putting my mouth on her cunt. "Oh fuck, Theo." She moans my name as I swirl my tongue around her and suction my lips around her clit.

God, it fucking sounds good on her lips.

I find myself thinking about her calling my name in just a normal day to day routine.

No. Stop that. Dangerous territory.

"Theo," she moans again. "Fuck, you're going to make me come so hard." She grabs my dick with one hand and wraps her lips around me and I groan, which I'm guessing sends a vibration through her because she squeals and lets out the sexiest, breathiest giggle that almost makes me explode down her throat.

"Fuck, baby. You already know my dick so fucking well," I tell her as she pulls me out of her mouth and takes long slow licks up the shaft and swirls her tongue around the tip. One of her hands is on my balls, rubbing them gently and *fuck* I want her mouth on them.

Next dare. My mind thinks.

"Don't stop," she cries as she begins to move her hips up and down slowly in time with my licks.

She's so sexy, holy fuck.

She cries out again and I feel like her orgasm must be close because she pulls me out of her mouth and continues to hump my face. "Fuck fuck fuck, Theo, I'm coming! Oh God, right there!" She screams out her orgasm and I'm thanked for my service by the most explosive orgasm leaking out of her and down my chin.

"Fuck." I growl, as I lick her cunt through her orgasm even as she quivers around my tongue.

"Mmmm, baby, too sensitive." She moans as she tries to pull away from my tongue and there's a spark in my dick over the first time she's called me something other than Theo. I know it's a part of the sex high, but I want to hear it again.

Fuck, I'm in trouble.

I grip her hips, keeping her on top of me and I drag my tongue through her slit one more time. "Theo!" She gasps and squirms and I finally let her go with a gentle slap to her ass.

She pulls off of me finally and kneels between my legs before leaning up to press a kiss to my lips. "I love seeing your face covered in *me*."

"I love being covered in *you*," I tell her. She sits back on her heels and leans over my dick and wraps her lips around it. "I don't want to come in your mouth."

"Please." She looks up at me with what I think is her attempt at giving me puppy dog eyes. *And dammit, it's working.*

"I want to come in your pussy," I grunt.

"But, I want to swallow your cum."

"Avery," I warn through gritted teeth, "don't do this to me, baby."

"I can get it up for us again, don't worry." She winks before she sucks me into her mouth, fucking me with it like that night in the car when she deep-throated me.

"Put your mouth on my balls."

"Mmmm, you didn't roll." She says with a sassy look that tells me she'll probably do it anyway she just wants to be a smartass.

"You got like three in one." I laugh and she giggles before swirling her tongue around one of my balls before the other and then sucking it into her mouth all while she's jacking my dick.

"Fuck fuck fuck, Avery you're so incredible. You turn me on so much." She continues this assault for a few moments before she moves back to my dick, alternating between licking and sucking.

"Shit, right there. Right there, angel." I groan and then a blast of pleasure moves through me as she presses her finger to my perineum and gently massages it. "Fuck, Avery. You're a Goddess, fuuuuck." I groan as I begin to climax in her mouth. She fucks me through it, sucking me harder with each thrust. When I finally stop coming, she slides off of me, wipes the sides of her mouth, and licks her lips before giving me a devilish smirk. "That was fun."

I let out a breath. "An understatement." *Best fucking blowjob I've ever gotten. Jesus Christ. It's a clichéd saying but she may actually be able to suck the nails out of a floorboard.*

"I have something else I want to try while we are waiting for your dick to get hard again."

"Oh yeah?" I raise an eyebrow.

"You don't...I mean if you don't do it or don't want..." She stammers.

I grab her by her waist and pull her hard against me before moving us so that she's underneath me and I'm hovering over her.

"Are you getting shy on me?"

"No. It's just not something...conventional."

I sit up wondering what she's going to ask and reach for the dice before dropping them into her hand. "I'm not conventional. Roll the dice."

"Okay, well..." She reaches over to the nightstand and drains the contents of the glass, which was probably at least another shot, and looks at me. "If I roll a seven, I want you to get on your knees and eat my ass." I'm instantly fucking hard again at her words but she doesn't look at me after she says it or even wait for me to respond before she rolls them.

My eyes dart to hers, desperate to see one of the many ways you can make seven when I see it lands on snake eyes. *Two.*

"Well..." She shrugs. "You don't have—"

"Doubles," I grunt. "Roll again."

A smile pulls at her lips and she picks up the dice and rolls them again, landing on nine. She turns to me and I can still see her cheeks are a little flushed, either from her words or the alcohol or a combination of the two. "Okay, your turn."

I eye the dice, before turning to her. "Fuck it, I want to eat it anyway." I push her to her stomach, pull her up on her knees, and press her face into my pillows.

"Theo." She gasps when I spread her cheeks and spit on her hole. She clenches and I see her sexy cunt wet and begging me to lick it and fuck, do I want to taste her there again.

She lets out a cry and I lay a smack on her ass eliciting a moan out of her. "You going to let me put my dick here," I ask as I rub her hole with my index finger before circling it with my tongue.

"Fuck…" she moans. "Yes." She turns around and looks at me. "Smack my ass again."

"Damn." I bite my bottom lip and lay a smack on the other cheek. "You like that?"

"Love it." She moans as I go back to swirling my tongue around her puckered hole, squeezing her cheeks as I eat her like the starving man she's turned me in to. The last week I haven't had her I've been fucking desperate for her taste and her scent and *Christ*, that fucking smile she gives me when we're alone. I slide my hand forward to rub her clit and she gasps, trying to pull away from my mouth as she reacts to the blast of pleasure. I hold her tighter, keeping my mouth on her and my fingers on her clit.

I do this for several more minutes, my dick hard and leaking precum and ready to be inside her. I pull back, pressing a kiss to one of her ass cheeks before sinking my teeth into the flesh. She lets out a squeal and then a moan worthy of porn. "Theo. Fuck me, *please*."

"I'll fuck your ass next time. I don't have any lube and my dick could cut glass right now." I swipe two fingers through her slit. "I need to fuck you here."

She giggles and pushes her ass up against my groin and moves it against me. "Yes, please."

I haven't fucked her from behind which is usually one of my favorite positions and seeing Avery's ass up close and personal is not going to let me last long. She slides back onto my dick and immediately we find the perfect rhythm. I grip her hips, pulling her harder and harder against me and she meets me with equal thrusts.

"Oh God, Theo! Fuck, it's so deep."

Yeah, it is. Her cunt is like a vice around my dick she's clamped down so hard. "Baby," I let my head fall back as pleasure shoots through me, "I'm not going to last long."

"Shit, me either." She grabs a pillow and I see her bite down on it and a muffled squeal leaves her. "Just like that. Oh God, yes yes yes like that!" she cries, letting the pillow fall from her mouth. "Fuck, I'm coming!"

Those words falling from her lips and the feeling of her cunt squeezing and fluttering around my dick has my climax ripping through me and I come with a roar, growling her name through gritted teeth. "Fuck fuck fuck Avery. Yes, right fucking there." I fall over her, still holding most of my weight but my torso rests lightly on her back. She turns her head and I press my lips to her cheek as she gives me a dreamy smile. We stay like this for a few moments even as I'm softening, our bodies connected and a thought floats through my head that I want more of her and *this*.

"You are…a God Theo Graham, wow." She slides down to her stomach and I move to the side to spoon her, pulling her against me so her back is to my front and wrap an arm around her stomach. I press a kiss to her shoulder. "I wish I could stay," she murmurs as she reaches for the hand that I'd snaked underneath her and drags her teeth along the finger gently.

"I wish you could too."

She turns in my arms and looks up at me, her gorgeous face still has a light sheen of sweat and her eyes are a little hazy. "Maybe I could stay over Saturday? I'll come up with a reason to be out of the house?"

Lucas leaves Saturday which means she could stay over and the idea of going to sleep and waking up with her in my bed sounds fucking phenomenal.

We lay like that for a few more minutes, but we can both feel our time together getting shorter. When she gets up to pull her dress on and grabs her underwear she asks with a sexy look on her face, "Want to keep these?"

I yank them from her hand before she has a chance to say she's kidding. I pull on some sweats and a t-shirt because even if she is next door, I'm going to make sure she gets inside safely.

"You know…" she starts, "I do still have my college apartment until the end of June." She runs her hands up my chest. "And at some point, I do have to go pack it up." She looks up at me. "You don't have to help, but you could come with me…we could have some privacy."

"Of course, I'll help you." I press a kiss to her forehead. "Let me know when." She nods as we begin walking down the hall and down the stairs. It's nearing two in the morning and I know Lucas will be home soon but at this point, even if he walked in right now, we could say she fell asleep and just woke up and it would be believable.

Soon, Lucas will be in New York and it'll be much easier to navigate whatever this is between us. "I'll be at the café tomorrow," she says as I disarm the alarm to open the door. "You should come by." She shrugs. My office is only about a five-minute walk from *Avery's Café* and we often ordered coffee and lunch from there. "I'll buy you lunch." She taps my nose and presses a light kiss to my lips before she opens the door. I follow her out as she darts across my front yard and between our houses to hers. She waves from her front porch and then she's safe inside.

I close the door behind me, and the skittering of my pulse at the thought of seeing her tomorrow sends up about a hundred red flags. I feel the exact moment my mind starts to shift and I realize that this is definitely not just a fling and I am in a whole lot of fucking trouble.

Chapter
TWELVE

Avery

DESPITE ALL OF THE ALCOHOL I CONSUMED LAST NIGHT, I'm not terribly hungover, though I am very fucking sore, in the best possible way. I've been replaying last night, also known as the hottest night and the best sex of my life, on a loop since I woke up this morning. My mom leaves for the café at five in the morning, but I won't be getting there until closer to nine every morning, so I have time for a cup of coffee before I get ready.

Around eight-thirty, just before I get in the car to head over there, I get a text from Theo and I immediately smile.

> **TG: Good morning, just thought I'd let you know my sheets smell like you. Had to put them in the washer this morning.**
>
> **Me: Shame. I smell good.**
>
> **TG: Yes you do, but it's also very noticeable if anyone were to go into my room.**
>
> **Me: Ah, fair. How are you feeling this morning?**
>
> **TG: Tired as shit, and a headache but I'll manage. You?**
>
> **Me: Fine, but I'm 21.**
>
> **TG: Ha—Ha. Well, have a great first day. I'll text you when I plan to come by.**

I totally forgot I let my love drunk and *actual* drunk brain

convince me to invite him to the shop last night like some cute little lunch date.

Ugh, Avery, you have no chill!

> **Me: Oh! You really don't have to.**
>
> **TG: You're uninviting me now?**
>
> **Me: No! I just meant I didn't want you to feel obligated
> since I asked you. I understand you're busy**
>
> **TG: I'm not too busy to come see you.**
>
> **Me: *heart eye emojis***

I press my phone to my chest and I know that I am visibly
swooning right now.

I make it to the café and find street parking pretty easily despite
the morning breakfast rush. While *Avery's* is by far the best *and* most
picturesque café, there are a few others down the block that compete
for customers. There are six tables outside of the entrance that are full
right now. Two moms with their strollers, two girls that look about
college-aged, a guy on his laptop, a man and a woman who look like
they may be on a date, and a girl reading a book all occupy tables with
various drinks and breakfast dishes. I make my way inside and there's
a long line leading to where my mom is behind the counter along
with the two college students she hired for mornings in the summer.

She has a staff of six, including someone who helps with cooking *when my controlling mom feels the need to release some responsibility,*
two of the most chipper college students, an assistant manager, and
an accountant. My job, for now, will be to assist everyone where they
need help as I learn the ropes. Eventually, when my mom wants to
step back and only work one or two days a week, I will fill her shoes.
We also are talking about expanding so I would probably promote
the assistant manager and assistant chef to higher positions.

I move to the back office and set my stuff behind my mom's
desk. I smile thinking about all the times I came here as a child and
would sit here coloring or doing my homework as I got older while
I waited for her.

"Hi, honey!" My mom pops in and presses a kiss to my cheek. "I saw you come in. You want some breakfast?"

"Maybe just a croissant. I drank the coffee you left in the pot."

"Oh good, I was hoping you saw it. I do think Jordan is going to go on break in a few, so if you want to come help for a bit that would be great. I think you kids getting home from college has made us a little busier this week."

"Yep. Let me just wash my hands." I knew that there was a chance I was going to be getting my clothes a little messy today, so I opted for cream linen pants and a black v-neck wide-strapped tank top. My mom wanted the place to have a very Parisian feel so everything is black and cream, including the dress code. I pull my hair up with a claw clip and make my way out to the main floor.

It's nearing almost two in the afternoon and I haven't heard from Theo. Lucas has texted about having dinner later so I'm hoping that means we are moving past last night without rehashing it. *Fine by me.* But I haven't had a chance to respond. We've been pretty busy all day and this has been the first lull in the rush. I'm actually sitting at a table with my laptop open doing some market research when the door flies open and the person I was definitely not expecting to see walks through the door.

My mouth drops open when I see Rebecca float through the room dressed like she'd just stepped off the runway at Milan Fashion Week. She's wearing black shorts over a pair of sheer tights with her long lean legs attached to a pair of loafers, a black blazer with a white chiffon bow tied under her neck. *God she is so fucking chic and it pisses me off.* She's been in Italy for the past few years, and has rarely come back, and even gave Lucas some half-assed excuse as to why she couldn't even make it to his college graduation. She pushes her sunglasses to the top of her head and I notice her dark hair has been chopped into a short sleek bob and even that looks fucking good. She turns her head away from the counter to look in my direction, and when I try to avert my gaze she sees me and then she's moving towards me.

Great.

"Avery! Oh my gosh!" I stand up just in time for her to wrap her arms around me. "Mwah, mwah." She kisses my cheeks. "My God, you are more gorgeous every time I see you. You must have the boys fighting over you."

"Rebecca! What a nice—surprise!" I laugh nervously as I cock my head to the side because I would definitely know if Lucas or Theo for that matter knew she was coming. *They are both going to flip.*

"I know! I figured it was time to come spend a bit of time with my babies."

"Oh! Wow...that is...wow!" I put on my best fake smile because *oh fuck.*

"But I couldn't come to town without stopping to get coffee first. I swear, the food here is just like it is in Europe. Your mom knows her stuff." She scrunches her nose. "So, what's new with you!?"

I'm sleeping with your ex-husband?

"Nothing!" I shrug. "I just graduated and now I'm going to be working here. Rebecca, you know Lucas is moving like...tomorrow, right?"

"I know. New York! So exciting. I actually have to pop up there before I go back to Italy. But I figured with this revelation regarding Raegan, we needed to have a family meeting."

Family...meeting? Since when is that a Graham family thing and since when do you even consider yourself a part of their family? "Right..."

"I'm sure you know by now?"

"Well...I'm not sure." *What does she know?* "I only know she's seeing someone."

"Oh my gosh, and she wants to marry this guy? I swear, if she's pregnant, I am going to lose it," she says with a huff. "Oh, Camille!" She waves and my mother gives me a look before giving her the infamous Camille Summers smile.

"Oh my gosh, Rebecca! Hiiiiii." She smiles and I immediately drop to my table and text Theo and Lucas in a group chat because now is the time for everyone to be on the same page. I add Raegan as well.

Me: Hi! This is 100% not a joke. But Rebecca is here at the café.

Lucas: Excuse me???

Raegan: OMG

My phone immediately starts ringing and when I see it's Theo, I answer it before slipping out the front door. "Hi."

"What the fuck?"

"I...yeah."

"Why?"

"To, and I quote, 'spend time with her babies and for a family meeting about Raegan.'" I look over my shoulder to make sure I'm still alone.

"What the fuck?"

"You said that." I wince.

"FUCK." He growls and I hear the slam of a door. "I don't think Raegan has told her yet and this is not going to end well."

"Well, given that she also said and I quote 'I swear if she's pregnant, I am going to lose it,' I would say that's a fair assessment."

"I'm coming over there. I'm sorry I haven't had a chance to before now. It's been a hell of a day."

"And getting better, it seems."

He chuckles and I hear him telling his assistant that he's stepping out for lunch and will be back, and to let him know if she needs anything.

"This is not how I wanted to spend my time there. I wanted to stare at the gorgeous new girl that works there and flirt with her, not deal with the wicked witch of Milan." He sighs. "Fuck. I shouldn't have said that. I...shouldn't talk about her like that in front of you."

I frown. "Why?"

"I don't know...because..."

"I think in this situation I can be the woman you're sleeping with and not your son's friend that lives next door, don't you think?" I turn around again, before turning back to face the street. "Look she cornered my mother, but I should get back in."

"See you in five."

"Okay."

"In case I can't tell you when I see you, you look beautiful today."

I fucking *melt*. "Bye Theo." I giggle.

⁓

Theo looks so good it hurts to not stare at him when he steps into the café. He's wearing a white button-down and navy slacks, and I wanted to rip them off right the fuck now.

"Oh. Well, good news travels fast!" Rebecca's eyes fall to mine and she gives me a fake smile that I give right back. I am still standing with her as my mom goes back to work but for the past five minutes, she's just been scrolling on her phone as she shows me pictures of shit I care nothing about and people I don't know.

"I was just confused as to why Lucas didn't tell me you were coming to town," I explain.

"Let's not place false blame here," Theo starts. "Why didn't you tell anyone you were coming? You know your son is moving to New York tomorrow. Odd time for mother-son bonding?" Theo blinks at her and she pulls her to-go cup of cappuccino to her lips.

"Hello to you too, Theodore." She smiles. "For your information, I felt so far and out of the loop."

"What else is new?" He snaps and I realize it is definitely my cue to leave.

"You know, you guys can have this table." I grab my laptop, my notebook, and my iced coffee. "Theo, can I bring you something?"

He doesn't even look at me as he speaks. "Uh, yeah. Coffee would be great."

I nod. "Rebecca, anything else?"

"Oh no, honey. Thank you." She takes my seat and Theo sits across from her. I move away not wanting any part of that.

"What is that about?" My mother asks as she peers at them over the counter.

"None of them knew she was coming."

"You called Theo?" She asks me.

"I texted all three of them in a group chat—him, Lucas, and Raegan and he called me," I explain.

"Hmm. Well, why do you think she's in town?"

"Supposedly, 'to spend time with her children,'" I say using air quotes.

"A little late for that, no? I mean never too late to spend time with people but…she's got quite a few years of making up to do. And isn't Lucas leaving tomorrow?" I pull my mother into the back office, knowing that the girls can handle the front for now.

"Okay, you cannot repeat this to anyone."

"I won't! Oh, you've got tea!" My mom's hazel eyes light up as she claps her hands together.

"I'm only telling you because…well, I don't know why I'm telling you, because you're a gossip!"

She puts her hands on her hips and narrows her eyes into slits. "I am not."

"Okay, evidently Laura Wilder, you know Natasha's mom?"

"Yes, yes of course! Pops pills like Tic Tacs," she says waving her hands as if to say *okay out with it.*

"Mom!"

"Well! Go on!"

I roll my eyes. "Apparently, she told Rebecca that Raegan's boyfriend has a ring. She called Theo hysterical when the three of us were out at brunch last weekend. So, I feel like *that's* why she's here." I leave out the part about Raegan being pregnant because that is definitely not my place to tell.

"Ooooh." She nods and puts her hands on her cheeks. "A ring. Wow. So, I guess they're serious."

"I don't know the details. I don't think he's planning to propose tomorrow but…I suppose it's in the works. Now, don't go spreading that around."

"If Laura knows, I'm sure I'll hear it from Macey at tennis." She pulls out her phone and I immediately grab it from her hands.

"Okay well, don't *you* go spreading it. Come on, Mom, they

know if they hear anything about the Graham family from you it's true because you have a reliable source."

"Fine." She zips her lips before unzipping them. "Except your dad." She zips them again and I chuckle before following her out.

Fuck, Theo's coffee. I quickly make him a cup and take him the cream and sugar as well and I see the conversation is not going over well based on their body language.

"I wasn't sure how you took it so I brought—"

"Black is fine," he says and I nod. *Okay, then.*

"Right, well, I'm going to step out for a minute, so if you need anything just ummm…" I point at the girls. "They can help you."

"Always good to see you, Avery." Rebecca stands and gives me a kiss on the cheek. "I hope I see you before I leave."

"I—maybe!"

I look at Theo who has just now looked at me and gives me a curt nod. "See you later, Avery." He waves and I make my way into the back to grab my bag. "Mom, I'm going to survey the block, I'll be back," I tell her. Once every couple of weeks, I like to walk through the city and see what the competition is doing. Main Street is several blocks long so I'm hoping I can be gone long enough that my *situationship* and his ex-wife will have dispersed by the time I get back.

What was that anyway? He barely looked at me.

You know that was about Rebecca. Not about you.

Still.

Relax. Stop overthinking. He told you that you looked beautiful five minutes prior and he ate your ass last night. He's still interested.

My phone vibrates before I'm even at the end of the block.

TG: I'm sorry. Forgive me.

I contemplate letting him wait for a response for about half of a second before I realize I don't want to play games and I really want to know what he's thinking.

Me: Care to tell me what that was about?

TG: I don't know how well Rebecca can still read me.

I didn't want her to see anything in the way I looked at you. She is the last person I want in my business about anything. Let alone about you.

I tilt my head to the side because the reasoning does make sense.

TG: But I'm sorry. I suddenly couldn't remember how I used to act around you. All I could think about was the past week.

Me: Okay. Understood.

TG: Do you really?

Me: Yes

TG: Alright.

Me: Is she still there?

TG: Yes. On the phone.

Me: Is she staying with you while she's in town?

TG: What do you think?

Me: I don't know!

TG: She didn't stay with me when our kids lived there, you think she will now?

Me: Okay.

TG: I feel like this should go without saying since you've been around a minute and you know my relationship with her is less than pleasant, but you have nothing to worry about in regards to Rebecca.

Me: I'm not worried

TG: Good. You shouldn't. No one should worry you.

I narrow my eyes at his words, not wanting to read too much into it but also wanting clarification because that sounds like something a man would tell his girlfriend, not the woman he's casually sleeping with.

Not casual. This is serious. I can practically hear Theo saying in my ear.

TG: Tell me something good.

I smile at this question that he's asked before. I think about it for a second before I type out a response.

Me: I had a lot of fun last night.

TG: So did I. How about something that doesn't have to do with how much I made you come?

I giggle and roll my eyes.

Me: Well my first day is going well. I really love working with my mom and being a part of the business that she built from the ground up.

TG: I'm really glad to hear that. I'm sure she's happy you're there.

My phone starts to ring and I half expect it to be Theo when I see it's Raegan.

"Hey."

"Oh my God. Does she know I'm pregnant?" She basically screams and I have to pull the phone away from my ear.

"I don't think so." I wince. "I'm not sure if your dad is telling her? I left the café. It is *frosty* in there."

"I'll bet. My parents are like cats in a bag. She texted Lucas and me that she wants to have dinner with us." She groans. "Lucas is pissed because he doesn't want to deal with this on his last night at home. He wanted to have dinner with you, me, and dad."

"I know."

"Maybe you and dad should come."

I chuckle nervously because *absolutely not.* "Uhhh…"

"Come on, I'm bringing Wes."

"Really?"

"Sure. He knows about all my mommy issues and he never lets anyone bully me and he knows how manipulative my mother can be.

I need my guard dog." She giggles. "Besides, if I bring him, she's less likely to be too unhinged." She sighs. "Which is whyyyy you should come!"

"No thanks, Rae, I'm good."

"Ughhhh." She groans. "I knew I shouldn't have called her."

"Wait, you talked to her?" I ask confused.

"I called her after I found out she called Dad. I told her that it was true and Wes does have a ring but that it isn't happening tomorrow. I should have known she would take that to mean it was time for her to hop on a plane and come make my life difficult."

"Are you going to tell her you're pregnant while she's here?"

"I suppose that depends on how she acts at dinner."

My phone starts to buzz indicating I'm getting a call and it's the one I've been expecting. "Call you back, your brother is calling."

"Oh good, maybe he'll convince you to come!" I roll my eyes before clicking over.

"Don't ask, the answer is no," I say as soon as I answer the phone without giving him a chance to speak. I'm still walking down the block, but I decide to stop and sit on a bench.

Lucas chuckles. "And you claim to love me."

"Not that much."

"It's my last night in town, Avery!"

"You aren't moving across the planet. You'll be an hour train ride away. I'll come visit in a few weeks."

"Not the point!"

"Lucas, I'm not coming to dinner with you and Rae and your mom and maybe your dad? No."

"Why? You're practically family."

I wince thinking about the very not family-like things I've been doing with his father the past few years. "And I love that you want me to feel included, but no." *Even if I didn't already feel like it wasn't my place, there is a zero percent chance, I'm going to willingly have dinner with Theo and his ex-wife.*

"Wes is coming," Lucas offers.

"Wes is in a relationship with your sister."

"And you're my best friend," he argues.

"This family dinner is about said relationship, Lucas. It makes sense for Wes to be there."

He huffs. "I would do it for you."

"I wouldn't ask and also Camille Summers resents the comparison to your mother," I say because even on my mother's worst day, she could never be like Rebecca.

"Ave, in all seriousness…" He pauses. "Please."

I sigh, remembering what it was like becoming friends with Lucas fresh off his parents' divorce and witnessing that trauma firsthand through his eyes. Rebecca packed up and left Raegan and Lucas in the midst of turmoil at the beginning of their teenage years to go traveling around the world with calls once a week and a bi-annual visit that usually left Raegan in tears.

I definitely didn't want to go to dinner with Theo and his ex-wife, but I'd go to dinner with Lucas and his parents because I've always been there for him over this. Feeling abandoned and unloved by your mother isn't something I understand on any level, but I've tried my best to be there and listen. As of late, I probably haven't been the best friend to Lucas with everything going on with Theo, but I still care about him. He's not only been my best friend for eight years but he's also my person and although things are slowly shifting, I suddenly feel desperate to hang on to this part of our friendship that made us more like family.

"Okay, I'll be there." I sigh. "Text me the details."

Chapter
THIRTEEN

Avery

TG: Heard you got roped into this shitshow tonight.

Me: Not how I expected to spend my Friday night haha

TG: I'm sorry.

Me: It's okay. Lucas asked me to.

TG: I'm sorry if I can't be as attentive as I want to be with you tonight.

Me: Theo, it's fine. I get it.

TG: I don't.

Me: What do you mean?

TG: Nothing, I'll see you soon. Do you want to ride with me and Lucas?

Me: No, that's okay. I'm going to drive myself. It will also keep me sober in case I have to drive any of you home

TG: As much as Rebecca makes me want to drink, I need to keep that in check. The last thing I need is to have one too many and spend the night staring at you like I want to fuck you.

Me: Yes, keep your eyes in check, Theo.

TG: I'll try my best. See you at eight

After a few moments of staring at our conversation, I text him again.

> **Me: Hey**
>
> **TG: Yes?**
>
> **Me: Tell me something good.**

He doesn't respond right away and I read over the conversation again, wondering what he meant by *I don't. What's there not to get?* I contemplate this thought, obsessing over it the entire way to the restaurant as I try to calm my nerves and convince myself that there is absolutely nothing sexy about seeing Theo tonight. I opt to wear black flowy pants and a high-neck sleeveless black backless top, trying not to show too much skin so Theo doesn't have to struggle with keeping his eyes off of me. I get to the restaurant with about ten minutes to spare and see I have a message from Theo.

> **TG: I can't stop thinking about you.**
>
> **Me: Neither can I.**

I'm beaming at my phone when I hear Lucas' voice as soon as I enter the lobby so I put my phone away.

"Hey, they sat us already," he says as he pulls me into a hug. He's wearing a black polo and dark blue jeans and I'm suddenly very grateful that I didn't dress up too much. "Just wanted to make sure you knew where to find us."

"Is everyone here?"

"Hell no. My mom will probably be at least thirty minutes late and Raegan will be either right on time or a little late herself. It's just me and Dad."

Awesome.

"Okay." I reach for his arm as he goes to walk away and tug on it gently. "You okay?"

"Yeah." He shrugs. "I was just thinking I haven't seen my mom in almost two years. That can't be right?" He narrows his eyes. "I remember last year she came to New York for Fashion Week in September and we somehow missed each other." He shrugs. "It's always got to be on her terms though, right?"

I wince, remembering that. He wasn't dying to see her or anything but I remember hearing the disappointment in his voice when she told him that she was "swamped while she was in town" and that he should definitely come to Italy over winter break. "Lucas…"

"I'm glad you're here." He gives me a smile before he ushers me in front of him towards our table, guiding me with his hand on the small of my bare back to a private room. It's a round table and I see Theo sitting and scrolling through his phone. His eyes lift to meet mine when I walk in and I give him a small smile as Lucas takes the seat next to him.

"You look very nice, Avery." He's a little more dressed up than Lucas, in a button-down and slacks and I try not to focus too much on the skin exposed from where he left a few buttons undone.

"Thank you." I smile, trying my best not to swoon in front of Lucas.

"Yeah, you do. I rarely see you in pants during the summer." Lucas chuckles before he takes a sip of what I think is bourbon.

I sit on the other side of Lucas and we have a few moments of silence before Theo breaks it.

"Your sister said they will be here in five. Any word from your mother?" Theo looks at Lucas in question and Lucas rolls his eyes.

"She said ten minutes, but I'd bet a million dollars she hasn't left her hotel yet."

"Alright, no one is less pleased about this than me, but she's here and she's your mother. Don't spend the whole dinner making jabs at her." Theo lightly scolds.

Lucas scoffs. "How is that a jab? That's a fact."

"You know what I'm saying Luke." Theo gives him a look and Lucas rolls his eyes before taking another sip of his drink.

"Fine, whatever."

The door opens and Raegan walks in with a tall man at her side. He has sandy brown hair, a little peppered with gray, and blue eyes behind sleek square frames. I've never met Wes; I've only seen pictures, but he is definitely better looking in person.

Yep, I definitely have a thing for older men.

"Dad, Lucas, you remember Wes." She points at him and they both shake his hand and extend polite pleasantries before she turns to me. "This is Avery, Lucas' and my childhood friend. More Lucas though. They've always been attached at the hip. She's his buffer," she whispers loudly, causing Lucas to shoot her a look.

I stand and hold out my hand. "It's nice to meet you. Raegan has had nothing but lovely things to say about you." He shakes my hand and gives me a warm smile revealing dimples on each cheek.

"Lovely to meet you as well, Avery. Raegan has told me about you also." His voice is low and deep and very sexy. *Good for you, Rae.*

Raegan immediately takes the seat next to Theo and Wes sits next to her, leaving the only open seat between Wes and me. While it's not my ideal seating arrangement, I can understand why. Wes and I inadvertently serve as the shield to both Raegan and Lucas.

The conversation flows for the next twenty minutes or so and although everyone is tense, the air is breathable. It's like we're all bracing ourselves but we want to enjoy it now before the storm begins.

When Rebecca finally walks in, she's dressed to the absolute nines in stilettos and the most stunning Fendi dress. *God, how is she always so perfect!?*

"Oh my gosh!" She squeals as she scoops Raegan into her arms. Theo stays put but Lucas stands and makes his way towards them and she grabs him as well, holding them both in her arms. "I've missed you guys so much."

"Missed you too, Mom," Lucas says.

"Yeah, ditto," Raegan says.

Lucas lets go but Raegan stays holding on to her for a little longer and I hate how much Raegan gets hurt by this. Lucas definitively chose sides and has clung to Theo his whole life but a girl needs her mother and Raegan was deprived of that during the most quintessential time in her life. Now she's pregnant and she'll more than likely be denied her mother again.

"You look so beautiful." She smiles at her and gives her a squeeze. "Now, who is this?" She gives Wes a once over with her eyes and I can immediately see Raegan preparing her defense.

"Mom, this is Wes Beckham."

"Very nice to meet you, Rebecca," he says and she gives him a smile before shaking his hand.

"Charmed." She moves her gaze around the table before landing on me. "Well, I wasn't expecting a full party, just for little old me." She giggles as she takes her seat between Wes and me. "Avery, darling." She leans over and kisses my cheek in the same fashion as earlier.

"Good to see you again."

"Well, isn't this just wonderful?" She claps.

Lucas snorts into his glass and I wonder just how much alcohol he's put away, especially if Theo drove here and he had any drinks at home.

"So, Lucas, you're leaving tomorrow?" She asks.

"Yep, bright and early."

"Well…I am taking the red eye out of New York on Monday morning so I was going to come to New York Sunday and maybe we can have dinner?"

"I don't know…I have some things to do Sunday to prepare for work Monday." He's living in the same apartment he lived in during college and doesn't really have much to move, so I'm guessing this is partially an excuse.

"So proud of you, honey." She gives him a look that I'd almost think was genuine. "I searched your company and your position on *LinkedIn*. You are going to have a very healthy salary." *And there it is.*

"Of course, you did." Lucas laughs, but I hear the sarcasm lurking beneath. "Yes, it'll be great."

"So, Mom, how are you?" Raegan interjects. "How's everything and…Garrett?" she asks, referring to her husband.

"Oh fine, he's in Greece right now on business, but he'll be back in a few weeks." She flicks her wrist before picking up her water. "Where's our waitress? I would love a cocktail." She looks around the table and notices that only Lucas is drinking. "No one else? That's shocking for everyone at *this* table." She laughs. "Sorry dear, I don't know you that well," she says to Wes with a hint of condescension.

"Yeah, I wonder where Raegan and I get it from." Lucas snorts and Rebecca's eyes pin him with a glare.

"Nice." She gives him a look as she puts her menu down. "Wes, hon, tell us about yourself. What are your intentions with my daughter?"

I internally cringe at the names she's giving him when I'm fairly certain she's younger than Wes.

"Becca," Theo warns and the nickname reminds me of the painful familiarity between them and it feels like a punch in the gut.

"What? I am not one to beat around the bush. I didn't fly forty-five hundred miles for idle chit-chat."

"No one asked you to fly here," Lucas says, giving his mother a look. "You didn't even call to let anyone know you were coming. You just show up and expect everyone to drop everything and cater to you just like you always do. Never mind that I had plans tonight. It only mattered that you wanted to have some awkward ass dinner under the ruse that *anyone* cares what you think about Raegan and her boyfriend."

I sit back in my chair, ready for Rebecca to say something back and not wanting to be literally between them while they argue when she flits her eyes to Theo. "And you have nothing to say to that?"

"Say to what?" Theo asks and I already know he's not going to get involved with their back and forth unless Lucas really crosses a line.

"Of course, you don't care what he says to me."

"Mom," Raegan speaks up, "look, I am sorry that I called you. I thought talking to me instead of continuing to engage in random gossip with Nat's mom would make you feel better. I certainly didn't expect you to fly here on a whim."

At that moment, the waitress enters and takes Rebecca's sole drink order and we order some appetizers of mini crabcakes, calamari, and bacon-wrapped scallops.

"I just felt so out of the loop. I had no idea what was going on," she says when the waitress leaves the room.

"But you've chosen to be out of the loop, Mom. You call me once a month, and yeah, the phone works both ways but there was a long stretch of time when I used to call you and you either wouldn't answer or couldn't talk or I would get you on the phone and I could tell you were distracted and not listening to a thing I was saying." Her eyes well up with tears and Wes' hand immediately moves to rest on her thigh. "No, you weren't my first call when things got serious with Wes because, frankly, I didn't think you'd care." She shrugs. "I wasn't going to get married without telling you. That's more *your* speed."

I wince thinking about how Lucas and Avery weren't even at Rebecca's second wedding because it was spur of the moment and 'just the two of us on a beach!'

"That's not fair!"

"Oh? You flew across the country because you heard that he *might* have a ring. Lucas and I found out you got married in a two-line text message with a picture of you two in all white."

"Honey—"

"I'm over it," Raegan interrupts. "But please don't give me a hard time just because you haven't been around to get to know the man I love."

"Love? Oh, honey…"

"Yes, Mother. Love. I love him." She pulls her eyes away from her mother to look next to her at Wes and a smile tugs at my lips at how she looks at him.

Fuck, it's how I look at Theo when we're alone.

Nope, absolutely not the time.

Rebecca's eyes flit to Theo's and then Lucas' who's still staring at his drink before turning back to her. "You hardly know him."

"No, Mom, *you* hardly know him and you hardly know *me* for that matter."

The table is silent before Wes speaks up. "To answer your earlier question, Rebecca, I am very much in love with Raegan and I do intend to marry her." His eyes pan to Theo's. "I had all the intentions to talk to you about it before things escalated to this. Raegan stressed the importance of it and I value what's important to her." I realize now that they're holding hands because when he moves his into view, it's clasped with hers and he brings it to his mouth. "I understand the apprehension around all of this. Our age difference and maybe the speed in which things moved, but as I believe Raegan told you and Lucas," he says, still talking to Theo, "we've been together for about a year now."

"Why wait so long to tell us?" Rebecca asks.

"Because of all of this," Raegan says. "This production over what? I'm twenty-three."

"And he's not." She responds.

"So?" Raegan snaps, her blue eyes narrowed and annoyed.

"Honey, he's too old for you."

I wince, hearing those words because even if Lucas wasn't a factor, is that what people would think about me and Theo?

Yes. My mind thinks instantly.

"I think that's my decision."

Rebecca sighs just as the waitress sets down her drink. "Thank you, dear," she says as she pulls the dirty martini to her lips. "Oh!" She cringes. "No no no. This isn't right." She hands her back the drink. "Can you have them try again? I think they forgot the vermouth or something."

"Of course, my apologies," The waitress says before leaving the room.

Lucas chuckles and drains his glass. "Some things never change."

Her eyes snap to his and she glares at him. "Sorry, I like my drink made correctly?"

No one says anything before Rebecca turns to look at Theo. "You're certainly quiet."

Theo, who's been staring at his glass, meets her gaze, but not before floating past my eyes quickly. "What did you want me to say? I don't even know why I'm here. I've talked to Raegan about it. We're good."

"Of course, always had to be the good guy so I had to be the bad one."

"Rebecca, the kids are grown. There is no good guy or bad guy anymore. Part of having grown children is you parent them differently. What, do you think we have the power to forbid her from marrying him? Ground her?"

"No, but we can advise…"

"Yes, of course," Theo says. "But for one, you give your advice once and that's it. You don't force it on them. Two, they have to ask for it and I don't think either of our children would ask you for advice for much, and three," he points at her. "Now pay attention because this is a big one, you support them anyway even if they don't take your advice. Because they are now at the age where they have to make their own decisions, mistakes, whatever." He gestures towards Raegan and Wes. "I'm not even saying this is a mistake. I've been around them so few times and I can see how much they care about each other and I want that for Raegan."

She sighs. "Well, fine. If everyone is just so on board." She rolls her eyes just as the waitress comes back with her drink. Another server follows behind her with our appetizers and disperses them around the table. "Oh, much better! Thank you." She smiles as she sips her drink. She opens her napkin. "Well, at least you're not pregnant, I suppose," Rebecca says flippantly.

Nobody says anything until Wes clears his throat and chuckles. "Well, that's a really unnecessary and quite frankly, rude thing to say." He looks at Raegan who's staring down at her hands and shakes his head. "You know, Raegan has been really happy about the fact that we are having a baby until she realized she had to tell you. Ever since she talked to you, she's been anxious and nervous and upset and I have no tolerance for that. She's twenty-three years old and she's nervous about telling her mother who she barely has a relationship with that she's pregnant? What does that say about you?"

I sense movement in my periphery and I notice Lucas' nodding in approval. "Wes, you and I are going to get along just fine." He laughs and gets up from the table. "I have to take a leak."

Rebecca looks at Raegan, tears flooding her eyes. "You're pregnant?"

"Yes."

"So that's the reason for all—" Rebecca starts.

"Let me stop you right there," Wes interrupts, holding a hand up. "I was talking to Raegan."

"Well, now you're talking to me. Let's get something straight. I've wanted to marry Raegan since about five minutes after I laid eyes on her. We've been together for over a year, and we first discussed marriage about three months into our relationship. We've been living together officially for six months, so no, her *very* recent pregnancy is not the reason for anything." He looks around the table. "In the spirit of transparency, Raegan would like to be married before the baby is born and more specifically before she's really showing so that does move things up some, but let me be very clear to everyone here, and then I don't want to talk about it again, we are *not* getting married just because she's pregnant." He looks at Raegan and I melt at the look they share.

He loves her so much.

"We are getting married because we love each other. The fact that she's also pregnant just makes us more excited to be tied together forever."

I think my heart and uterus just skipped a beat.

⁓

Two hours later, I'm in the bathroom with Raegan after the awkward dinner where Rebecca was basically on her phone the whole time. "Well, that was...something."

"Did you expect anything else?" Raegan asks.

"I did not expect your guard dog." I giggle. "He is..." I whistle. "That was sweet and hot and I think triggered my Daddy issues a little bit." I laugh nervously, as I play with the ends of my hair and Raegan giggles in response.

"Yeah, he's like that."

"Love that for you."

"Hey, he's an only child but he's got some nice cousins? Or maybe a friend? I could set you up!" She claps her hands.

I chuckle, hoping it doesn't sound forced and nervous. "That's nice, but I'm okay."

"Okay," she says as she begins to touch up her lipstick. "Thanks for being here. I know you came for Lucas, but it made me feel good too."

"Of course."

"You're a really good friend, Avery." She hugs me. "And the closest thing I've ever had to a sister." She gives me a smile that reminds me so much of Lucas. "And I'd really like it if you'd be one of my bridesmaids."

I put a hand over my chest as I try to calm the euphoria coursing through me that causes my heart to flutter. "Really? Me?"

She nods as tears flood her eyes. "Of course. You're family." She wraps her arms around me and I feel the tears prickling in mine as well. But the overwhelming feelings of happiness and honor are quickly cut short when I realize that she probably wouldn't ask me if she knew about what her father and I have been doing behind everyone's backs. I've spent so much time focusing on how Lucas would take it that I didn't even think about Raegan's feelings and she's asking me to be a part of the biggest day of her life.

I am the worst.

She pulls back and wipes under her eyes and then mine before laughing. "We should get back out there. Wes can only serve as a buffer for so long."

When we get back to the table, Theo is signing the check for dinner while Rebecca is touching up her lipstick and Lucas is scrolling through his phone. He nods at me and when I sit down next to him, he grabs my hands in his. "Want to get a drink?"

Theo isn't looking at us but I know he's paying attention. "You don't want to hang out with your sister and your dad on your last night?"

"Oh," Raegan interjects, shaking her head, "I'm going to bed. I love you Lucas, but I barely make it past nine-thirty right now. It is ten-fifteen and I have to be up in seven hours to start puking." She groans. "We'll be in New York for work in like two weeks." She points back and forth between her and Wes. "We'll go to dinner?"

Lucas gets up and I notice he's moving a little lethargically making me wonder if he stopped off at the bar when he went to the bathroom and consumed even more alcohol than the two stiff whiskeys he had at dinner.

"I love you, Rae." He hugs her.

"Oh, you're drunk. How did I miss that?" She chuckles before kissing his cheek. "I love you too."

"Shut up." He nudges her shoulder. "Big brother, I guess?" He shakes Wes' hand and when they share a look of respect, Raegan beams at them.

"Look at this! Two of my favorite guys. Just missing one." She looks at Theo who stands up and says goodbye to them as well.

We make it outside and while Rebecca is saying goodbye to Raegan and Wes, Lucas wraps an arm around me. "I'm going to go with Ave," he says to Theo.

"Lucas, maybe we should just go back to your house."

"It's my last night in Philly!"

"Okay, we talked about this earlier," I joke as I rub his arm. "It's literally an hour train ride. People commute from Philly to New York every day."

"You know what I mean. I'm going to be working all the time. You're going to be working. It's going to be hard for us to see each other, you know?"

"We'll make time," I tell him. "I'll always make time for you."

"Awww," he pinches my cheek. "Fine, yeah let's just go to the house. That way you can actually indulge with me."

Chapter
FOURTEEN

THEO

LUCAS SLAMS HIS TRUNK CLOSED, TAPPING HIS HAND ON top of it a few times before turning to me and Avery who are standing next to his car. "Well, that's it." It's barely nine in the morning and Lucas is already packed up and ready to head back to New York. "I know it's close, but it's still weird." He looks at the house behind me and then over at Avery's house. "Keep my dad out of trouble, will you?" He says, wrapping his arms around Avery and it takes everything in me not to react to that.

"Sure thing." She smiles.

He turns to me and gives me a look that I can't quite read. "Give us a second?" I nod, before heading back to the house. I've never known Lucas to like any kind of dramatic goodbye so I wonder what he's going to say to her and I try not to watch from the window but I can't seem to move away. He pulls her in for a hug before kissing the top of her head and when they pull back, I see him rub her face making me wonder if she's more upset than she let on about him moving. I hate the pang of jealousy that flares in my veins in response.

I finally pull away from the window not wanting to encroach on their moment or annoy myself further. A buzzing in my pocket breaks my thoughts and when I reach for it, I see it's from an unknown number.

It's Saturday at nine in the morning, who the hell is this?

"Theo Graham."

"Theo. Hey, it's Wes."

Well, I know what this is about. "Wes, what can I do for you?"

"I hope I'm not bothering you too early, but Raegan said you were probably up."

"It's not too early, I just finished saying goodbye to her brother. You caught me at the right time."

"Great, I just wanted to talk to you if you have a minute? I know we didn't really get to talk much last night."

"Yeah, I thought I would let Rebecca run the show."

"And as much as I thoroughly enjoyed that," he laughs sarcastically, "Raegan does value your opinion about everything, so I wanted to at least make sure you and I are good."

I take a sip of the half-drunk coffee that I'd made this morning. "We're good."

"Great, would you mind if I stopped by? I would just prefer to talk to you in person."

You knew this was coming. "Sure, when were you thinking?"

"Maybe an hour?"

"Works for me, you know where I live." Just as I'm hanging up, Avery appears on the back patio, before she slides open the door and slips inside.

"Did he leave?" She nods. "Are you okay?"

"Yeah, I didn't think it would hit me like this. It's like when he left for college all over again." She chuckles. "I cried for two days when I got to school." I don't respond and she moves around the island to stand next to me. "It doesn't mean I have feelings for him, Theo."

"I know. I get it." I put a hand over my eyes and let out a sigh. "It just reminds me how close you two are and how this," I say pointing between us, "affects him."

"It's not going to affect him. He's not going to find out." She looks up at me and her eyes look a little glassy which means the green in her hazel eyes is shimmering.

I try to ignore the uncomfortable feeling caused by her words. *This can't ever be anything real until he knows.*

I touch her cheek and her eyes flutter shut at the touch before she moves closer to me, pressing her body against mine. I drop a kiss to her lips making me realize that I haven't kissed her since she left my house two nights ago at two in the morning. I pin her to the island with my groin, pushing harder against her and she responds with a whimper and puts her hands behind my neck as she pushes back against me. I lift her into my arms with ease and carry her to the couch in the living room, our lips never breaking once. I sit with her in my lap and I groan as she begins moving around on my lap.

"Can we go upstairs?" She asks against my lips before she moves to my ear and bites down gently.

"Fuck." I let out a breath, my dick trying to overtake any reason I might have over whether that's a good idea. "Where," I groan as my dick jerks against her, feeling the heat through the flimsy spandex shorts she's wearing, "do your parents think you are?"

"I don't know," she says against my neck.

"Okay, but your car is parked at your house, they know you haven't gone far and Lucas is gone. There's only so many places you could be."

"Stop worrying so much." Her tongue drags up my neck. "Can you just relax?"

Despite what my dick is begging me to do, I pull her lips away from my skin and give her a look. "You don't think it's going to raise a hundred questions if you're here just hanging out with me?" I give her a look and she bites her bottom lip and narrows her eyes before shifting in my lap, very purposefully.

"I went on a walk." I eye her warily because while that could work, it could only work so many times. "Please stop worrying so much, okay?" She gets off of my lap and kneels in front of me reaching for my shorts and unbuttoning them. I don't say anything as she pulls them down and frees my dick.

Fuck. "Avery."

"Hmmm?" She asks as she strokes her hand up and down my shaft slowly without breaking eye contact. "Should I stop?"

"No." I grunt. "But…" I grab her wrist, keeping it on my dick but stopping it from moving. "I want to fuck your pussy not your mouth."

She swats my hand away and wraps her lips around the tip before pushing herself all the way down to the back of her throat. Her lips lightly brush against the base of my dick before pulling back slowly as she glides her tongue over every ridge of my dick. She does this a few times, finding that sexy rhythm that has me lifting my hips in time with her strokes, making me forget my earlier request.

My head falls back as her sinful mouth and tongue pull me under just as the feeling disappears and I immediately want to be back inside her. I look up to see her standing in front of me, pulling her shorts off before she climbs back into my lap.

I wonder why she didn't take her panties off when she pulls them to the side exposing her slick cunt to me. I resist the urge to push her to her back and put my mouth on her because it seems like she has other plans for us. She hovers just above me, letting my dick ghost through her wet slit gently and a shiver snakes through her that has me wanting to push my hips upwards into her.

"Don't be a tease, baby. Let me inside you."

Still holding her panties to the side, she sinks down on top of me and the fabric of the lace drags down my shaft with every slow tortuous inch.

Fuuuuuck, that feels good.

She moves up and down and I look down between us, watching me bottom out inside of her.

I grip her ass, pulling her harder against me just as her hands find my shoulders and she begins to move faster. "You're so deep."

I pull her to me, pressing our lips together and sliding my tongue against hers. I weave my hands through her dark tresses, pulling gently every few seconds eliciting a moan from her which just makes my dick harder. She pulls away and lets out a low moan in my ear letting me know she's getting close and hearing how good I make her feel furthers my climax as well.

"You drive me so crazy, Avery. Your little noises when I'm inside you, fuck. They make my dick so fucking hard."

She responds with another one of her sexy little moans and presses her lips to my neck. "Fuck," she gasps. "I'm close."

She's still wearing the oversized t-shirt she came over in and I wish I'd ripped it off of her because I want to bury my face in her tits and run my tongue over her nipples. I reach under the shirt and lower her bra so I can rub them having figured out how sensitive they are before she comes.

"Oh God, yes. You know just what I like." She whimpers. "I'm going to come." She lets out a cry and a squeal that may have been a version of my name as she continues to ride me through her orgasm. "Yes yes fuck yes, that's so good." She pushes her lips to mine, still moving up and down to milk my orgasm out of me which happens moments later.

"Fuck, Avery, you take my dick so well."

I don't know how long we stay connected, her body pressed against mine and locked together in the most intimate way but she eventually pulls out of my arms and slides her underwear back into place. She doesn't put her shorts back on and I try not to fixate on how it makes me feel that she's not leaving yet. I pull my shorts back up and she pushes me onto my back resting her head on my chest as she snuggles against me.

"Was last night hard for you?" She speaks up after a few minutes of silence.

"You mean having you there?"

"All of it. Rebecca, Lucas, Raegan." She perks her head up and rests her chin on my chest. "It was a lot."

"Yeah."

"You didn't say much, that's all."

I didn't say much because I was fighting the line between being annoyed with Rebecca and being turned on every time my eyes floated past Avery. *And then annoyed again with myself every time I looked at Lucas.*

"Rae knows how I feel. I like Wes. But also, she's an adult and she doesn't really *need* my approval for anything but I know she wants it."

"Do you? Approve, I mean?"

"Makes me a bit of a hypocrite if I don't, I think? If Wes were ten years younger, this wouldn't even be a question. He seems like a good guy who loves my daughter and that's all a father wants. The large age gap between them is why there's all this conversation and given that I'm in somewhat of a relationship with someone *younger* than my daughter, I don't think I'm allowed to hate the difference in their ages."

"Fair."

We lay like that for a while, her running her fingertips over my chest while I stroke her back and it feels comfortable, intimate, *easy*. It lulls me into a false sense of reality that things could be this simple between us all of the time.

"So, for tonight…" I start. "I know we talked about you coming over, but I think I'd feel better if I got us a room again."

She sits up and gives me a look while dragging her fingers along the waistband of my shorts like she wants to take them off again. "You want to get a room every time you want to fuck me? That's not going to be cheap," she sings.

"One, I can afford it. Two, not every time. I just want to relax and I don't want to feel like anyone could just show up and catch us or…" I want to tell her that I'm beginning to hate all of this sneaking around. That I'm forty-five years old and I'm being forced to sneak around with a girl like a teenager. But my thoughts are stopped by the ringing of my doorbell and the dread that floods me when I remember Wes was stopping by. Her head snaps to the door and she narrows her gaze at me.

"It's Wes, I forgot he was coming over." I groan as she gets off the couch and pulls her shorts up.

"Awww! To talk to you about Raegan." She claps her hands excitedly and I swear I see the stars in her eyes. "They are so cute." She puts a hand over her chest. "Be nice."

"I am nice." I run a hand through my hair and she swats it away before running her hands through it herself.

"You're a little grumpy sometimes."

I glower at her just as the doorbell rings again. "You have to go."

"Okay, see you later." She stands on her toes and presses her lips to mine gently. It takes everything in me not to deepen the kiss, but I refrain to let her go and she slips out the backdoor.

I make my way to the front door and open it to find Wes standing there with his phone to his ear. He pulls it away and gives me a nervous smile. "Sorry, I was just calling you. Thought maybe I missed you."

"No, uhhh," I stammer, "I was just upstairs. Sorry about that. Come on in." He walks in and I follow behind him suddenly, very aware of the possibility that my clothes could be wrinkled or I could smell like sex or look like I'd just had a naked woman bouncing in my lap less than an hour ago.

Even if he did pick up on something, it's not like he'd ever guess it was Avery.

"Want something to drink?"

"No, I'm good, thanks," he says as we enter the kitchen. "I assume you know why I'm here."

"I have an idea, but I never like to assume."

He fishes something out of his pocket and slides it slowly across the island to where I'm standing and I stare down at the gray suede ring box before looking up at him. "Has she seen it?"

"No."

"You sure she'll like it? My daughter is very picky." *Picky and spoiled with expensive tastes.*

"If she doesn't like it, I'll get her something different." He shrugs as I reach for the box and open it. I keep my face impassive as I stare at the stunning ring that my daughter will definitely fucking love. It's a nice-sized emerald-cut ring with diamonds around the band.

"She'll like it," I tell him as I shut the box, and the smug grin that crosses his face should irritate me but it actually makes me laugh.

"I know."

"Well, you handled yourself well with Rebecca which is impressive. She can be tough to take sometimes."

"I was thoroughly prepared," he says. "I didn't mean to overstep."

"She'll get over it." I cross my arms over my chest and lean against the countertop. "I don't want to talk about Rebecca. I want to talk about you and my daughter." He nods and for the first time, I see a bit of nervousness cross his face. "There's a significant age gap between you two."

"Yes."

I narrow my eyes at him. "How old are you exactly?"

"Forty-Three."

"At least you're younger than me," I grumble and I hate that in another life that didn't involve him defiling my daughter, we could have been friends because he's actually pretty likable.

I do, however, take some comfort that he has more gray hair than I do.

He leans forward over the counter and gives me what I think is a sincere look. "I know I'm significantly older than her, but I can assure you that I love her more than anything and will do everything I can to be the best husband I can be."

I eye him warily because he's saying all the right things but I am curious why he hasn't been married before or why he's not interested in a woman his age.

You want to go there? my subconscious adds.

"Any reason why you haven't been married before?" I ask him, trying my best to not sound judgmental.

"I was engaged once. We broke it off." He sighs. "I don't know, I haven't been interested in marriage."

"Why now?"

"I met the right woman."

"You understand my apprehension, right? An age gap of this size—" I start. "She's impressionable—"

"I'm sorry, impressionable?" he interjects. "Are we talking about the same woman?" I'm a little bit irritated and impressed at his response. "I just mean...I can't convince Raegan to do anything she doesn't already want to do." He lets out a breath and rubs his forehead. "I don't know if you know anything about dating a much younger woman, but they have all the power."

Avery's face immediately flashes through my mind. "I can see that," I tell him. I know I'm projecting a little and I find a feeling of jealousy shooting through me that Wes has it so easy. Nothing is standing in the way of him getting what he wants. No one who'd potentially be destroyed over him being with Raegan. In theory, his biggest obstacle is me and I've barely made him jump through a hoop.

Don't make him jump through a hoop. Be nice! I can hear Avery's voice clear as day. *He loves her and she's pregnant.*

Right. Pregnant, I think.

"I assume I would know if you had kids. You don't, right?"

"No, and I'm pretty excited about her being pregnant. I'll be honest, I didn't see myself having a baby at this stage of my life but I want to give Raegan whatever she wants. Another thing about getting involved with a girl in her twenties." He gives me a look like he thinks I understand and I look away in case it's written all over my face.

"Well, I'm happy for you both. Raegan is my first born and my only daughter, so I don't think I need to tell you what she means to me."

"You don't." He shakes his head.

"Well, as long as you treat her right, you and I will never have any issues." He nods. "When are you planning to ask her?"

"Soon. She wants to get married before she starts showing so we are working with a small window."

"Can you give her the wedding she wants in that time frame?"

"I'm going to try my best." I don't respond and he narrows his eyes slightly. "You know," he starts and I already know I'm not going to like what he has to say, "Raegan worries about you."

"What? Why?"

"She thinks her mom messed you up."

I shake my head. "No. I'm fine."

"She wants you to meet someone." I swallow nervously wondering if this is a trap because surely Lucas told Raegan that I supposedly have a 'girlfriend.' "But the way you're looking at me, it makes me think that Raegan may be left out of the loop."

Alright, time for Sherlock Holmes to go. "Tell Raegan not to worry. I'm fine. I'm good. I'm happy." I try to ignore the fact that Avery flashes through my mind the second the word *happy* leaves my mouth.

He nods, standing up. "Good. She'll be glad to know that." He shakes my hand and gives me another look like he knows all my secrets and I usher him towards the door before I unleash all of them on my daughter's soon to be fiancé.

Chapter
FIFTEEN

Avery

I KNOCK ON THE DOOR OF THE HOTEL ROOM, EXCITEMENT coursing through me over spending the night with Theo again. We haven't spent the night together since the night of my graduation party and while that was only a week ago, I feel like it's been months. He's right, the thought of being together without the worry of someone turning up unannounced at his house makes me breathe easier. He'd even booked a room further out of the city, over an hour away from where we lived so that we could go out to dinner and it would be less likely anyone would recognize us.

The door opens revealing Theo in nothing but a towel wrapped around his waist and I raise an eyebrow at him before pressing a hand to his chest and pushing him back into the room. "Are you trying to seduce me?"

He narrows his brown eyes curiously at me as he shuts the door. "You got here very quick. How fast were you driving?"

"My question first."

"No, *my* question first. I was not expecting you already. I figured I'd be dressed by the time you got here. So again, how fast were you driving?"

"I was excited to see you." I tell him as I grab his towel by the knot and pull it from him leaving him completely nude in front of me. *This man is a fucking God.*

"We have dinner reservations at seven," he tells me and I'm

vaguely aware that it's just after six. I am not dressed for dinner but he's also naked and hard and as far as I'm concerned that takes precedence.

"I'll be quick," I tell him with a devilish grin before sinking to my knees.

⸺ ❧ ⸺

After dinner, which felt more like foreplay than anything, we decide to go to a bar nearby. We are far enough away from where we live that we can actually go out and we figured we should capitalize on the opportunity of not running into anyone. We are seated at the bar, sitting next to each other which is actually a shame because I have been openly ogling him all night and it's harder at this angle. He always dresses well, somehow effortlessly stylish and appropriate for every occasion. The black polo shirt he's wearing hugs his biceps so deliciously, every time he reaches for something and they flex, I feel a flutter between my legs. The gray pants looked custom-made with the way they were tailored to him and every time he gets up, I stare at his ass shamelessly.

I am truly no better than a man.

"What?" He narrows his eyes at me, catching me staring at him.

I shake my head and pick up the glass of wine I ordered. "You're just…very nice to look at."

What I'd really like to say is I want to lick every fucking inch of you.

The bar is dimly lit but I can still see the look on his face as he leans against the back of the barstool and preens. I giggle into my wine, starting to feel the drinks from dinner and the two I've had since we got here. "You are the most beautiful woman here." He rubs a hand slowly down my arm and lets it land on my thigh. I try my best not to react by squeezing them together. "I've caught more than one man staring at you."

"You sure they don't recognize you and they're just trying to place you?" I know Theo still gets recognized from time to time even if it's not as often as he used to.

He sits up and leans forward, his face barely an inch from mine.

"They are definitely not looking at me." He leans closer, ghosting his lips against mine, and a sigh escapes my lips in response to the spark that shoots through me. My heart is racing by the time he pulls back and I turn my eyes to the glass in front of me draining the contents in one gulp because *fuck fuck fuck.*

I absolutely cannot be falling for Theo.

It's just the alcohol. And the great sex, I try to tell my brain and my heart that seem to be getting more confused by the second.

The feeling of my chair moving breaks my thoughts and I notice that Theo has dragged my stool closer to him so our thighs are almost touching.

"What are you thinking about?" He asks and I glance at him nervously, trying to calm my racing heart. "You seem nervous." His voice is low and moves through my whole body causing a dull pulse between my legs. His cologne, sexy and masculine swirls around me, and combined with the low lighting of the bar and the light music playing, it's the most carnal aphrodisiac.

Maybe I could just climb into his lap.

"Do you want me to tell you what I'm thinking?" He asks and I realize I never answered his question. I nod, not knowing what my voice will sound like or if the words that leave my mouth would be, 'Fuck me on this bar right now, please.'

"That I wish we'd just gone back to the room after dinner because I can't stop thinking about fucking you in only those sexy as fuck heels." My toes attempt to curl in my shoes in response to his words. "That I want to eat your cunt until you fucking scream."

Jesus Christ.

"And that I really want to fuck your ass tonight." My eyes widen just as the bartender approaches us.

"Can I get you some more wine?" he interrupts and I'm grateful for it.

"Tequila," I blurt out because the wine is making me feel warm and clearly nasty Avery has to make an appearance tonight. "Please."

"Make it two, whichever is your best," I hear from next to me and I turn my gaze to his.

"Did you bring lube?" He nods, just before he drains the rest of his whiskey. "Someone's presumptuous."

"I like to think of it as prepared."

"I've never done…*that*."

His eyes soften and the lust leaves them filling instead with sincerity. "Baby, we don't have to if—"

"No, I didn't mean that. I just mean, be gentle." I giggle nervously.

His eyes look serious and he doesn't laugh with me. "I would never hurt you." I bite my bottom lip at the double meaning I swear I hear in his words. "I'll make it good for you." His promise is laced with sex and I'm grateful for the tiny glasses of the clear liquid placed in front of us.

"Should we take these?"

"It's your world." He smiles as he lifts the glass, removing the lime from the side. The salt is already on the rims of both making it easy to take the shot without dumping salt everywhere. We take them and I scrunch my face before sucking the lime into my mouth. I drop it into the glass before turning to Theo who's watching me intently and I lean forward, wanting to taste him instead. His lips meet mine after no more than a second and my hand moves up his thigh slowly, trying my best not to alert the whole bar that I plan to rub my hand over his dick.

"Avery," he warns.

"Mmm, yes, Daddy?" I graze my knuckles over his covered cock, and I feel it jerk under my hands. The word falls from my lips with ease making me wonder if the tequila has hit me already.

He growls against my lips but he makes no effort to move my hand. "We should go."

"Why? I'm having fun." I pull away from his lips and trail them down his neck before pulling back, dragging my hand along his thigh before putting it back in my lap.

He rubs his forehead before dragging his hand down his face. "Fuck, I don't think I've ever been this hard." He half laughs like he's shocked at himself and a smile spreads across my face.

"Alright, just let me use the ladies' room and then we can go back to the hotel?"

His eyes just drag over me, lingering on my chest for a second before meeting my eyes. "Whatever you want, baby."

Him. We want HIM, my entire body practically screams.

"Be right back." I get off the stool and press my lips to his before making my way towards the bathroom, very certain that his eyes are glued to me as I walk away.

A few minutes later, I am staring in the mirror as I reapply my lipstick for whatever reason knowing that it's about to be smeared everywhere.

I'm grateful for the moments of peace in the bathroom because I'm starting to pace thinking about how things are changing between Theo and I. I'm getting in fucking deep and pretty soon I'm not going to be able to pull myself out of it.

Lucas may not take it so bad...?

Yeah, fucking right, Avery. He's going to lose his shit.

I put a hand to my chest, my heart beginning to race at the thought of losing my best friend. Losing him but still having to see him all the time because I'm. Dating. His. Dad.

You know what, this whole argument might be pointless because Theo will never tell Lucas. So, this is just a fun little secret that I'll be keeping until the end of time.

Ugh.

I make my way out of the bathroom, not looking where I'm going, and walk right into a wall of very hard unfamiliar muscle. His hands find my forearms and I look up to see a guy that's probably in his mid-thirties.

"Oh, I'm sorry." He's attractive objectively and if I wasn't so obsessed with my best friend's dad, I may be able to appreciate it more. His brown eyes are warm and a smile finds his face.

"No need for apologies. A woman as gorgeous as you bumping into a guy—well, I should be thanking you." He lets me go and I give him a polite smile.

"Thank you." I go to move down the hallway when he speaks again.

"The guy you're with..." he starts and when I turn around his eyes drop to my hand, "I don't see a ring on your finger, so I assume he's not your husband."

"Not yet." I hear Theo's voice from behind me and then his hand snakes around my waist, pulling me closer to him. Theo moves to stand next to me and rubs my waist, holding me tighter against him. "Everything okay here?"

I nod, my voice having left me after hearing him say, *"Not yet."* *Not yet?*

"You ready to go?" He looks at me before his eyes turn to the guy, looking him up and down once. The guy clears his throat and moves around us leaving us alone in the hallway outside of the bathroom. Theo narrows his eyes, following after him. "I told you everyone was looking at you," he says before he turns his gaze back to mine.

"Not yet?" I blurt out, not giving a shit about who's looking at me.

His lips find my neck as he whispers in my ear. "I was making a point." Goosebumps instantly pop up all over my flesh.

"Which is?"

"That you're spoken for."

"Am I?"

He narrows his eyes with a look of confusion and maybe also a little irritation. "Are you what?"

"Spoken for."

"We've been over this. Yes. You're fucking mine, Avery, just like I'm yours."

"But no one knows that." I blink at him.

"Okay...?" He boxes me against the wall, pressing his strong hard body against mine with his hands above my head. "We've talked about this."

"I know." The tequila is starting to settle in and the course of this conversation is going to push me to tears if I don't change it.

"Why do I get the feeling you want to talk about it again?"

A flicker of hope washes over me and I do my best not to fix-ate on it because this wasn't the plan. "Are you open to talking about it again?"

His eyes trace my face and then his hands find my cheeks. "Do you know what that means?"

I nod again, the tears finding my eyes. I feel like he might be telling me this is over because no one was ever supposed to know. *That was the deal.*

"I just know myself and…I'm just going to get," I swallow trying to rid the ball of emotion sitting in the back of my throat, "attached." The tequila is making me honest and I capitalize on the moment. "I won't be able to hide my feelings forever." And even though we are in a bar where anyone could turn the corner and witness what's happen-ing, a tear begins to slide down my face despite my efforts to stop it.

"Please don't cry." He presses his forehead to mine and rubs his thumb gently along my cheek to collect the stray tear. "Fuck, how did we get here?"

I sniffle. "I don't know."

"We should go," he says, sealing his comment with a kiss to my lips and guiding me out of the restaurant.

⁓

We didn't say anything on the five-minute walk back to the hotel and by the time we are alone in the elevator, I feel like I could climb out of my fucking skin. "Say something," he says as he reaches for my hand and clasps it with mine.

"Like…?" *I want to be with you and that scares the shit out of me?* I reach for the lapel of his shirt and bring him closer. "I want you in-side of me."

"Don't you think we should talk before we do that?"

"We can talk after," I tell him because if this is the end of us, we should at least go out with a bang, right?

He picks me up again, reminiscent of that first night when he carried me out of the elevator and sets me on my feet when we get to the door. He pushes me against it and stares down at me. "Avery."

"Theo."

"I'm already fucking attached."

"What does that mean?" I whisper, wanting to make sure I'm not misunderstanding.

"It means we're going to fuck now because my dick is hard and your pussy is wet and we need a clear head for this conversation. Then we're going to talk and *then* we're going to fuck again."

Chapter

SIXTEEN

THEO

THE DOOR HAS BARELY SHUT BEHIND US AND I ALREADY have her pressed against the wall, my hands touching every inch of her skin that's exposed. I lift her into my arms and her legs immediately move around my waist. I rock against her, pushing my dick against her barely covered cunt feeling the heat of her against me. "Theo." She moans just as I drag my tongue over the tops of her tits. With her legs wrapped around me and the way I'm holding her against the wall with my body, I have a free hand to lower one of the straps of her dress exposing her breasts and her gorgeous nipples. I press my mouth to one of them, sucking it into my mouth and biting down gently causing her to cry out. "Oh God!"

I suck harder, palming the other one all while still rocking against her and she moves her hips against me, trying to hit my dick with each jerk of her hips.

I drag my lips from her nipple and drag my nose up her skin, her perfume and the scent of her arousal surrounding me and making me feel even more drunk than I think I might be.

I want her so fucking bad and it's to the point where I don't know if I care about the repercussions that come with it.

Fuck.

I reach under her dress, which is so fucking sexy I don't think I took my eyes off of her the whole night. *Much like every guy at that fucking bar.* Red and molded to her, the dress matches the color on her lips and had me picturing my dick the same color all night.

I caught the guy that approached her staring at her for half the fucking night and then when he followed her, I almost broke the glass I was holding with the force I slammed it down on the bar before I followed. I'd never been a jealous person. My guess is that's how Rebecca got away with her affair for as long as she did, but the thought of anyone touching Avery, triggered a response I'd never felt before.

She is mine and I wanted to fuck her on top of the bar, to prove it to everyone who dared to look at her.

I pull off her underwear with a rough snap and she moans against me as she watches them fall to the floor when I toss them over my shoulder.

"Theo, please fuck me." Her eyes are filled with lust, and coupled with the desperation in her voice has me wanting to give her whatever she wants.

I keep one hand underneath her as I push harder against her, pressing my dick against her bare cunt.

"You are so perfect." I pull her away from the wall, carrying her through the suite and into the bedroom with the king-sized bed that we'd already broken in before dinner. Her arms and legs are wrapped completely around me as she seals her lips to mine. I press her into the bed and reluctantly pull my lips from hers. She whimpers at the loss of contact and sits up on her elbows to watch as I slide her dress down her body slowly leaving her completely naked except for the shoes I told her I wanted to fuck her in.

There's always an ache in my dick when I see her like this but now, I feel something else washing over me as I watch her rub her thighs together. I grab them, separating them, and push my fingers through her slit. "Fuck, you're so wet."

"I've been wet since dinner." She bites her bottom lip and I can see the excitement in her eyes when I lower my mouth.

"You've been thinking about this since dinner?"

She nods and lets her head fall back with a groan as I blow on her gently. "I'm never not thinking about this."

"Same." I tell her as I trace the seam with my tongue before pushing my mouth completely against her. I slide my hands beneath her to grip her ass as I fuck her with my mouth slowly. I look up at her again, expecting to see her head thrown back but I meet her gaze and my cock jerks at the look she's giving me. Her fingers are on her nipples, rolling them between her fingers, her teeth digging into her bottom lip, and those gorgeous eyes are trained on me as I continue to lick her needy cunt. She stares at me so intensely I wonder if she can see everything I'm thinking.

About her. Us. This.

"Oh God, that feels good." She moves her hands from her nipples to run her fingers through my hair and each pull feels like another spark to my dick. "Fuck me."

"Come in my mouth first and then I will." I place a loud obscene kiss on her clit, before running my tongue over it and she tugs my hair harder this time.

"No, now," she argues and I shoot her a questioning look while still continuing to fuck her with my mouth. I flick her clit with the tip of my tongue and she cries out. "Oh my God, please!" She begs. I pull back slowly and a strand of her wetness mixed with my spit connects my mouth to her cunt before I run my tongue along my lip to break it.

I'm still dressed, so I pull off my clothes, my eyes not leaving hers once even as she runs her fingers against her clit and shudders against them. I drink her in from her feet to her eyes and the thump in my chest that matches the one in my dick tells me that everything is getting more complicated with every second that passes.

I'm on top of her a second later, dragging my dick through her slit without pushing inside and she lets out a shaky breath. "I don't like being interrupted while I'm eating your pussy, Avery." I bite down on her shoulder and she wraps her arms around my neck and lets out a giggle.

"You'll live." I push inside of her in response to her sassy comment. "Oh God." I pull back and push inside of her harder and she lets out a delicious moan that almost makes me lose it inside of her especially when I feel the pierce of her heels at my back. "Just like that, fuck…me…" She sputters as she struggles to get the words out.

I pull out of her to get on my knees and she whines in response. "Don't stop!"

I grab her thighs before raising her legs up towards her ears and I lean down to spit on her pussy. Her mouth drops open in response, her thighs tremble under my grip, and her sex clenches. "I wanted to make you come all over my face and you stopped me, so now you have to wait to come on my dick." I tap her clit with the tip of my cock, letting it glide against her and her nipples pebble into rosy hard points.

"Theo, *please*," she cries. "I can't take it." She reaches down and wraps her small hand around me and moves it up and down my shaft and closer to her entrance. The tip grazes it and she clenches around my dick and I'm powerless against her, letting myself sink into her again.

"Yes, you can. I've got you, baby." I waste no time fucking her harder, holding her down as I rut into her, feeling my climax looming. "Fuck, you feel so fucking good. I'm going to come if you keep squeezing my dick like that."

"Good." She gives me a lazy smile as she drags her fingers slowly up my torso. I press my thumb to her clit, wanting her to come with me.

"Fuck, Theo right there." Her eyes flutter shut and I move my hands to her waist, pinning her down while I continue to thrust into her. "I think I'm going to come!" she cries. "Oh fuck, fuck, I'm never not going to want this." She moans at what I think is the peak of her orgasm before moaning my name and *God* and *yes* as she shakes beneath me.

Hearing her confession and how much she wants me shouldn't turn me on as much as it does but it pushes me closer to the edge. I continue fucking her through my frustration over letting things go too far with Avery and now I'm addicted to her and I have no intentions of giving her up.

I come hard, shooting my load deep inside her. I fall on top of her, while keeping most of my weight off of her, but still resting against her luscious body. I've stopped thrusting but I'm still inside of her even as my dick slowly softens. She's looking up at me with a sexy lazy smile and I lean down to kiss her. "I can't let you go," I whisper against her and she gasps.

"I don't want you to."

I press my lips to her collarbone and then her neck and then a final kiss to her lips before I pull out of her. "We need to talk."

We're sitting on the balcony of the suite, both of us in bathrobes after the shower we took together, neither of us saying anything and somehow everything at the same time. After ten minutes of silence, she finally speaks up. "Who's going to tell him?" She winces, referring to Lucas. "I do not think we should do it together."

"Absolutely not." I shake my head because that awkward conversation you have with your kids when you're dating someone new is something you do when they're under the age of eighteen and definitely not one of their closest friends. "I think it should come from me."

"Are you going to tell him and Rae together?"

"No." I shake my head. "I think Raegan will be irritated, but I think she'll take it better. I also don't think we should do it before her wedding." I don't want anything to take away from what should be the happiest time in her life, let alone the tension that this situation will inevitably bring.

"That's a good idea. Get through all of this and let the focus solely be on Raegan." She snaps her finger. "I don't know if I told you, she asked me to be a bridesmaid."

"You didn't, but I'm not surprised. I know you're not as close with her as you are with Lucas but Raegan adores you."

"Not sure how much she will now." She moves closer to me and settles so her back is against my chest.

I wrap my arms around her and drop a kiss to her shoulder. "So, we get through the wedding. That's only a few months."

She nods. "It also gives us some time to make sure this is really what we want and get to know each other past…the sex." She giggles.

"I want to make sure I'm definitely keeping you before I blow up my whole life."

I grip her jaw and tilt her face to look up at me. "You're keeping me, Avery." I know she was making a joke, but it doesn't stop the involuntary feeling of inadequacy from creeping in caused by being in a marriage with an unfaithful partner.

The last thing I want to do in this moment is unleash all my baggage on Avery but I'd be lying if I didn't feel just a little bit insecure at times. And while I do realize that women are attracted to me, I also know that feelings change and also that Avery is twenty-one and I am *not*.

What if it all becomes too much for her?

I don't realize how much I've spaced out until I feel her hands on my face and her lips brushing gently against mine. "I was just making a joke…but this is really big," she says, "and once we open this door, we can't ever close it again, so I only meant that I want us both to be sure."

"I know."

Her eyes are filled with sincerity and I wonder if she can see where my mind went because she snuggles against my chest and rubs her hand over it. "I want you," she says quietly. "I want this." She presses her lips to my neck. "We'll make him understand. He won't be upset forever."

"Are you going to be okay if he never understands?"

She turns in my lap to straddle me. "Will you?"

"I…I don't know." She looks down and the sadness is painted all over her sweet face. I hate that I put it there. I raise her chin with my index finger to make her look at me. "I know that I want to be with you."

"You're his dad, Theo. He'll eventually forgive you." She bites her bottom lip. "There's a chance he'll never forgive me." She sighs. "But, I was running that risk regardless," she says. "Whoever I chose to be with was always going to be a sore subject."

"And that's the problem, Avery."

"I know. I know." She puts her hands over her eyes. "It's not my fault, I didn't…I don't lead him on, Theo."

The guilt of what I'm doing feels like it's taking over at her words and I sigh before removing her hands from her face and kissing her fingertips one at a time. "I know. I never thought you did." I pull her towards me and begin to rub her back gently. "I just can't believe you're you." I sigh. "In another life, it would be so easy."

"In another life, I probably don't live right next door, so maybe we would never cross paths," she teases.

"I'd find you in every lifetime."

We spent the rest of that night trying not to think too much about the future and just enjoying our time alone. It felt like a turning point for us. This is more than just exclusive sex.

We are…together.

I look down at the picture I snapped of her while she was sleeping and part of me wants to make it the background of my phone. She looked so peaceful and happy and fucking stunning and I've looked at it no less than a hundred times since I took it. I lean back in my chair at my desk, and part of me wants to call her just so I can hear her voice. It's been two days since that night and I've woken up without her in my bed the past two mornings and I am already fucking over it. We are supposed to have dinner tonight and I want to broach the subject of her moving out of her parent's house just so it's easier for us to see each other.

I pull up my phone, deciding that it might be time to tell someone what's going on and my brother is the only person who will give it to me straight and *probably* not give me too much shit for it.

"Little bro, to what do I owe this pleasure?" Bryan is four years older than me and lives in Arizona with his wife and two kids after selling his tech company for a shitload of money. He also spends more time at the golf course than anywhere else so I know he's got nothing but time.

"You busy?"

"Of course not. I'm supposed to tee off in thirty minutes so I'm just at the clubhouse having breakfast."

I sigh. "I have to tell you something. I haven't told anyone and it's...kind of a big thing."

"Well, you have my attention." He clears his throat. "First off, do I need bail money? A shovel? That fucker didn't do something to Rae, did he? Do we need my lawyer?"

I roll my eyes. "You and I have the same lawyer, which is dad, and no." I hadn't talked to Bryan in a week or so which means he also doesn't know the latest about Raegan. "Speaking of Rae," I lean back in my chair and look towards the ceiling. "She's getting married."

"WHAT? To that old dude?"

I roll my eyes. "You do know he's younger than both of us, right?"

"You okay with this?" He asks, ignoring my comment. "Be straight with me."

"I...think. I don't know. My judgment is a little compromised right now which is why I'm calling."

"Oh...kay?" I hear the sound of a can opening and I look at my watch wondering if he's having a beer this early.

"Isn't it eight in the morning there?"

"You know it's never too early to mind your business. What is the reason for this call?" He asks with a bored tone.

I chuckle. "She's also pregnant, by the way."

"Oh, wait what!? That's why they're getting married?"

"Apparently no. I guess they've been talking about it for a while. I mean they do live together."

"That sounds like grade-A bullshit. Which is fine, I respect a man who wants to do the right thing when he gets a girl pregnant, but let's call a spade a spade here."

"I don't know. I like him, and part of me thinks he'd tell me the truth." Maybe it was the romantic in me, but I believed Wes when he said he's been in love with my daughter for months.

"Well, you know I can spot some fuckery a mile away. I can't wait to meet this guy. Tell him you're the nice one, but I'm the black sheep of the family and I've got friends in low places that will kill him for nothing and make it look like an accident. But is this why you called?"

"No. I was just keeping you informed. They want to get married before she starts showing, so the wedding will be kind of soon, I expect."

"Would not expect anything less from a shotgun wedding."

I laugh because my brother always says the things people think but don't say out loud. He has no filter. Half the time it pisses people off and half the time it comes off as lovable; one hundred percent of the time, though, Bryan doesn't care. "I'll let you and Rae argue that out. The reason for my call is I'm seeing someone."

"Oh, fuck yes. Fucking finally. And for you to be telling me means it's not just sex and it's serious."

"It's not just sex and it's...moving towards serious."

"But wait, you said no one knows. How can it be serious if Lucas and Rae don't know? Oh God, please tell me you're not getting back with Rebecca." He groans.

"What? Hell no. You know me better than that."

"Well, I don't know who else you'd be keeping from your grown-ass kids. Why would they care?" He pauses. "Oh shit, don't tell me it's one of Raegan's friends." He chuckles. "I mean actually please *do* tell me that, because respect. But... Rae will absolutely freak the fuck out even with her current situation." I don't respond even as he continues to laugh and he lets out a whistle, taking my silence as admission. "No fuckin' way. One of her friends?"

"It's even worse than you're thinking."

"What could be worse than—" He stops talking and at this moment, I'm fairly certain he's put it together. "No." He sighs. "Of all the people in the entire fucking world, tell me you are not sleeping with Avery." I swallow guiltily, knowing that I'm about to endure a long fucking lecture about this. I don't speak, and I hear him again. "Theodore."

I groan. "My full name. Really?"

"Yes, you absolutely get your full fucking name. THEO, WHAT

THE FUCK?" He yells into the phone and I pull it away from my ear with a groan.

"I know. I KNOW."

"You know!? Your son's best friend that he used to have feelings for?" He yells, his tone is laced with judgment.

"It's been…a long time coming I guess you could say."

"What? How long?" And I can hear the emphasis in the question because I've known Avery a very long fucking time.

"Stop it. It's not what you're thinking. It's only been a few years. We kissed once when she was twenty." I stand from my desk and begin to pace the length of my office to my couch. "Last winter when she was home, we went a little further, and then about two weeks ago we slept together."

"But how exactly did this happen?"

I launch into the whole story starting with the night I kissed her for the first time, to last winter, her graduation party, and the last few weeks and learning how she's had a crush on me for years, and when I finish, my heart is racing and I feel like I need a drink.

"Well, shit. You're fucked, you know that?"

"And now things have gotten more serious and now…" I lean against my desk. "I want to be with her and I don't know how to tell Lucas."

"This could potentially destroy your relationship with him, you know."

His words are expected but not what I want to hear and I feel sick at the thought of not having a relationship with my son. "I want to think he may come around? Yes, he'll be pissed but…"

"But what? He held a candle for her for years which you knew and now you're fucking her? Come on."

"Don't make me feel like shit."

"Don't do shitty things then and stop thinking with your dick. I am *sure* the sex is amazing and I will admit I am jealous because Avery is a fucking smokeshow, but…"

"Watch yourself, Bryan," I snap. I already have to deal with half the men in Philly lusting after her, I'm not taking that shit from my brother.

"Oh Christ. Unlike you, I wouldn't go after my nephew's girl."

"She's not his girl," I groan.

"Semantics! You know what I'm saying."

"Can you say something helpful?"

"Call it off?" He offers and it feels like the wind has been knocked out of me. I've gone too far down this road and now that no longer feels like an option.

I sigh. "Got any other ideas?"

"I don't know. Are you willing to part with a significant amount of money? Maybe for a cool mill, Lucas won't hate you as much."

"I'm serious."

"I was also serious, but okay, no to the money." He's silent for a second before he speaks again. "What would you do if one of your friends…or I went after Rebecca?"

"Wish you good luck? And also, that is very different. We were married and we have two children. Lucas and Avery have never been romantically involved."

"Fine, but you get the point I'm making. This is a bad idea and it's going to change your whole relationship with your son. Is that what you want? Not to mention what happens if and when things get more serious. What, Avery is going to be Lucas and Rae's stepmom? Or if you two have a baby? He would have been in love with the mother of his half-sibling? Is that incest? It feels incest-y."

"We are a long way off from marriage and a baby." Even though the thought of her walking around with a cute little baby bump and my ring on her finger is triggering my possessiveness.

"But it's something you're thinking about. That's the only reason you're considering telling Lucas." I sigh, not knowing what to say to that when he speaks up again. "It sounds like you've already made up your mind about this and there's no way I can talk you out of it, so what I am going to say is tell him before he finds out on his own. If he catches you, it'll be ten times worse."

"He's in New York now."

"Okay, but you and Avery are still in Philly, where he still has connections. What if it somehow gets back to him if you two are spotted out somewhere?"

"We are avoiding going public for now."

"Because you know it's shady."

"You know for someone who rarely gives a fuck what anyone thinks, you're being awfully tough on me," I scoff.

"One, you're not me, and two, I always gave a fuck what my immediate family thought." I snort, remembering more than one screaming match between him and our dad. "Don't bring up Dad; he can be a dick and you know it."

"Because you're cut from the same cloth, but we are digressing."

"The point is, you want to be able to be with Avery and also maintain a relationship with Lucas. There's a good chance you can't have both. And let's say you tell Lucas and he fucking loses it and you decide it's not worth it so you break things off with Avery, your relationship with Lucas is still forever fucked because you stuck your dick somewhere it did not belong."

I sigh in frustration because none of this is helpful. "So, the trade off is what? I don't get what I want?"

"What, young pussy? Theo, don't bullshit me. Find someone else."

"It's not like that."

"What's it like then? Enlighten me." I swallow the words sitting in the back of my throat, not wanting to speak them aloud in fear of what it means. "Oh shit," he says. "You're falling for her, aren't you?"

I sit on the couch in the corner of my office and place my phone on speakerphone before lying on my back and closing my eyes. I was not expecting this conversation with Bryan, although I should have and I'm suddenly exhausted. "I don't know...maybe."

"Not good enough."

"Get off my back, Bryan," I snap at him. "I haven't been serious with anyone since Rebecca. I don't even know how this shit works anymore."

"Sure, you do. You've always been a hopeless romantic and all that shit. That's why Rebecca fucked you up." Bryan has never been quiet about his feelings for Rebecca or his distaste for how she treated me. I'm pretty sure he told her off more times during our divorce than I did. I think about them seeing each other for the first time at Raegan's wedding and I know that's not going to be pretty. "How does she feel about you?"

I think about our last weekend together, how she looked at me, and the things she said and did and I want to believe she feels the same. "I think she wants me too." I clear my throat. "Beyond the sex." I stare up at the ceiling, trying to put my very confused thoughts into words. "I haven't felt this way in a long time. Maybe I've never felt this way." I confess, because this feels different than it did with the only other woman I've been serious with. "Maybe because I'm older now. She's just different. I don't know exactly what it is, but I just fucking *want* her."

"Uh huh," I hear the skepticism in those two syllables and I roll my eyes. "She's a good kid and cute as hell. Speaking as your older brother, good for you. Speaking as Lucas' uncle, you kind of suck." I roll my eyes just as I hear a knock on my door.

Very fucking grateful for the interruption, I sit up. "Listen, thanks for nothing. I got to go, I'll call you later."

"Alright, talk to you later." He hangs up and I open the door to find Avery looking fucking delicious holding a coffee in her hand and a bag in the other.

"Special delivery." She smiles and hands them out to me.

"What are you doing here?" I ask, trying to hide the smile and also prevent my dick from getting hard as I stare at her bare legs under a black mini-skirt.

She turns her head slightly to make sure no one is within earshot and I'm grateful my assistant isn't at her desk. "I thought I could see you under the illusion of bringing food for your team."

I grab the coffee and the food and pull her into my office. I start to close the door but I don't know how that would look so I just turn around, leaving the door open and she frowns. "We shouldn't," I tell her as I set the food and coffee on my desk.

She pouts and tucks a dark strand behind her ear. "Fine, I should get back anyway."

I lean against my desk and let out a sigh because after the conversation with Bryan, I could use a distraction. I pull her to stand between my legs and she gasps as she peeks over her shoulder before turning back to me. I trace my finger up her thigh slowly and run it over the hem of her skirt, wishing I could push it up to play with her cunt. "You said we shouldn't."

"I'm not good at listening to my own rules," I tell her as I bring her so that she's pressed directly against my dick.

"Theo." She gasps when she feels how hard I am and I reach around her to give her ass a squeeze. I slide my hand around to her front and under her skirt and drag my fingers along the edge of her panties.

"Don't start something you can't finish," she tells me as she runs her knuckles gently over my groin.

Fuck, I want to finish. More importantly, I want *her* to finish. I want to close my door and let her ride my dick until she comes all over it but the sound of laughter just beyond my office door stops me from doing anything reckless. "You should go before I bend you over my desk without a care as to who's here." I stand up and gently move her back a few steps.

She smirks, before dropping her gaze to my dick and then back up with a smirk. "Okay, I'll see you tonight? Meet you there at eight?"

I nod, hating that I can't even drive her without that causing question. "I'll be there." She gives me a smile before reaching up on her toes to press a kiss to my lips that if I were anywhere else, I'd deepen. She pulls back after a second and bites her bottom lip before walking out of my office, leaving me hard, and thanks to the conversation with my older brother, like complete shit.

Chapter
SEVENTEEN

THEO

THE CALL WITH MY BROTHER HAS ME ON EDGE FOR THE rest of the day, his words sitting in the back of my mind like a pesky conscience I've been trying my best to ignore.

"Is everything okay?" Avery asks from across the table. She cocks her head to the side and leans forward to run her fingers over my hand and strokes it gently. "You're so quiet tonight."

I sigh and run a hand through my hair, knowing I should probably tell her what I'm thinking instead of keeping it from her. "I'm sorry, I just have something on my mind." She nods at me as if to say, *well out with it.* "I told my brother." She stops stroking my hand and slowly slides it off of me. I immediately hate the loss of her touch so I reach for her hand before it's completely out of my reach. "Hey." I lean forward and press my lips to her fingers. I don't say anything else but I hope my eyes say it all.

I still want this.

"What did he say?" She asks and her voice is soft and quiet before she sinks her teeth into her bottom lip, assumedly nervous over what I'm going to say.

"What you'd expect." I squeeze her hand. "He thinks this is a bad idea for reasons I'm sure you can guess."

"Are you having second thoughts about…us?" She doesn't have tears in her eyes but I can see the sadness written all over her face.

"I don't think so," I tell her honestly. "I spent a year trying to ignore what I was feeling for you and now that we're here…" I trail off as I mindlessly trace her hand. "I don't know how to just turn them off. I'm in too deep now."

"Same." She sighs and laces our fingers together. "Lucas and I have been friends for a long time and I think he wants me to be happy. It will be tough at first, but maybe he'll eventually understand that *you* make me happy." She winces. "Or maybe I'm being really naive."

I'm about to respond when I hear my name.

FUCK.

I knew we should have gone further out of the city.

"Hey, I thought I saw you," the familiar voice of my daughter's boyfriend breaks through our conversation. Dressed in a suit, with a smile on his face, Wes' voice is calm and light and I try not to look at Avery because I know she's freaking out and he hasn't looked at her yet.

"Wes, hey...are you here with Raegan?" *First and foremost.*

"No, I had a meeting." He turns toward the table behind him where two other men are seated. "I'm heading out though. Rae wants a very particular ice cream that is not in our freezer." He chuckles before adjusting his glasses and turns his eyes toward Avery. "I'm sorry, forgive my rudeness, I'm—" He stops when he realizes who it is. "Avery?" Although he's not facing me, I can tell he looks confused at first and then a flash of realization crosses his face.

"Wes!" She stands and gives him a polite hug like it's the most normal thing in the world that the two of us would be out at a restaurant on what looks like a romantic date.

"Uh, hi!" He collects himself quickly even though I'm guessing he knows what's going on and he turns his head back to me. "I will let you guys get back to your dinner. It was great seeing you both." He clears his throat, clearly uncomfortable. "Avery, you look lovely. Nice to see you again." He nods at me. "Theo." And then he's gone moving towards the exit.

Avery is staring at me with a panicked expression and I nod. "Relax, baby. I'll handle it," I tell her before I'm out of my chair and moving in the direction that Wes went. I'm grateful he didn't go back to his table which would force me to engage in a bunch of football related pleasantries. I find him just outside the restaurant waiting for his car. "Wes."

He turns to look at me and then back to the restaurant. "I—It's none of my business," he says as he holds his hands up.

"What you saw in there…"

"You were having dinner. Nothing out of the ordinary to me." He turns back to the road assumedly looking for his car and I wonder if for the first time I'm the future father in law making him nervous.

"You can't say anything to Raegan and I hate that I'm asking that of you but…"

"What's there to tell?" He asks.

"Wes, I'm serious."

He sighs. "Look, it's not my business and I don't want it to be my business. I don't want to be forced to keep things from Raegan and I'm certainly not going to be the bearer of *that* news." He points towards the restaurant. "But if this blows up? Do not take me down with you. This never happened." He lowers his face and looks at me over the top of his glasses. For a moment I feel like I'm being scolded. "I didn't see anything. I don't know anything."

I let out a sigh of relief because I actually believe him. I don't think Wes has any interest in telling his pregnant future wife who happens to be my daughter that her father is having an affair with a girl she grew up with. I hold out my hand. "Thank you, Wes. I appreciate it." I nod, grateful that I don't have some asshole future son-in-law that could have used this situation to his advantage. "Have a great night." I turn back towards the restaurant when he speaks again.

"What I will say, however," I turn to face him, already not liking where this is going. *I knew that was too easy.* "I've done the whole sneaking around with a younger woman that should have been off limits. You need to come clean before you get caught. Tell Lucas. I can help you with Raegan a *little bit*, when the time comes, but tell your son. Because if you're out at a public restaurant, that means it's more than…" He gives me a look and holds his hands up. "Out in public in Philly no less! Come on. Even I took Rae to another state when we went out on dates." He rolls his eyes.

"Mr. Beckham, your car." One of the attendants gestures towards the black Maserati that pulls up and I eye it briefly in appreciation before turning back to him.

"I know what it's like to fall in love with someone you shouldn't," he continues. "While our situations are different, they are similar in that we both had something to lose. There are no fraternization policies in place for a reason and I broke all of them and some that didn't exist before that certainly do now." He chuckles. "Get in front of it before you get caught. It's much easier, I promise."

"I don't think—"

"Don't even say you're not in love with her." He gives me a look. "It's written all over your face." He moves toward his car. "Hers too for that matter," he calls over his shoulder and then gives me a wave before getting in his car.

And again, I'm annoyed at how much I fucking like him.

～⌒～

Avery

Theo still isn't back from talking to Wes and I'm starting to get a little worried. *Maybe it's not going well? Maybe they're arguing? What if he threatened to tell Raegan?*

No, Wes is so sweet. He would never.

From the two times you met him? my subconscious sneers.

My thoughts are interrupted by a FaceTime call from Rory. It's only eight-thirty so I'm sure she's not drunk but I'm also surprised that she's FaceTiming me. She moved to New York this week also, so I'm wondering if she's calling to show me the *Dior* showroom. *In which case, just kill me now.* I end the call and shoot her a text.

> **Me: At dinner, what's up?**
>
> **Rory: Ah! I'm at this party and I'm not supposed to have my phone but I wanted to show you these new shoes we**

are launching this fall that are to DIE for. Who are you at dinner with?

Me: Oh send a pic!

Rory: I will! Also, there are so many celebrities here, not going to lie. I'm starstruck as fuck. But dinner…? Guy?

Fuck.

Me: My mom

Rory: Oh tell Camille, hey girl hey!

Rory: By the way, I feel like something is going on with Lucas

Me: What makes you say that?

Rory: I don't know, he's just been weird ever since we got here. He's been drinking a lot and sleeping with a lot of women.

Me: Well…that's normal? He's always drunk a lot.

Rory: More than usual! And he's never been a manwhore.

Me: Okay…well, what can we do? He's grown lol

Rory: I think he's going through something.

Me: Liiiike?

Rory: I don't know! You're his best friend?

Me: You live there with him!

Rory: He doesn't open up to me the same way he does with you

Me: Okay, I'll talk to him.

Rory: Don't say I put you up to it!

Theo slides back into his seat and I put my phone down. "How did it go?"

"Everything's fine. He's a good kid."

I give him a look and he chuckles before rubbing his forehead.

"I think of him as a kid because he's dating Raegan. You know what I mean." He takes a sip of his whiskey, draining the full glass before sitting it down. "He's not going to say anything." He moves his chair around the square table so that he's closer to me and holds my hand in his. "He did say I need to tell Lucas soon." He presses his lips to my fingers and I melt at how romantic he is all the time. "I know that's not the plan, so we just need to do better about lying low for now." He looks around the restaurant. "We're still too close to home."

"Okay." I agree. He leans forward and captures my lips with his, sliding his tongue through them and rubbing it against mine. I moan and he pulls back slowly, his eyes tracing my face as a smile pulls at his lips.

"Your little noises are going to be the death of me, Avery."

⁓

Later that night, we are back at Theo's place where we are finally spending the night for the first time. My car is parked at my college apartment, and in the morning he's going to take me there so I can drive it home under the illusion that I stayed there tonight. Yes, the whole plan is risky and convoluted, but I'm dying to stay the night with him in his bed and I don't want to wait any longer. We're still naked from multiple rounds of sex, lying on our sides facing each other. The room is mostly dark, other than the few candles he'd lit around the room when we got here.

"You're so incredible." He strokes my cheek so softly that I could cry, and part of me wants to after the orgasm I just had. It was the first time we had sex that felt like more than just frantic fucking where we didn't feel like we were rushing against time or in fear that someone was going to call looking for one of us. It felt slower and more intimate and not at all like the times we were racing to our climaxes. "I just can't believe you're *you*." He turns onto his back and stares up at the ceiling. "I still remember the day we moved in." He sighs. "Rae and Lucas had been arguing for two days. I don't know if they were taking their anger towards their mother out on each other or what, but they would not stop yelling." I prop my head up on my fist as I listen to him because I don't think I ever knew this. "And then you just showed up at the front door bouncing up and down like you'd just consumed a mountain of sugar."

I do remember that. I remember my mom sending me next door with some food because my mother's love language has always been feeding people and that was how she welcomed all of our new neighbors.

Eight Years Ago

I can't even stop the blush from creeping onto my face as the hottest guy I've ever seen in my entire life answers the door. I don't know much about the people that just moved in, only that I saw two kids that look about my age and I'm excited to finally have some people to hang out with or ride the bus with. There was no one close to my age in this neighborhood, a bunch of elementary school and high schoolers but no one I could suffer through the middle school years with.

"Hello! I live next door," I tell him, trying to keep the squeak out of my voice as I point to my house. "My mom wanted me to bring these. She owns the best bakery in town, so the brownies are great. The lasagna?" I hold out the hand not holding the food and give it a little shake as if to say meh. *I hold the food out for him with a bright smile and he takes it while giving me a look of confusion. "I'm Avery Summers." I smile as I hold out my hand.*

"Theo." He shakes my hand with a smile before setting the food down on top of a table set amidst a sea of brown boxes. "Thank you very much for this."

"You're welcome. But what's your last name? I can't call you by your first name; my mom will have a fit."

He chuckles. "Graham."

"Great, now that we have that settled, Mr. Graham. Do you have kids? Preferably a girl around thirteen?" I point at myself, excitedly.

"Well, she's fifteen actually, but I have a son that's thirteen."

"Hmmm, that'll do. Can they come out?"

"Please, take them." He laughs before he calls into the house. *"Rae! Lucas!"*

"I don't think they came home for two days." He laughs. "Well Lucas did, but I think Raegan stayed at your house for the next two nights."

I smile at the memory of finally having what felt like a big sister. "It was so nice having a girl around and she was older and cooler than me. She probably thought I was so lame." I chuckle, although if I can remember, Raegan loved hanging out with me and my mom and it didn't take a therapist to understand why.

"No, Rae has always loved you like the little sister she wanted instead of Lucas." He laughs and I frown thinking about what it could mean now. "You were the best thing to ever happen to Raegan and Lucas and at the best time." He turns back towards me and pulls me closer. "And now you're...." He moves us so that I'm beneath him and though he doesn't say the words explicitly, I hear the implication. "What are you doing to me, Avery?"

"The same thing you're doing to me," I tell him. "I used to fantasize about being here with you and now I'm actually here." I pull my eyes from him to look around his bedroom.

"I never thought you'd ever be here. Honestly, there's been so few times I've had a woman here at all."

I raise an eyebrow, curious about this particular conversation and the women who came before me. "Yeah, about that. You never dated anyone seriously. At least no one you brought around Rae and Lucas. How come?"

He shrugs. "I never felt like I met the right woman that I would feel comfortable introducing to them." He looks me over. "This is not to say I didn't date, it was just harder. Rebecca wasn't here, so it's not like I had weekends or days where they could be with her and allow me to really spend an extended amount of time getting to know someone. I was always running one of them here or there. I couldn't stay overnight at a woman's place and I wasn't allowing just anyone to come here. If they were both sleeping at a friend's house, I could or before Bryan moved to Arizona and they'd stay there for a night I could have someone over but I don't know. Meeting someone was never my focus. I guess I felt like Rebecca robbed me of that in some ways. I didn't want them to feel like they had two parents that didn't put them first. That I valued a relationship with someone else more than I did with them." He shakes his head. "And now I wonder if that's exactly what I'm doing with Lucas. Am I just as bad as Rebecca? Or hell, worse because he expects that kind of selfishness from her and doesn't from me?"

I am at a loss for words, hearing him unload all of his fears and when his eyes dart to mine, he winces at the look of shock on my face. "Shit, Ave. I shouldn't have said all of that."

"No!" I press my lips to his as I try to calm the anxiety taking over that comes with sharing too much. "Of course you should." I sigh, unsure of what to say. "It's messy." I nod in agreement. "Especially when you phrase it like that."

"I'm fucking crazy about you and I'm not taking into consideration how that fact now affects him. Does that make me selfish?" He rubs his hand down my shoulder gently and goosebumps pop up in response.

"I think the fact that you're having these thoughts means you're not selfish at all… I feel the same guilt." I've wanted this man for years, but I never thought I would ever get here and now we are and he feels the same but never in my fantasies did I ever picture how we'd ever tell people about us. *How we'd tell Lucas.*

I bite my lip as I prepare to tell him about what Rory said. "Rory texted me while you were outside talking to Wes," I tell him. "She's worried about Lucas."

He frowns. "Why?"

"I don't know. She says he's drinking more than usual and…" I clear my throat. "There have been a lot of girls." I sigh. "She thinks he's going through something and I really hope it doesn't have to do with me."

He turns onto his back and I immediately hate myself for

making us have this conversation. He turns on the light on his nightstand and sits up. The sheet is still covering his lap but his naked torso is on display, shiny from sweat and glistening and I can't help but notice how gorgeous he is and how much I want him even amidst this slightly uncomfortable conversation.

"Sorry," I whisper as I sit up too and wrap the sheet around my chest. "I shouldn't have said anything." I push my thoroughly just fucked hair out of my face.

"No, I'm glad you did." He reaches for me and pulls me closer to him. "Don't keep anything from me."

I nod. "She wants me to talk to him and if I'm being honest I do too. Just so I know what's going on." I bite my bottom lip as I prepare to speak my biggest concern. "I hope he's not doing all of this to get any feelings he may have for me out of his system." I frown. "I want him to be completely over me if he's not already but not by being self-destructive."

"Hey, this is not your fault." He strokes my cheek before tucking a hair behind my ear. "Maybe this has nothing to do with you at all and Rory is just overreacting."

I don't know if he's trying to make me or himself feel better, but I hear the skepticism in his voice.

What am I going to say if it comes out that it actually is because of me?

"Okay, and on that note, I'm dating your dad."

I hadn't even noticed the tears in my eyes until I feel Theo's hands beneath them. "Please don't cry. We'll figure it out." He pulls me into his lap to face him and begins to rub my back slowly, and even though there is not much between his dick and my pussy, it's not remotely sexual.

"What if *figuring it out* means I can't have you?" More tears form in response to my words and my heart begins to race at the thought of not getting to be with Theo. The thought that Theo and I would be over before we even had a chance to begin. "And I hate the friend that it makes me that being with you is becoming a bigger concern."

I meet his warm brown eyes that are filled with so much sadness and confusion. "I know. I knew this was fucking dangerous." He grimaces. "Going down this road with you." He clears his throat. "I spent so many years just focusing on being a good father only to finally be ready for more with a woman and it's...you." He chuckles darkly. "Which probably negates everything."

Chapter

EIGHTEEN

Avery

TG: We have plans tonight.

It's six in the morning and I'm sitting in the kitchen of *Avery's* watching my mother pull out a batch of her infamous blueberry muffins when I open Theo's text. A smile pulls at my lips seeing the words on the screen and I shift my body away from my mother so she doesn't start an inquisition as to what has me grinning at my phone before the sun is barely up.

Me: Oh? What kind of plans?

TG: It's a surprise.

Me: I don't particularly like surprises, you know.

And while this is true, I have a feeling I'll like whatever he has planned.

TG: I do know but you'll like this one. Leave your car in the garage on Main Street and I'll pick you up at five.

Me: What should I wear?

TG: Casual, we'll be outside.

Me: Okay…Do I need overnight clothes?

TG: Since when do you sleep in clothes?

Me: Lol I meant do I need to bring things for the morning?

TG: No, I'll have you home at a respectable time tonight.

Me: Okay. Can't wait *kissy face emoji*

TG: Have a good day, beautiful.

The excited nerves are coursing through me all day as I go through a million different things Theo and I could be doing tonight. I leave the café around three which is enough time for me to go home, shower, and change. After changing my clothes ten different times—because really what the hell is *casual* anyway?—I decide on a black short strapless sundress under a chambray shirt in case it gets a little chilly tonight. I make it to the garage at five minutes to five and am not shocked to see Theo already there. The garage has mostly cleared out from the day, so I find him easily, parked in a corner away from most of the cars and I wonder if that's on purpose.

Another reason why I wore a dress.

I park my car next to his and before I can even open my door, he's there opening it and holding his hand out for me. "Hi." I smile and the sexy smile he gives me heats me all the way to my toes.

"Hi, gorgeous." He pulls me into his arms and slowly slides his hands down my body. He cups me underneath my dress, giving my ass a gentle squeeze, and I gasp just as his lips connect with mine. His tongue licks his way into my mouth and dances with mine as he pushes me up against my car. I don't know how long we're kissing when he pulls back and presses a kiss to my nose. "We should get going, we have a bit of a drive." When he opens the passenger side door of his Mercedes for me, I notice he's wearing dark blue jeans and a black v-neck shirt and I want to laugh at our matching attire.

I look him up and down and then down at myself and he realizes what I'm looking at. "Well, now there won't be any question that you're mine," he says as I slide into the car.

We've been driving for about twenty minutes south on the highway when I realize we are probably leaving Pennsylvania. "Can you tell me where we're going?"

"Maybe when we get a little closer."

"How long until we get there?" Even with his dark sunglasses, I know what kind of look he gives me and I let out a sigh. "Fine. How was your day?"

"Good. A pretty easy day. How about you?"

"Nothing out of the ordinary." I shrug, thinking about how normal this feels, talking about our days like a regular couple. His hand finds my thigh and I want to melt at how warm and strong it feels and how large it looks against me making me feel feminine and sexy. He squeezes it gently and my pussy flutters in response.

I look down at where his hand is resting and then up at him and lower my sunglasses to the tip of my nose to shoot him a warning look. "I wouldn't unless you're prepared to pull over somewhere."

He laughs and it's one I can see myself hearing for a very long time. He strokes the skin gently without removing it and I shake my head at his teasing. I put my hand over his, rubbing the skin with my fingers when he wraps his hand around mine and brings it to his lips to kiss my knuckles.

Oh my God.

"I had to actively stop myself from thinking about you today in order to get any work done." He's still got my hand encased in his, rubbing his thumb over everywhere it can reach. "You are a very present fixture in my mind these days."

"I think about you a lot too," I tell him because I can't remember a time since I met him that he wasn't somewhere on my mind.

We've been driving for close to an hour when I start probing for more details. "Are we going to Maryland?"

"Not quite that far."

"What's in Delaware?" I ask, referring to the only state between Pennsylvania and Maryland that's on this road. "Where we'd be outside?" I start thinking of all the possible places and none of them would make sense unless...

I gasp excitedly and turn to him. "Are we going to the fair!?" I clap my hands together because I fucking *love* the fair and if that is where we're going it warms my heart that he remembered that fact. He gives me a smile revealing his perfect teeth, and I squeal. "Oh my God! I was so mad that it left Philly before I could go! Theo!" I do a dance in my seat already thinking about the funnel cake I'm about to devour.

"I didn't say that's where we're going."

I purse my lips at him suspiciously. "So, that's not where we're going?"

He chuckles. "Yeah baby, that's where we're going."

I bite my bottom lip. *Oh yeah, I am so glad I wore a dress.*

～～

Thirty minutes later, we are pulling up to the fairgrounds. It's almost six-thirty so it's still light out and I'm so excited to see everything when it gets dark. One of my favorite things to do is to ride the Ferris wheel at night and see everything lit up with neon bright lights.

"Theo, this is so great, thank you for this." I tilt my head back to offer him my lips which he takes as he holds me tight against him. "This is already the best date ever," I tell him when we pull apart.

He gets our tickets and soon we are pushing through the turnstile to let us onto the grounds. "So," he looks around, "what do you want to eat first?"

I laugh because I was always into all the fair food and I used to be very serious about what we should eat at what times so we didn't get sick on any rides. I tap my chin and look around. "Well, are you hungry? If so, turkey legs first. We are very close to Maryland though so waffle crab fries are also a great idea if they have them. If you're not hungry, we can start with dessert." My eyes dart between all the food vendors near the entrance and I don't see any of those. "Snow cones? Pass," I say waving my hand. "Oooh! Fried pickles?" I point to the stand a few yards away.

"God, you're fucking cute." He wraps an arm around my shoulder and kisses my temple. "Whatever you want."

We get an order of fried pickles and a boozy lemonade which I'm really not sure what that consists of and we start walking around.

"So, I know you're staying in Philly for the foreseeable future while you're helping your mom, but do you see yourself anywhere else?" He asks as we walk amongst the crowds. It's a weeknight, so while it's a little less busy than I'm sure it is on the weekends, there's still a good number of people and more children than I'd expect for a school night.

"I don't know. I haven't given it much thought except for when I was considering moving to New York with Lucas and Rory, but the thought of anywhere else seems scary. I've lived here my whole life. I didn't even go away to college." I cock my head to the side. "What about you?"

"I don't know. I suppose if there were a reason." He takes a sip of the drink and immediately coughs. "This is awful by the way." He scrunches his face and I snatch it from him.

"What did you expect? Top-shelf liquor? Don't be a snob." I laugh. "This may or may not have been concocted in someone's bathtub." I take a sip of it. "Just ride the wave."

"I want to make sure I can get us home." He laughs. "Maybe you ride that wave alone." He points at me. "Back to your question though; Rae is here and Lucas isn't far. My parents are still in New Jersey. I don't see why I'd leave if practically everyone I know is here unless I had a real reason to move." We make it to a row of different games and I can already feel my competitive side coming out. "Like maybe the woman I was seeing needed to move and we were serious and I wanted to go with her."

His eyes trace my face and though the implication is loud, I don't respond to it. I look at the first game, the high striker, which is the one where you have to slam the large hammer down to ring the bell and I nod my head towards it. "If my memory serves me correctly, you're pretty good at this one."

"It's been a while." He hands me the bag of fried pickles and wipes his hand on a napkin. "Let's see."

"I want a big stuffed animal," I say, holding my arms out. "The biggest."

He raises an eyebrow at me. "That I'm going to be stuck carrying around the park?"

I give him a fake pout. "Okay, a smaller one, but this is what happens when you don't tell me things, I would have brought a backpack to make it easier to carry a bunch! Now I can only get like two." I pout jokingly as he steps up to the game and pays the attendant who can't be older than eighteen. The guy hands him the oversized hammer and I take a step back to give him some space. Just as he raises it up and he's about to hit it, I scream. "Don't miss!"

He stops just before it hits the metal plate and he turns around and glares at me for breaking his concentration. The attendant snorts. "You're funny."

"Hush, Avery," Theo growls over his shoulder before he does it again, slamming it down so hard that I hear the bell a second later. The visual of his strength makes my knees weak and I bite my lip.

God, what can't this man do?

"And you didn't even break a sweat! See I was trying to give you a challenge." I giggle as I move into his arms and wrap mine around him.

He presses his lips to my temple. "Which one?"

"Hmmm." I look around and spot a cute little yellow dragon and point at it. "That one!"

Theo laughs as the attendant hands it to me. "It looks like that dragon from that book you love."

I pull away, giving him a curious look because while I know why I picked it, I'm surprised he does. "How did you know?"

"I listen." He shrugs as he hands the kid an extra five dollars with a nod and guides me toward the next game.

"Yeah, but we weren't together...I mean..."

He brushes his lips against mine gently. "I've been very aware of you for the past year."

I don't know if it's the rail liquor lemonade making me emotional but his words make my heart flutter in my chest. "Come on," he says as he tugs me toward another food vendor. "I think I want fried Oreos now."

After a few more games, including one involving a football that he was obviously way too good at, it's starting to get darker. I now have another stuffed animal, a cute giraffe that is bigger than my dragon and almost half my height.

So yeah, Theo is carrying it.

He won even more, but he ended up giving them to whatever young kids were around which made their night and me very turned on.

We're walking for a bit longer when we run into a funnel cake stand that has a long line of people. "This was really fun," I tell him. "Thank you for this. It was so thoughtful."

"Of course," he says, like it's the simplest thing he could have done. "I would do anything to keep you smiling like you have tonight."

I grab his jaw, tugging his face closer to mine, and press my lips to his. I don't know how long we're kissing when we hear a throat clearing behind us. We turn to face them and we see three teenage girls who are probably around fifteen staring at us with the goofiest expressions. "You guys are so cute," one of them says with a grin.

"Thank you." I smile as we move forward.

"He's hot," I hear one of them whisper causing both of us to chuckle.

"You hear that, babe? You're hot," I whisper and he rolls his eyes as we move up in the line. "Hey, I was once their age thinking the same thing."

"Please don't remind me." He grabs my hand and laces our fingers.

We order our funnel cake and sit at a picnic table to eat it. "Can I stay over tonight?" I ask him as I take a bite of the funnel cake and the powder flies everywhere.

"You never have to ask. I want you in my bed whenever you want to be there. I just didn't know how easy it was for you to keep staying over." He leans forward. "You have powder here," he says just before his tongue darts out and licks the tip of my nose.

I gasp, touching the wet skin on my nose. His tongue is very acquainted with my pussy and a lot of other places and somehow that has me turning into a fucking puddle. "Theo."

"Mmmhm?" He looks at me through hooded eyes and if there weren't children everywhere, I'd climb into his lap and rock against him a little bit. I turn my head towards the main attraction of the fair and then back to him.

"I've never fooled around with anyone on a Ferris wheel before," I tell him with a sexy smirk.

We finish the funnel cake and make our way over to the ride and after a few moments, we slide into one of the cars. It's fully dark now and the whole ride is lit up with turquoise, purple, and pink lights. I sit next to him and drape my legs over his knees, not wanting to alert the guy controlling the ride that I plan to climb into his lap.

"You going to climb on my dick and ride me?" Theo whispers in my ear and a delicious shiver runs through me. I look up and around as we start moving and I shake my head. "I don't know how sturdy this ride is for me to bounce up and down on you." I giggle as we make our way a fourth of the way to the top.

He pulls me into his lap so that my back is resting against his chest and lifts my dress to my waist. He pushes my hair to one side and presses his lips to my neck as he wraps an arm around me and drags his fingertips down my stomach. He glides his fingers over my panties, stroking me gently and I let out a sigh.

"I would put my tongue here if there was room. I'll have to settle for just touching your pretty pussy for now." He presses a wet kiss to my neck as he pushes his fingers inside of me, swirling his fingers around my clit.

"Fuck, Theo." I moan as we keep moving to the top.

"Shhh, baby, do you want people to know what you're doing? That you have your man's fingers shoved down the front of your panties?" He slides two fingers into my opening. "You want my third finger?" I let my head fall back and nod against him, my body already humming as it chases my release. "You look so pretty like this. Squirming and panting in my lap. Fuck, you're so gorgeous. We're almost at the top. How close are you, baby?" he murmurs in my ear.

"Close," I mumble out. "Oh fuck, that's good." He continues fucking me with three fingers and rubbing the heel of his hand against my clit every few strokes.

"I want you so fucking much, Avery." I realize now that my

moving has caused his dick to start rising underneath me and I let out a whimper. "You feel that? The power you have over my dick, Avery. Fuck. Just the thought of you makes me hard."

"Oh God, I'm going to come." I moan as I let my head rest against him and he presses a kiss to my cheek.

"Come all over my fingers, baby." I clench around him and he lets out a groan. "Oh fuck. I know you're close." I clench again and just as our car comes to a stop, I feel myself falling over the edge.

"Oh my God, Theo!"

"Oh, that's a good fucking girl, coming all over my hand." His voice is low, gruff, and sexy and I sigh in response as the intensity of my orgasm doesn't allow me to speak yet. "Open your eyes." He tells me and when I do, all I see are all the stars in the night sky and it makes me feel like I'm floating. A tremor skates through me and I squeal, grabbing his hand to stop him from rubbing.

"Theo," I whisper.

"Hmm?" he says against my jaw just as his tongue darts out to trace the skin.

"Oh my God," I say as he pulls his hand out of my panties, and when I turn to look up at him, I see him running his tongue over his fingers lasciviously. I get up and turn around to straddle him.

"We don't have time, don't start." He chuckles and I bite my lip as I move around on his lap and press my lips to his. He tastes like my pussy and funnel cake and powdered sugar and I moan as I drag my tongue against his.

"You are so sexy." I pull away but keep my face a mere inch from his. "I want to take your dick out and sit on it," I tell him. "Just for a second, I want to feel you inside me."

"Angel." He starts to protest as he looks down while we start to descend.

"Two seconds."

"You think either of us can stop after two seconds?" He gives me a look but I'm already fumbling with his belt to undo his jeans.

"Don't deny me what's mine, Theo Graham." I smirk and he shakes his head.

He lets out a deep exhale through his nose like an angered bull. "Be fucking quick." He growls just as I pull his hard dick out and stroke it once before I pull my panties to the side and slide down on him.

"Oh." I breathe out as I let my head fall back. I clench around him hard and move my hips in a circle, careful not to rattle the car too much, and when I bring my head back up to meet his gaze his brown eyes are dark and hungry. He grabs my hair at the root and pulls my lips to crash against his and I moan into his mouth.

The kiss is aggressive and passionate and consuming and I don't think I've ever been kissed like this. "You are fucking mine, Avery," he tells me as he lets my hair go.

"Yes yes yes. Yours, Daddy."

"Damn, you're going to make me come. Don't call me that." He groans as he lets his head fall back.

"Why, because you like it?" I purr. "Daddy." I press my lips to the space behind his ear and nibble gently. "I won't tell anyone you like it. Our little secret." I trail my tongue down his neck. "We're almost at the bottom though, so if you want to come in my pussy, you better do it fast or else everyone is going to know. They'll know that under my dress, your dick is wedged inside me ready to fucking blow."

"Fuck fuck fuck." I'm not even moving up and down, I'm just clenching around him and I feel like he's ready to come.

"Are you going to fuck my ass tonight, Daddy?" I ask in my most innocent voice and then he presses his face into my neck.

"FUCK, right there, baby. Your cunt is so fucking warm and tight. Squeeze me again." He says in a choked whisper. "Just like that. Oh fuck," he says through gritted teeth as I feel him expanding inside of me. He bites down on my shoulder and I gasp at the sharp sensation. Then I feel his tongue running over the space to soothe the sting. I scramble to pull off of him and slide my panties into place. "Oh my God, Avery." He shakes his head while giving me the sexiest smile. "What am I going to do with you?"

He's just finished tucking his dick back into his jeans when we make it to the bottom and I give him a wicked smile. "You want to ride it again?"

Chapter

NINETEEN

Avery

One month later

THE PAST MONTH HAS BEEN NOTHING SHORT OF PERFECT. I've been in relationships before but this just feels different. Theo is romantic and attentive and patient and far more mature than anyone I've dated while still being exciting and so much fun to be around. I find myself wanting to spend all my nights with him after spending most of my days thinking about him and us. While I've always known he was kind and generous, it's so different being in a relationship with him. He calls when he says he will, plans dates, and it's the healthiest relationship I've ever been in.

Even if I do have to hide it from everyone in my life.

I find myself falling deeper every time I see him and it's a bittersweet feeling. I'm happy being with him and with every realization that this could be the real thing, I find my heart fluttering in my chest, and then moments later comes the anxiety of having to tell Lucas the truth. *But what is the alternative? Never telling anyone about me and Theo?*

At this point, we've developed a system, and while I'm pretty sure my parents suspect I'm seeing someone, I'm even more sure that they have no clue that it's the man who lives next door. We've spent every moment together we could the past month and in a few weeks, I'm moving into my own apartment which will give us even more freedom.

TG: Come to room 403

The text breaks my thoughts and I narrow my eyes suspiciously because we already had a very long conversation about not getting reckless tonight.

Tonight is Wes and Raegan's engagement party in New York which means practically everyone in attendance got a room for the night. Most of us are staying at the same hotel so Theo and I cannot afford to do anything crazy. I'm not sure Lucas is here yet and the last thing I want to happen is to get caught coming out of his father's room.

Me: Didn't we say we had to behave this weekend?

TG: It's still early, no one is here. Lucas is still at his apartment.

Me: We aren't just looking out for Lucas. There are a lot of people here that know us both.

I wince thinking about his brother who knows about us and I wonder if I'll be able to see the judgment all over his face. Then I think about Wes and I wonder if he really has kept this secret from Raegan.

TG: Fine

TG: I'm coming to you.

My eyes widen and dart to the door like he's already there. I look down at my state of undress, as I'm not completely sure what I want to wear tonight between the four dresses I brought. I sigh knowing he's not leaving this room without being inside of me if I answer the door half-naked. I'm freshly showered and glowing from the oil I use after and I'm wearing nothing but a strapless bra and a thong that I already know he's going to try and pull off with his teeth.

A knock startles me and I already know it's going to be dangerous that he and I are on the same floor. I rush towards it, peeking through the peephole to be sure it's him before opening it, and usher him in quickly. He's already dressed in a navy suit but without a jacket and he smells as delicious as he looks. He must have showered because the ends of his hair look a little damp and he smells like the cologne he always wears with a hint of the soap he uses.

His eyes rake over me salaciously as he scratches his jaw and before I know it, I'm up against the door with his hard body pressed against mine. "You must want to get fucked."

I press my nose against his neck, getting a whiff of whiskey, and I wonder if he's already had a drink. "You smell really good." I inhale deeply and let out a moan when I feel his strong, firm hands massaging my ass as he wraps one of my legs around his waist. *Yes, I do really want to get fucked but we shouldn't.* "Ah, Theo, we can't," I gasp, but I already feel my resolve crumbling as he presses himself harder against me.

"Why the fuck can't we?"

I move around him when I feel a smack on my ass and I have to focus on putting one foot in front of the other so my knees don't buckle. "Because someone may start looking for us and it'll be really hard to explain why you're in my hotel room."

"Then we should be quick." He crosses the room quickly, his long legs eating the distance between us until he's on one knee in front of me. "All this talk, and I could have made you come already."

"Theo," I warn, as he presses his face to my covered pussy and grabs the fabric with his teeth before letting it snap against my skin. He does it again, this time letting his teeth graze my sensitive skin and a whimper escapes me.

"Avery." He grunts as he hooks his thumbs in the waistband of my panties and slides them slowly down my legs. His eyes don't leave mine as he moves them down, almost like he's daring me to stop him. I step out of them, all the while my mind is screaming at me that this is a horrible idea despite how good it feels. "I don't know when I'm going to get another taste this weekend." He pushes me gently towards the small loveseat in the corner. "Sit," he commands and I do, spreading my legs obscenely as I put my bare cunt on display for him. "Damn, you're beautiful. I'll never get enough of this," he says just before he takes one slow lick through my slit. "Enough of *you*," he says and butterflies flutter in my stomach.

My hands immediately go to the back of his head as I push my hand through his strands. "Oh God," I cry out and my eyes slam shut as his tongue begins to move rapidly over my clit.

"Look at me, baby," he commands and when I finally manage to open my eyes, his brown irises are staring at me. "I don't care what happens while we're here," he says as he pushes two fingers inside of me, hooking them upwards to rub the spot that will have me coming very fucking quickly.

"Theo," I moan.

"Listen," he grits out. "You are mine, do you understand me?"

Wait huh? I'm too far gone at this point, so I'm not sure what he means. *Of course, I'm yours, just keep doing what you're doing, please!*

"Answer me, Avery." He pulls his fingers out of me and his tongue disappears from my sex that is tingling with the anticipation of my climax.

My eyes fly open. "Don't stop, please!" I beg. His face is right in front of mine, his eyes full of lust and his mouth wet and shiny. I lean forward to kiss him and he pulls back. I pout at the fact that he's denying me his lips.

"Do you understand me?" He asks.

"Of course, I'm yours, who else's would I be?" He stands up and suddenly I'm very confused, *and still horny for that matter.* "Wait," I whisper. "You didn't finish." I'm wound up and so close to the end that even the faintest brush against my pussy will send me over the edge. He looks back at me and I take the moment to run my fingers through my wet slit as a way to entice him.

It seems to work because he moves back to settle between my legs. "I can't touch you." He pushes a digit through my folds and I shudder against it. "I can't claim you. Can't let anyone know that you're fucking mine and it pisses me off." He leans back down and brushes his lips across my pussy and his facial hair tickles the sensitive flesh. "I'm going to have to watch men hit on you with the taste of your cunt on my tongue and I can't do a fucking thing about it."

"No one is going to hit on me." I bite my bottom lip, wondering where this sudden bit of insecurity is coming from. I thought he was just being possessive but it seems deeper than that.

He shoots me a look. "You don't even believe that."

"Okay, take off your clothes," I tell him as I reach behind myself and unsnap my bra. I start unbuttoning his shirt to get him started before I press a kiss to his lips. "You are very worked up, and I think fucking me will calm you down." I stand up, grabbing his hand before leading him to the bed. He toes off his shoes and takes off his pants and his shirt and I'm grateful that he realizes that leaving anything on while he fucks me is very risky.

He wastes no time pushing inside of me and he lets out a feral groan as he starts to work himself in and out of me. "Just because you can't claim me, doesn't mean I don't know who I belong to." I wrap my hands around him, dragging my nails down his back. I look up into his eyes. "I'm yours, Theo." I see something in his eyes I don't recognize. Something different than the usual looks he gives me when he's inside of me.

"Yes. Fuck." He presses his lips to mine as he begins to fuck me harder, more urgently like he wants to seal my words with an orgasm. "Mine." He growls before sinking his teeth into my neck and biting down hard like he doesn't care if he leaves a hickey I'll have to explain.

"Oh God, right there." I moan just before his lips find mine again. His tongue slips between my lips and kisses me in a way he hasn't before. It's intense and passionate and frenzied as he ruts into me like it's the last time he's ever going to do it. "Let me on top," I whisper against his lips and he rolls us to let me on top of him. I move up and down slowly, a swift change to how he was just fucking me. "Nothing changes between us," I whisper as I begin to move faster, bouncing up and down on his rock-hard cock. "If a guy hits on me, they'll know immediately that I'm not interested." I lean down to drag my tongue over his lips before trapping his bottom lip between my teeth and nibbling gently. "How could I be when I have you?" I drag my tongue over his bottom lip. "You're the only man that I want."

"Shit, Avery." The two words come out shaky and he grips my hips as he begins to thrust upward into my aching cunt.

"Are you mine? When some random woman flirts with you because they don't see a ring on your finger, are you going to tell them your dick belongs to someone else?" I press my lips to his neck. "That *you* belong to someone else?"

"Fuuuuuck." He groans. "Yes, baby. I'll tell them."

"Good," I purr in his ear. I circle my hips, rubbing my clit along his hard length as best as I can. "Now, say something nasty," I tell him and the smile paired with the wicked gleam in his eye lets me know that he's less tense than he was minutes ago.

He opens his mouth to speak when his phone begins to blare through the room. I snap my head towards the noise, slowing my thrusts as I panic thinking about who could be calling, potentially from where they are knocking on his hotel room door looking for him.

I go to pull off of him when he grips my hips holding me in place. "You haven't come yet."

"You can't be serious, Theo. It could be someone here at the hotel looking for you."

"I don't care," he says as he thrusts upwards.

"Because you're thinking with your dick." I smack his hand, to remove it from me as I climb off of him. "We smell like sex, your mouth is still wet from my pussy and now," I pull his phone out of his pocket. "Excellent, your ex-wife is calling," I say with an eye roll as I toss him his phone. I didn't mean to spit it out like that, but the way he's looking at me, I can already sense where his mind is going.

"Hold that thought," he says to me. "What's up?" he says as he answers the phone. I'm retrieving my discarded underwear when I feel him behind me and one hand wraps around my waist as he keeps me in place against him, my back to his torso. His lips find my shoulder and he kisses it gently. "I'm on a call, I can meet you guys in the lobby in twenty minutes." His tongue darts out to trace the skin as he rubs his fingers through my sex. I put a hand over my mouth, to stop any sounds from leaving my lips and I can't deny how hot this is. Theo on the phone while he touches and pleasures me. The fact that it's also his ex makes this even hotter. "I said twenty minutes. I have to go," he snaps and then he tosses the phone towards the bed. "We aren't leaving this room until we both come."

"Are Lucas and Rae here?" I ask, wondering who he's meeting in the lobby.

"I think Rae is, but Rebecca meant her brother. I guess he's looking for me." He pulls me into his arms and sits on the couch, pulling me to straddle him.

Jealousy flares through me at the thought. *They were a family. Her family is still Lucas and Rae's family and thereby makes Theo family on some level.*

"None of that." He points at me and I frown.

I scoff. "You were just freaking out about random guys hitting on me and I can't feel a little uneasy about the woman you were married to for fourteen years?"

"No, because you know that Rebecca and I are anything but amicable."

"That's not the point."

"What is the point then, huh?" He whispers as he stares up at me with eyes full of sincerity. His full lips turn slightly downwards. "You have no reason to be jealous."

"I'm not jealous of Rebecca. It's just…the familiarity is throwing me a bit, I guess."

"I get it." He lets out a sigh. "I hate that I've had similar feelings." I nod in understanding without him having to explicitly say it.

"I meant what I said," I whisper as I press my hand to his chest. "I am yours." My cheeks heat, saying this during a time when I'm not chasing the high of an orgasm. It feels more intense and I feel more vulnerable. "If you want me to be."

He cups my face and his lips brush against mine. "Avery, it's a fucking honor that you want to be mine." I press my lips to his, feeling the words on the tip of my tongue and not wanting to blurt them out. "Put me back in your pussy," he tells me. "Or do you want to come on my tongue?"

I let out a moan as I slide back down on him, taking each inch slowly. We find a rhythm easily, and just as I find myself getting closer to my orgasm, my phone starts to ring.

"For the love of God," Theo grits out. "Don't answer it."

"I have to."

"No." His fingers dig into my hips, and the force of his grip sends a spark to my clit as I keep riding him.

"But…"

"If we stop, we'll both be worked up and won't be able to get through the night without…" He looks up at me before darting his gaze down to my tits. He palms one before running his tongue over the other nipple. "If you want me to behave tonight, come for me now." My phone has stopped ringing at this point and I just pray it's not anyone that's looking for me. "Give it to me, Avery. I need you to come all over my dick."

"Theo…" I whine, when he bites down gently on my nipple. "Oh fuck!" I cry out as I feel the orgasm starting at the base of my spine.

"This will not be the last time I fuck you this weekend." My mouth drops open at the thought of sneaking off somewhere with Theo amidst Raegan's engagement party. "It may not even be the last time I fuck you tonight."

Chapter

TWENTY

THEO

SLIP OUT OF AVERY'S ROOM WITH EASE AND BREATHE A SIGH of relief that no one is around to see me leaving. I get in the elevator after giving myself a once-over in the mirror to make sure I'm somewhat put together. I know I'm being reckless but I can't fucking help it.

I wanted Avery so much that I *almost* didn't care.

I make it to the restaurant inside the hotel where we're having the party. Raegan spots me first and moves towards me instantly, dressed in a white, short backless silk dress that I'm sure she picked because soon she won't want to wear anything like it. I meet Wes' gaze over her head and he gives me a nod that I'm pretty sure doesn't have a hidden meaning but I can't be sure.

"Thank God, you're here," she says as she hugs me. "Lucas just got here, but he's showering." I almost tell her I know because that's who called Avery, but I catch myself before it slips out. "Thank you so much for setting all of this up." She beams up at me and squeezes me for another second before she lets go. "You really pulled all the strings." She giggles. Wes offered to take care of everything, but I wanted to do this for Raegan. I'm her father, and I always assumed I would be paying for her entire wedding. I wanted to do more for her big day, but Wes wouldn't hear of it.

The room does look amazing and exactly like Raegan. *Completely over the top.* There are white and gold balloons floating along the ceiling, a large lit neon sign with their initials hung on the wall along with the words, *And so it begins.* There is a champagne tower set up in the corner and candles on every table along with a bouquet of white roses.

"Anything for you." I press my lips to her cheek.

"Oh my gosh!" She says, her eyes no longer looking at me. "Avery, you look so amazing!" She squeals and I try not to stiffen, but just hearing her name sends what feels like a bolt of lightning through me. I follow Raegan's eyes towards Avery who is a few steps away from us and I try not to react to how gorgeous she looks. She wasn't dressed before I left her room, so seeing her in this sexy off the shoulder black dress with a long slit up the side that stops mid-thigh shocks me for a moment.

"Thanks, Rae! You look amazing." She hugs her tightly and I'll admit it warms my heart to see the two most important women in my life hugging like this. I have a fleeting thought that hopefully it will always be this way. "Let me see the ring!" She says and Raegan holds it out for her, beaming with excitement. I'll admit I don't think I've ever seen her so happy.

"Gorgeous. It's perfect! He did great."

"Right!?" She puts a hand to her chest and her blue eyes glisten. "He knows me so well." She looks at me with a smile. "Thanks again for giving him your approval."

"He's not bad, that one." I nod towards my future son-in-law who's standing in the corner talking to some people I don't recognize. They invited just under a hundred people and most of them RSVP'd they were coming, so I anticipate quite a few people I've never met. Wes' eyes look up and find Raegan and I almost feel like I'm intruding on the look they share so I turn away from her just as he makes his way over to us.

"Avery." I nod, turning my attention towards her. "You look beautiful."

I see the faint pink in Avery's cheeks and she gives me a smile that isn't the usual smile she gives me when I compliment her. It's shy and polite and yet it still makes my dick hard. My fingers touch her elbow as I lean down to press a kiss to her cheek and I hear the sharp intake of breath as she stiffens against me.

"Thanks, Theo." She narrows her eyes playfully and moments later she's blocked from my vision as Lucas scoops her into his arms and lifts her off the ground.

"There she is." He sets her down after no more than a moment and I try not to pay too much attention to them to avoid getting jealous of his hands on her.

"Hey, Lucas." She returns his hug. "Not like you to be late," she says, taking a peek at the gold watch on her arm.

He scoffs. "I am not late."

"Your mother beat you here, I'd say you're late." She scrunches her nose and he puts his hand up.

I slowly move away from them, not wanting to feel like an awkward third wheel, and make my way to the bar set up in the corner. I've just ordered a scotch when I feel a hand on my shoulder. "How ya doing, Theo?" I turn to see Avery's father, Shawn, giving me a curious look. "I don't know what it's like to have my only daughter get married, but I imagine it's a little tough." He nods towards where Wes and Raegan are taking pictures. "You like him?"

"Yeah, he's a good guy and he really seems to love her."

"You good with the age thing?" He says and I hope the universe is getting a kick out of forcing me to have this conversation with my girlfriend's father. My eyes find her instantly like they're trained to do it.

"Yeah," I tell him honestly. "It was a little difficult at first, but all a father wants for his daughter is for her to be happy." I take a sip of my drink before turning back to him, selfishly hoping that one day he'll have those same thoughts about his own daughter.

"Well, I'm happy for you, and Rae is glowing."

"There you are, finally I've been looking for you!" Rebecca's voice rings through the air just as she comes to stand next to me. "The photographer wants us to take pictures with Raegan and Lucas." I give her a look and then down at the dress she's wearing.

"What?" She asks, her brows furrowing like she's already annoyed.

"Why are you wearing white?"

"Umm hello, I'm not. This is cream." She looks down at herself and then back up at me as if to say *obviously.*

I narrow my eyes at her, disappointed at the thought that even on one of the most important days of her daughter's life, she couldn't resist making it about her. "Looks white."

"Because you know nothing about fashion! God," she looks at Shawn. "You should have seen how he dressed before I got to him." She giggles and I take a sip of my drink, not nearly drunk enough to deal with her bullshit. "But anyway, pictures with her parents? You know, both of us? Come to think of it, I don't think the four of us have many pictures," she says with passive aggression dripping from her words.

Because you were never around? I think and Shawn clears his throat, giving me a look like he had the exact same thought. "Rebecca." He nods with a polite smile.

"Shawn! How are you?" She touches his shoulder. "Great to see you." She flashes her flirtatious smile that she uses on every man she encounters.

"You as well and I'm great. How are you?"

"Never better!" She gushes and I roll my eyes internally at her usual response.

He nods at me as if to say *good luck* before he slips away.

"Do not wear anything white…or *white adjacent* to her wedding, Rebecca. Contrary to what I'm *sure* you're thinking, the day is not about you," I tell her as I begin walking towards Raegan who's now with Lucas and Avery.

She scoffs from behind me. "Can you go five seconds without being a dick to me?"

I turn around before we get to our kids and I'm grateful there isn't anyone close enough to hear us. "I don't know. Can you go five seconds without being a narcissist?" I don't wait for her response before I keep moving towards Raegan and Lucas and yet they can both sense it as soon as I reach them.

"Ah, it feels like old times." Lucas chuckles as he takes in my annoyed expression.

"Your mom says we should take pictures," I say, ignoring my son's usual comedic response to our arguing.

"Yes, the four of us hardly have any!" She says as she links her arm with Raegan and pulls her towards the corner where they were previously taking pictures.

"Correct me if I'm wrong," Lucas points towards them as they walk away, "but aren't you not supposed to wear white to any wedding-like functions unless you're the bride?"

Avery's lips form a straight line and Camille lets out a sigh before turning to Avery. "I would never."

"I know." Avery nods and our eyes meet briefly before I look away.

I hate that I'm standing with Avery's mother and my son, and I can't just touch her for five seconds or even look at her for too long.

I nod at them both before following Lucas towards the photographer when I feel a vibration in my pocket. I reach for it and I'm surprised to see the name on the screen. I discreetly turn around to see Avery with her phone in her hand. A small smile finds her face before she looks back down.

> **Heart Eyes: Breathe please, baby. You look so annoyed. Don't let her get to you. This is a happy time!**
>
> **Me: I know. I somehow forgot how much she gets under my skin.**
>
> **Heart Eyes: If you're a good sport for the rest of the night and don't get into it with her, I'll come to your room later. *kissy face emoji***

I'm typing out a reply that she definitely has herself a deal when I hear Rebecca's voice, "Honestly Theo." I look up just as I make it to where the three of them are standing and see the disapproving look she's giving me.

"I know you're not talking," I snap back at her as I close my phone and slide it into my pocket. It is *rare* that she doesn't have her phone in her hand.

"Give him a break," Lucas says as he slaps my back. "He's probably talking to his new lady friend." He raises his eyebrows up and down and I know he's just trying to irritate his mother on my behalf but this is absolutely not where or how I wanted Raegan to learn this news.

"Lady friend? Dad!" Raegan turns towards me with an excited grin. "What!? How is this the first I'm hearing of it? Where is she? Why didn't she come? Why didn't you invite her?"

"Smile!" I hear from in front of us and Raegan turns towards the photographer.

"One second, please!" she says before turning back towards me with the biggest smile. I remember Wes' comment about how she's worried about me so I'm not surprised she's excited for any potential love interest. "Dad, how are you telling Lucas things and not me!" She stomps her foot and I roll my eyes.

"Your brother is nosy, I haven't *told* him anything," I correct before shooting a glare at him.

"But there is a lady," he says as he wraps an arm around my shoulder. "They had a sleepover and everything while I was home," he says to Raegan like I'm not standing right next to him. *For the love of God, Lucas.*

Her blue eyes snap from mine to his. "You've met her!?"

"Nah, he slept at her house."

"Hello, can we talk about this later?" Rebecca says as she picks at her nail beds, her tone bored and annoyed, and I'll admit I'm glad, at least it succeeded in irritating her.

We take a series of pictures over the next few minutes and Raegan turns to me as soon as we're finished. Wes also joined the last few so he's standing next to her trying not to react to anything.

"You absolutely should have invited her! What's her name?"

"Can we not do this now?" I ask her, suddenly very nervous even though there's no way in a million years that Raegan would ever conclude that Avery is the woman in question.

"He's so secretive about it. Like we're kids." Lucas rolls his eyes before taking a sip of his beer.

"I'm totally asking Avery if she's seen her," she says before fleeing the circle and as much as I want to go after her, I turn my annoyed gaze to Lucas.

"Really?"

"What? I don't see why it's such a big deal that you're seeing someone. You do know that Raegan and I are actually not kids anymore and we just want you to be happy." He laughs and I cast a glance toward Raegan and Avery. I'm not surprised to meet her eyes for a second before she turns back to my daughter. Avery laughs and shakes her head and while I know Avery can handle it, I wish I knew what they were saying. I decide against following Lucas when my phone starts to ring. I see it's my brother so I step out of the room to answer it.

"Hey, are you here yet?"

"Just landed. I could not fucking tell you why my flight was delayed. This is why I need my own jet."

"For what? You don't leave Arizona."

"Well, when I do, I do not want to worry about this fuckery. I should be there in thirty minutes or so. I just want to shower and change."

"Well, we'll be here all night. No rush."

"You get caught making eyes at your girlfriend yet?" he jokes.

"No, and I hope you're not going to spend the night fucking with me."

"Of course, I am."

"Also," I look around the lobby to ensure no one that I know is close enough to hear me, "Raegan and Lucas know that I'm seeing someone and they are pressing me for details. If they ask, you know nothing, got it?"

"Hmmm, I might know something."

"You don't," I growl at him.

"Alright, take it easy. I'm not going to say anything. When are you going to tell them anyway?"

"After Rae's wedding. I just want it to be a happy time for her and for nothing to overshadow her big day."

"Well, fucking your son's girl aside, aren't you a great dad?" He chuckles.

"Okay fuck you very much, goodbye," I say, before hanging up. I rub a hand over my forehead, willing away the headache that is starting to form. When I start to walk back toward the room, I spot Rebecca sitting in a chair in the corner looking very agitated. She's on the phone and then she hangs up before her head falls into her hands. I know Garrett couldn't make it because he was somewhere on business, but I'm wondering if there's more to that story.

I sigh, hating that I'm about to ask and thereby insinuating that I actually care what's going on between her and her husband, but on the off chance it's something else, I do want to make sure everything is okay. "You alright, Becca?" I ask as I approach her. She wipes under her glossy blue eyes and looks up at me as her lip trembles slightly. I can remember a time long ago that this visual would have had me on my knees in an instant.

"Yeah," she says. "Great." She nods and it's one of those rare times that she allows herself to put her guard down. I find myself feeling bad for her.

"What's wrong?"

"You don't care." She sniffles before tossing her phone in her small handbag and standing up.

"I asked, didn't I?" Her father passed away years ago while we were still married but her mother is still alive, and from what Raegan told me a few months ago, she's not in the best of health. "Is it your mom?"

"What? No. She's fine." She fiddles with her bracelets, a telltale sign that she's nervous or uncomfortable. She looks up at me and I give her a look that says, 'Well?'

She rolls her eyes. "Fine, I might as well tell you since you're all going to find out anyway." I cross my arms over my chest. "Garrett and I are getting a divorce."

This is why I shouldn't have asked. "I see. Well, I'm sorry. That's tough."

"Yeah," she says, not offering up anything else.

"Did you try counseling? Nothing you can do to work it out?"

"He doesn't want to. He says he hasn't been happy and he doesn't want to be married anymore. Kiiiiinda hard to counsel that."

"I see." No one knows what goes on between a couple except those two people but as someone who was once married to Rebecca, she can definitely be... difficult and also has a bit of a complicated relationship with the truth.

"Don't say anything to the kids. I don't want this to be a whole thing while we are supposed to be celebrating." She gives me a sad smile. "Contrary to what you...*and Garrett* said, I don't think everything is about me."

I wince, thinking about how that probably stung. "Sorry I said that." *Even if there's some truth to it.*

She sighs and pulls a mirror out of her purse, running her fingers under her eyes. "Can you believe she's getting married?"

"I can." I nod. "She's always known exactly what she wanted and Wes is good for her."

"He does seem to really love her. The way he looks at her is really sweet. I just hope it's not all a show for our benefit."

"I doubt it. Raegan has never hesitated to call anyone out on their shit."

"Including me," she says and gives me a sad smile. "You did a good job with them." *Who is this woman and what has she done with my ex-wife?*

"Wow, hell must be frozen right now." I laugh and she shoves my arm playfully.

"This is why I never say anything nice to you!"

I'm just about to respond when I hear Lucas' voice. "Ave, how many drinks have I had that I actually see my parents laughing... with *each other*."

Avery and Lucas are a few feet away from us and it only takes one look at Avery's face to know that they've probably been witnessing this exchange for a minute and she is feeling territorial.

Rebecca begins fussing with Lucas' hair, pushing it back. "Mom, stop." He moves away and out of her reach.

"What, I'm helping!"

"Where are you guys going?" I ask, changing the subject.

"Rae needs something from her room and I offered to go grab it for her. Naturally, my shadow is tagging along." Avery laughs, earning a glare from Lucas.

And now it's my turn to feel territorial.

Not that I think anything would happen, but the thought of Avery alone in a hotel room with *any* man that isn't me is enough to piss me off. I keep my face impassive, trying not to let the jealousy show. They're gone a moment later, and I try my hardest not to stare after them like I wish I was the one with her.

"They are so cute. When are they just going to get together already?" Rebecca says and when I look at her, she's staring in their direction with a smile. "They would give us beautiful grandchildren. Can you imagine?" I'm trying not to react to her words but she frowns at me. "What?"

"She doesn't see him that way."

"I don't see why not. Lucas is a catch."

This is absolutely not the conversation I want to have. And I mentally curse whatever cosmic God is forcing me to endure it. "Of course he is. That doesn't mean every woman is going to be attracted to him. Sometimes there's just...no spark."

"Hmph," she says before she takes a sip of her champagne. "And what's this about you seeing someone?" She raises an eyebrow at me. "What's she like?"

My phone vibrates in my pocket and when I pull it out, I see it's from Avery.

Heart Eyes: I don't think I've ever seen you two be that friendly.

I raise an eyebrow at her message just as Rebecca's voice interrupts me. "Is that her? Why didn't you invite her?"

"Why the sudden interest in my love life? You barely had interest in it when *we* were married," I say half joking.

She scoffs. "Whatever, that is not true!"

I laugh as we make our way back towards the room. "It's new and I'm not talking to you about it."

"Do you love her?" She presses.

There's a sudden tightening in my chest at the thought; not over the fact that I may love her, but *how* can I love her without telling Lucas the truth? The second I admit that thought to myself, it becomes ten times harder to come clean about what I've been doing the past month. *Maybe I could give up the best sex of my life, if Lucas couldn't handle it, but if I'm in love with her? Could I give her up?* "We haven't said it yet." *Yet.* My mind fixates on that word like a warning.

"But you do..."

We make it back to the party and people are now on the dance floor and I'm reminded again of the secret I'm hiding, disallowing me the chance to dance with Avery. I realize I haven't answered her message when another one comes through.

Heart Eyes: Mine

Me: Yes, baby. No reason to be jealous.

Heart Eyes: Like you were when you saw me and Lucas?

Me: I was not jealous.

Heart Eyes: Cute that you think you can lie to me.

I smile at my phone, wishing that I could find her and kiss her smart-ass mouth.

Chapter
TWENTY-ONE

THEO

'M OUT ON THE BALCONY TALKING TO MY BROTHER SOMETIME later when Avery makes her way outside. She's alone and assumedly looking for me, but stops when she sees me talking to Bryan. There aren't many people out here, so I wave her over and she approaches with caution, knowing that my brother knows about us and I can sense her apprehension.

"Avery." He nods at her and she smiles.

"Bryan."

"You can do better, you know," he tells her with a cocky smile before he takes a sip of his drink.

"Fuck off," I tell him and Avery giggles. "Hey, gorgeous." I turn my gaze to her, running my eyes up and down the length of her as I can finally drink her in and she gives me a different smile than she gave Bryan, one that's reserved for me.

"Hi." I am trying my best not to openly ogle her but she's so fucking stunning in this black dress that I can't pull my eyes from her and Bryan standing with us makes it less odd to anyone paying attention.

"Oh, for the love of God." Bryan rolls his eyes. "You know I'm the better-looking one," he says to Avery as he points between him and me. I roll my eyes because Bryan and I do look really fucking similar, only I'm in better shape and he's about an inch taller, *something he never lets me forget.*

"Do you mind?" I look at him and he shrugs. "You know what?

Go away." I wave him off even if it makes me standing here with Avery look more intimate.

I lean over the railing and she stands next to me, but further than I'd like her to be as we both stare at the city skyline. "You look beautiful," I tell her because it's the first time I've been alone with her.

"Thank you. You look so handsome." She runs her gaze all over me. "You really wear the hell out of *everything*."

"I'm glad you think so considering yours is the only opinion that matters to me." There's a light breeze that blows her hair gently and I get a whiff of her shampoo and her lavender perfume that now has the power to make my dick hard. *God, she smells good.* "I want to peel that dress off of you later."

She shifts her face to look at me. "Okay." She looks over her shoulder and then up at me shyly. "I'm going to go to my room for a minute." She blinks her eyes several times. "Maybe I'll see you there?"

Mentally I'm already there, on my knees with her legs wrapped around my face and my tongue buried between her thighs. "Yes. Five minutes."

"Oh, Dad, I was looking for you!" Raegan exclaims from the doorway as she comes outside. "We're going to cut the cake." She links her arm with Avery. "Come." The two of them walk in front of me and I try to keep my eyes off of Avery's ass, but fuck me, if it isn't perfect. I'd already given my toast, so this time Wes speaks and he really does seem to be crazy about Raegan. He talks about how she's his soulmate and the love of his life. How he's never loved anyone the way he loves her and that he can't wait to spend the rest of his life making her happy. His arms wrap around her waist as he presses a kiss to her lips and my eyes immediately find Avery across the room only to notice her slipping out the door as everyone claps for Wes and Raegan.

I've been very aware of almost every move she made tonight and while we haven't had a chance to make it upstairs, I wonder if now is our chance. I wait a few minutes for Wes and Raegan to start dancing before I go after her and I see her waiting for the elevator. I check my surroundings before following her and just before the doors completely close, I force them back open and move into the elevator with her.

Her eyes are wide and I realize she wasn't actually expecting me to follow her when I see tears pooling in her hazel eyes.

"Baby, what's wrong? Why are you upset?"

"I'll be fine, we can't..." she starts as she wipes under her eyes. I pull her into my arms and swat her hands away to do it myself.

"What's wrong?" I ask her again as I collect a stray tear that's threatening to fall down her cheek.

"Wes' speech." She lets out a shaky breath. "It just got me thinking. But I'll be fine. I just needed a minute."

"Hey, thinking about what?" I raise her chin to look at me. The elevator dings and the doors open letting us out onto our floor.

"Tonight is just a little harder than I thought it would be. Not being able to touch you or even look at you for too long." She runs her hands up my chest and rubs the space over my heart. "Lucas is talking about going downtown later, and I just...want to be with you. I can't ever be alone with you without having to lie to everyone I know. What if we can never be together like that?" Tears form in her eyes but she blinks them away as quickly as they appear. "And then I feel like shit because we're here to celebrate Rae and we both said we didn't want to do anything to upset her and I know we have a plan..." She trails off.

"Hey, it's okay." I press my lips to her forehead and hold her tighter in my arms. "I feel the same. I wish I was able to dance with you and touch you and kiss you. Instead, I'm seething that someone else gets to do two of those things so freely."

"I wish it was you," she whispers as she rests her hands behind my neck.

I cup her face and press my lips to hers, pushing her against the wall behind her as she rubs against me. It feels like it's been days since I've pressed my lips to hers and not the few hours since I left her room. She tastes like cherries and it makes me want to kiss down her body to taste the sweetness of her pussy. I pull away but still keep my lips close to hers allowing us to breathe each other in. "We should get back," she whispers and I shake my head.

"Not yet. I need another minute."

I press my forehead to hers and shut my eyes, allowing myself to think of a time down the road when things will be easier. My hand wraps around her back, holding her tighter against me and she lets out the sexiest sigh. I press another gentle kiss on her lips when a voice interrupts us.

"What the fuck?" My eyes dart to the source of the voice to see Lucas staring at us, his face going through a range of emotions. Confusion, shock, hurt, betrayal, anger.

Fuck. Fuck. Fuck!

Avery and I pull apart just as he takes a step forward, his brows furrowing even more and his eyes darting back and forth between me and Avery. "Dad, what the fuck? Are you drunk?" He looks at Avery. "Are *you*?"

"Lucas..." Avery says as she takes a step towards him and holds her hand out to touch him, her eyes wide and unblinking.

"WHAT THE FUCK?" He repeats and she flinches, dropping her hand.

"Okay, you have about one more fuck, Lucas Daniel," I warn him. Not that I really care if my kids swear but they certainly weren't going to do it at me.

"You're shitting me, right? You...and...you have a girlfriend! And...Avery? What is going on?" He yells.

"Lucas..." Avery's worried eyes dart to me for help and I wish I knew what to say. I was supposed to have time to plan for this conversation. He was not supposed to find out until I told him and I curse myself for not waiting until we were behind closed doors before I kissed her.

"We should talk, Son."

"Talk about what? Why you're mauling my best friend in a corner like some horny old guy?" He says with an incredulous look.

"Lucas," Avery snaps. "Stop it."

"Stop what? This is fucking weird." He shakes his head. "I don't like it. Don't do this again." He points between the two of us and I realize that he thinks this was just a one-time thing brought on by too much alcohol.

Avery and I share a look before I turn my focus back to him. "Lucas..." I think about going along with it, but I don't know if that would just make things worse in the long run. "Avery and I have been...seeing each other," I tell him because the thought of insinuating that Avery was just a drunken accident or fling does not sit right with me.

He blinks his eyes several times. "I'm sorry, what did you say?" He takes a step toward me and I don't think I've ever seen the look he's giving me. "What?" His voice is low and angry and at this moment, I don't think he sees me as his dad but the guy that touched the woman he believes belongs to him on some level. *Fuck.* "ARE YOU KIDDING ME?" He screams. *Yes, screams.* "You're..." He points at Avery. "AVERY? That's who you've been seeing? You've been sneaking around my back with my best friend?" He spits through gritted teeth. "And on top of that, the woman I spent years being in love with?" He darts his eyes to Avery and I can only assume the anger there is brought on by hurt and maybe a little embarrassment. "And you? MY DAD? I wasn't good enough for you, so what, you decided to go for the older version of me?"

"It was never about you not being good enough—" Avery starts.

"Save it," he growls at her. "You are the fucking worst for this, Avery. I've been nothing but a good friend to you and you mess around with my dad? I can't even look at you."

"Don't talk to her like that," I snap at him. "I raised you better than that." I see her lip trembling and the devastated expression on her face. He goes to respond when I pin him with a warning glare that I hope he heeds. "You and I should talk alone."

"For what? So you can apologize for stabbing me in the back? I'm good." He puts a hand up before running a hand through his hair. "I've looked up to you my whole fucking life only for you to do... this?" His lips form a frown and he shakes his head. "How could you do this? OF ALL THE FUCKING PEOPLE IN THE WORLD?"

I sense Avery moving next to me and when I look over at her, her gaze is focused on the floor. "Avery, can you give us a minute?"

She nods before looking up at Lucas with tears shimmering in her eyes. "I never meant to hurt you," she chokes out and I hate that I can't comfort her right now. He doesn't look at her as his angry gaze is still trained on me. "I know that's not enough but...I'm so sorry." She sniffles before walking down the hallway toward her room.

"How did this happen?" He snaps when we see her enter her room. "*When?*"

"Last summer."

"A year? This has been going on for a fucking year?"

"We kissed last year and that was it and then winter break..." I tuck my hands in my pockets, not wanting to get into the details. "Things got more serious when she got home for the summer."

He chuckles as he looks at me with such disappointment. "You're the guy she met up with after her graduation party." He puts his hands over his eyes and lets out an angry groan. "You are unbelievable! How...you *knew* how I felt about her."

"Yes, *felt*, you've been saying for years that you don't have those feelings for her anymore." I point at him. "I am not trying to deflect blame but you said you were over her." I cross my arms over my chest. "How about you be honest with me about it?"

"Like you've been honest with me?" He argues.

"I wasn't expecting things to get this far. I thought..." I sigh. "Fuck, I don't know. I thought I just needed to get her out of my system. Once. One time." I lean against the wall. "But things changed."

We stand in silence for a minute before he speaks. "You could have anyone. Why *her?*"

I hear the sadness in his voice and this is what I was afraid of. Not his anger or the yelling, but the thought that I've hurt my son so deeply that we may never recover from it. That he feels betrayed.

"I don't want just *anyone.*"

"And when were you going to fucking tell me?"

"After Rae's wedding. I just…we wanted to be sure before we told you."

"Sure about what?"

That I love her? That she loves me? "That this…was real."

"Are you kidding me? So, you're not just sleeping with my best friend, you want to what…marry her? Make her my stepmom?" He spits out. "You've got to be joking. Jesus Christ, Rae and I really got screwed in the parents department. You're just like Mom. You don't care about anyone but yourself." His words are like a punch to the gut and I don't know if he's just saying them to hurt me or if he feels that way on some level. I hate that there's any part of him that thinks I don't care about his feelings.

"That's not fair," I growl because after everything, I'll be damned if he makes me feel like I've ever been a shitty father until this.

"Oh? You want to talk about fair right now?"

"Lucas, I didn't take Avery from you," I argue because while his anger is warranted, it seems like he's angry about the wrong things. "You guys were never together!"

"So, that makes it okay? You're my DAD." He shouts. "And you're screwing around with a girl who's way too young for you by the way, who I also had feelings for! You don't see anything wrong with that?"

"I didn't say that."

"Then what are you saying?"

"That I'm not just screwing around with her."

He doesn't say anything for a moment before his cold eyes go from angry to hurt. "Do you love her?"

I stare at him for a second, deciding if I want to tell him the truth. "Do you?" I ask him.

He crosses his arms in front of his chest and glares at me. "If I said yes, would it even matter?"

My heart squeezes thinking that I've misread this whole thing and Lucas is still in love with her thereby making this whole situation even more complicated. "Yeah." I nod, sadly. "It would matter."

His eyes soften slightly just before he averts his gaze and looks down the hallway. He turns back to me after a few moments. "If I told you I still loved her, would you let her go?"

I shake my head at him. "This isn't a fucking test. Answer my question. I would do anything in the fucking world for you, but if you're asking me to give her up, it better be for a reason other than she's your best friend."

He doesn't say anything. "I made myself fall out of love with her years ago and part of me thought she'd eventually come around. So, yeah it really fucking stings that my dad is in love with her now. But no, I don't love her and if I did, knowing she's been with you would have done the trick." He snaps. "Do you know how weird this is for me?"

"Yes, and I'm so sorry," I tell him.

"Not sorry enough to stop," he retorts.

"Is that what you want?"

"You're asking for what? My blessing to be with her? You don't have it."

"I don't know if I'm asking for your blessing right now. Maybe just…acceptance?" *That we can get through this?*

"You don't have that either!"

Anxiety and maybe a little misplaced anger shoots through me because *is he really telling me he doesn't want me to be with her?* "So, you just don't want me to be with her?"

"No, I don't," he says instantly.

"Why?" I grit out. "Because it's weird? I don't accept that."

"You know why."

"Because you had a crush on her when you were fourteen? Lucas, come on. She's had a serious boyfriend since then and you had a girlfriend in high school. Multiple, if I recall."

"Because I was trying to get over her!"

"For the love of God, we're going in circles."

"No, we're not. It's pretty simple, Dad." He takes a step towards me. "Avery is off limits." I swallow down the immediate reaction to his words which would be to tell him that he doesn't have a say in anything regarding the woman who'd said she belonged to me just hours before.

I let out a sigh because I am officially exhausted from this back and forth and I don't know any response that allows for Lucas and I to be okay. "Fine," I tell him and surprise flashes across his face. I pause as it sinks in what I have to do now. "For what it's worth, I do love her. But...I would never do anything to intentionally hurt you. So, if you're not okay with this...then fine. I'll end it." I don't wait for him to respond; I just move down the hallway toward Avery's room as I prepare to rip both of us apart.

Chapter

TWENTY-TWO

Avery

MY KNEE IS BOUNCING NONSTOP AS I CHEW ON MY thumbnail nervously when I hear a knock on the door. I rush to it, not knowing who it is when I fling it open without looking. I breathe a sigh of relief when it's Theo and he pushes his way inside. "Hey, what happened?" I ask immediately as I take in his defeated expression. He drops to the bed and his head falls into his hands and I immediately fear the worst. Though I'm not exactly sure what the worst-case scenario is here. He shakes his head and looks up at me with sad eyes and I already know what he's going to say. "I'll talk to him."

He shakes his head. "Come here, baby."

"No," I tell him as I turn towards the door, prepared to find Lucas and make him understand my side of this as well. I feel Theo's hand on my elbow and he pulls me towards his chest. He wraps his arms around me as I succumb to the tears I'd been avoiding every time I thought about this outcome.

He lifts my chin to meet his eyes. "Please don't cry. I hate seeing you upset."

"What did he say?"

"It's just too hard or weird or painful for him. I think maybe a combination of the three." He rubs my back and it just spurs more tears. I'm lifted off my feet and carried to the same couch where we had a very different interaction just hours earlier and he sits with me in his arms. I wrap my arms around his neck.

"So, that's it for us?" I ask him as I pull back to look at him.

"He's my son, Ave."

"I know."

"I can't...I don't want him to spend the rest of his life hating me."

I don't know what to say because I can't even argue with that. I can't be mad. If anything, a part of me actually admires Theo for sacrificing his own feelings for the sake of his son. "Maybe he just needs some time?"

"Maybe." He shrugs as he runs his finger over my cheek. "But then I need to give him time." He rubs his nose gently against mine and I take a second to breathe him in if I'll never be this close to him again. "And I can't have you while I wait."

"So, we can't see each other at all anymore?" The tears haven't stopped sliding down my face, even as he tries to wipe them away.

"No," he says sadly and the pain on his face is so evident it makes my heart hurt more.

"Theo... I..." The words stop before they come out because what difference would it make to say it now? "I just...I want you to know..." I look at him and he nods.

"Me too."

I press my lips to his gently. I stroke his jaw, feeling the light stubble under my fingertips and I drag my tongue along the seam, wanting access to his mouth and he opens finally. I move to straddle him as I kiss him for the last time even as the tears continue to slide down my face. He doesn't let this go on for long before he stops us and holds my face in his hands. "I don't want to get carried away. I should get back downstairs."

I lick my lips and nod. "I'm just going to go to bed if that's okay?" I offer weakly. I'm not sure if Lucas or Rae would want to see me and it's late. I'm emotional and I really don't want to see anyone. "Fuck." I sigh. "I forgot my parents are here."

He rubs his forehead and lets out an exasperated sigh. "So did I. I don't know that this news has made it to them though."

"No, my mom would have called me. I'll let her know I'm going to bed." I get off of his lap. "This really isn't fair."

"No, it's not." He tucks a curl behind my ear and presses a final kiss to my lips as he makes his way towards the door.

"Theo," I call after him and he turns to meet my gaze, "if there's ever a time that he is okay with it...will you come find me?"

"Wherever you are."

～∽～

THEO

I make it back to the party and it seems like nothing is out of the ordinary. It's nearing midnight so the festivities are winding down but people are sitting around talking and a few people feeling their drinks are still on the dance floor. I am grateful that I don't see Avery's parents so that's two less people I have to deal with right now. I don't see Raegan or Lucas either for that matter, so I'm sure they are somewhere together. I go out onto the patio where I see Bryan and Wes each holding a drink while my brother smokes a cigar. I make my way over to them and Bryan gives me a look.

"You got caught?"

"Lucas came down and...he's with Rae," Wes adds as he gives me a sad look that isn't judgmental or with any hint of *I told you this would happen.*

"I'm sorry this happened tonight. We were trying to wait until after the wedding to tell anyone," I tell him because I'm sure this is not what Wes wants to be dealing with on the night of their engagement party.

"Clearly, you weren't trying that hard," Bryan says with his usual sarcasm and I give him a look that I hope tells him I'm too tired for the back and forth.

"Now is really not the fuckin' time," I snap and he sighs.

"Alright, sorry," he says and I think he realizes I'm not in the mood. "So, what happened?"

"He's pissed. So, I told him I'd back off."

"You did the right thing," Bryan says as he holds out an unlit cigar for me and I shake my head. "Look, maybe he'll come around."

"Maybe, but I ended it with Avery anyway."

"That's okay. She knows why. I'm sure she understands," Wes interjects. "This whole situation is complicated, but you guys knew that going in. You knew that there was a chance that he wasn't going to be okay with this."

"I guess a part of me thought once I told her I loved her, he wouldn't be so angry." Maybe I didn't deserve that. Maybe he was right and there are just some things a dad can't ever do. Maybe I was kidding myself to think he'd ever be okay with it.

"Give him time. This is a lot," Wes says.

"He said I was just like his mom. I think that hurt more than anything."

"Okay, well he didn't mean that. Rebecca hasn't lived in the same state since he was fourteen and not in the same country since he was what, sixteen?" Bryan snorts and I know I must look like shit if even he's trying to be supportive.

"I almost wish he did love her." It would make me feel better for giving her up. But maybe I didn't deserve to feel better and maybe he was allowed to subscribe to the belief that I can't have the girl that he wanted once upon a time.

"He doesn't?" Bryan asks.

"No. He just said it's too weird."

"Well, it is weird, Dad." I hear Raegan's voice from behind me and when I turn around, I see her standing alone with a disappointed look on her face. Her lips form a straight line and she shakes her head. "Avery? Really?"

"Where is he?" I ask her.

"He left. He's meeting some friends." She takes a few steps closer to us and Wes immediately takes off his jacket and slips it around her shoulders. She gives him a smile before turning back to me. "He said that you said you love her. Is that true?"

"Yeah, Rae." I nod.

"Does she love you?"

"I think so," I tell her because although she didn't explicitly say it, I do think that's what she was trying to tell me before I left her room.

"Look, he probably didn't like what I had to say, which is that he thinks he has some hold over Avery and that he's under the impression that one day she'll wake up and love him back." She puts her hands on her hips. "This doesn't mean I'm on your side either. I'm Switzerland. Probably because of him." She points at her fiancé. "I know it was hard for you to accept me with someone so close to your age so in my eyes, her age is not the problem and I told Lucas that. It's not even the fact that it's a girl you've known for years." She scrunches her nose. "A little weird." She puts her thumb and index finger close together. "But it's more that it's *her*. I've watched him love her and then get over her but still stare at her with that look, you know?"

"I get that so I broke it off, Rae. I told her we couldn't be together."

She sighs and wraps me in a hug and I'm happy that at least one of my kids doesn't hate me at the moment. "I don't know that I think that's right either. It's not anyone's fault that she didn't love him back."

"Sounds like it's mine," I say as I drop to one of the patio chairs.

"It's not, Dad." She sits next to me and sighs as she runs a hand through her hair. "I'll talk to him again."

"I don't want you getting in the middle of it." I wrap an arm around her. "You've got a lot going on and I don't want you stressing yourself out over things that are definitely not your problem."

"You guys are my closest family. Your problems are my problems." She presses a kiss to my cheek. "And, Dad, you're not like Mom. I yelled at him for saying that."

"Thanks," I say hoping he didn't really mean it.

"Maybe just give him some time?"

"If Lucas is ever okay with it, will you be?"

She stands up and gives me a conspiratorial grin. "Sure. If you two get married and have a baby. In twenty or so years, I can tell my little sibling all about how I taught their mom how to use a condom." She chuckles. "It'll be fun. I'm psyched."

Chapter
TWENTY-THREE

Avery

I T'S BEEN A LITTLE OVER A WEEK SINCE RAEGAN'S ENGAGEMENT party and I've been fucking miserable. It's not bad enough to have gone through the worst breakup of my life, but the man still lives next door. I'm supposed to move out next week, so I'm grateful I'll eventually have a reprieve from staring out my bedroom window in hopes I get just the smallest glimpse of him. I haven't talked to Lucas, but I did talk to Raegan after she showed up at my house and forced me to talk to her since I'd been avoiding her calls. I wasn't sure how she felt about it and I'll be honest, she scares me a little bit. She told me to give it time and that she still wanted me to be a bridesmaid in her wedding.

I'm not sure if that's only because she still actually wants me to be in it or if it's also to punish me a little bit by forcing me into a room with Theo and Lucas.

Fuck me.

While I'm definitely upset and wallowing in the misery of not seeing the man I'd quickly fallen for over the past month, a part of me believes it isn't over.

Lucas couldn't stay mad forever, right? He would come around because he cares about me and his dad and he wants us to be happy.

I could be patient.

Or delusional.

Or a combination of both.

I'd called Lucas a number of times and he'd ignored all of my calls, something that he'd never done in the eight years we've been friends and while I understand why he's mad, I don't know how he expects us to move past this if he doesn't talk to me.

Maybe he doesn't want to move past this.

Well, that's fucking annoying. If he doesn't want to be friends anymore, why can't I date Theo?

"Ugh," I growl as I toss the towel I'm holding on the counter and look at my phone for the millionth time in the past hour praying that there's a message from him.

My mom is rolling some dough next to me and when I look at her she's giving me a curious look. "Care to share with the class?"

"Not really." I pull my vanilla latte to my lips.

"You want me to guess?"

I assume at this point she's figured that I've broken up with the secret boyfriend I've been sneaking around with, but again, I'm sure she has no idea who it was.

"I'm fine," I tell her dismissively.

"You're not fine. You're moping."

"Mom, can we not?" I sigh. Of all the people in the world I'd feel comfortable talking to about this it would be her, but I really don't want to get into it now. Especially if Theo and I are never going to be anything again.

What would be the point of telling her?

"You've been in a mood ever since Raegan's engagement party and I haven't been able to figure out why." She narrows her gaze before wiping her face with the back of her hand, successfully smearing flour across her forehead. "Did you have a fight with Lucas?'

"No," I lie, although on some level I suppose it's the truth. We haven't talked about it at all except for him calling me the worst. My stomach sinks just like it always does when I replay those words in my head.

"You have a fight with someone else?"

"I didn't have a fight with anyone. It's just...been a long week and I'm tired from packing."

"Hmmm." She purses her lips. "You know, I've known you for twenty-one years," she tells me.

"That's what my birth certificate says," I tell her as I wash my hands thoroughly so I can help her.

"You know, I know about things you haven't even done yet."

"Really." I deadpan.

"Mmmhm." She says as she continues to roll the dough. "I never really pegged you for someone with Daddy issues."

I snap my head to look at her. "What?"

"Give me a little credit, Avery Danielle. You and Theo are not slick." I blink at her, not confirming or denying anything so she continues. "Okay, so we're playing like you have no idea what I'm talking about. Obviously, I knew you were seeing someone but you were so secretive about it and I couldn't figure out why. Why not tell me about this mystery guy? You're an adult. So, I thought, there had to be a reason and then at the engagement party, he couldn't take his eyes off of you." She cocks her head to the side. "And you couldn't take your eyes off of him."

Here I thought, we were being careful. Did anyone else notice?

"How do you feel about it…?"

"I… don't know. How did it start?"

"Last year, we kissed, but it wasn't really anything until about a month ago and I know it sounds fast but, God Theo Graham has been…the man of my dreams for years."

"Hmmm," she narrows her gaze at me.

"It was nothing before I was twenty, I swear."

"No, I know, you had that knucklehead boyfriend for far too long." She scrunches her nose in disgust and I chuckle at her never-ending distaste for my ex-boyfriend. "So, Lucas didn't take it well?"

"He did not."

"And Rae?"

"Rae's sitting kind of pretty in a glass house right now. She's not really upset about it I think because Theo has really not given Wes a hard time."

"Oh, Wes is a gem. They are *so* cute. I absolutely need that story.

Rebecca told me he's her boss! Scandalous!" She giggles as she raises her eyebrows up and down.

"I'll tell you everything another time, I promise. Anyway, she's trying to be supportive to both of them but also stay out of it—" I stop when Jordan pops her head into the back.

"Hey, ummm one of your friends is here?" She looks at both of us.

"Who is it," I ask?

"I don't know." She shrugs. "I think your neighbor?" She doesn't say anything else before she heads back to the front and I look at my mother. Both of us walk to the main floor, me because I assume he's here to talk to me, and my mother to be nosy. I see Theo standing in the area where customers wait for their to-go coffees. He's wearing a black button-down and gray slacks and he looks so fucking good.

Meanwhile, my hair pulled back in a bun because I haven't washed it in days coupled with my bare minimum makeup does not make me happy for this encounter at all. *Of all the days.*

His eyes light up as soon as he sees me and his eyes rove over me like I'm wearing the sexiest dress and not a cream t-shirt and black jeans. "Hi." I stand next to Jordan who is making his coffee and I see she's got two carrying trays out that can hold four cups each.

"Hey. I'm just…uh…getting coffee for the office."

"Wow, the owner of the company goes on coffee runs." I smirk at him, wondering, *hoping* that he's just here as a way to see me.

"I…was out already and thought I'd pick up coffee for everyone." My mom slides up on the other side of me and looks at Theo. "Hello, Theo." She smiles, knowingly like the cat that ate the canary. "Lovely to see you."

"You too, Camille." He smiles.

"I just finished baking what I think are my best cinnamon scones. I'm going to send some with you for your office." She claps and points at him. "Avery will help you carry them over." I go to reject that idea when she looks at me.

"Don't be rude. He only has two hands." She begins putting some scones in a bag for him.

Eight coffees and five minutes of awkward silence later, we're walking out of the café in the direction of his office. "I told my mom," I say, breaking the silence. "Well, she kind of put it together."

"I see, so that's the reason for this?" He gestures as well as he can between us. "She...approves?" He raises an eyebrow.

"I don't know, I think she's tired of seeing me so sad."

He turns his eyes back to the sidewalk and away from me. "I hate that you're sad," he says finally.

"How are you?" I ask, wondering if he's as miserable as I am.

"I'm...okay. Have you talked to Lucas?" He responds.

I shake my head. "No. Have you?"

"Through Raegan some, but no, he's not taking my calls. I was thinking of going to New York this weekend to see if I can get him to talk to me."

I nod, having had a similar thought but ultimately decided to give him more time and space. "I miss you," I tell him. "Sorry, I probably shouldn't have said that—"

"I miss you too," he interrupts and gives me another heated onceover. "You look beautiful by the way."

I give him a smile, and for the first time since I've known him, I feel like I'm at a loss for words. "Thank you."

"So, you're moving soon, right?"

"Next week."

"Do you have movers? I mean...do you need help?"

"I have movers. I'm good. I think Rory is going to come down and help. Lucas was supposed to but...you know." I shrug.

"Right. Well, if I can help...or you need anything..."

"Besides you?" I ask him honestly and I watch his shoulders sag. He nods. "Yeah, besides me."

We walk the rest of the way in silence and when we finally make it to his office, he stops. "Can you just wait here for a second?"

"Sure." He takes everything into his office by himself, because he absolutely didn't need me to help him carry everything and he's back a few moments later.

He starts walking back towards the café but he stops when I'm not following. "I drove to *Avery's.*" He waves his keys. "Going to go get my car now."

"Oh! Sorry, why didn't you say anything?"

"I wanted five minutes with you. Well, ten."

He smiles and I reach for his hand, lacing our fingers. "Theo."

He shakes his head and takes a step back, letting my hand drop from his. "I want to, believe me. It is taking everything in me right now, not to throw you in the backseat of my car and fuck you in broad daylight." We start walking back towards the café. "I wish I was holding your hand." I stare down at our hands that are mere inches apart, wishing they were laced and I feel the tears building in my throat.

We walk in silence the remainder of the way back until we get to his car. "Well, it was good to see you." He says.

"You too."

"If I don't see you before you move," he starts and I wonder how he's going to end that. *See you around? See you never?* "I hope it goes well." I bite my bottom lip, hating this awkward but still very real tension between us. He doesn't wait for my response before he's in his car and pulls off.

⁂

I should have known Rory coming down to help me move wouldn't come without a hundred questions and tequila shots.

"I still can't believe I didn't realize it. Like…it was a shame that nobody had hooked up with Daddy Graham after all this time. What is the actual point of having a friend with a hot dad?" She sucks the lime into her mouth. We'd spent the last two days moving and had actually put a decent dent in my apartment. I have a couch, my bed is set up, and I have WiFi so everything else can wait as far as I'm concerned. My mom left about an hour ago after neurotically organizing my kitchen, and we'd opened a bottle of wine and then switched to tequila right after.

I'm lying flat on my back on my couch with my eyes closed, with an eye mask resting beneath my eyes in hopes it will get rid of the dark circles brought on by staying up all night packing and crying all week. "How pissed is he?"

Rory, who's sitting on the floor in front of me, takes a bite of the sausage pizza we ordered. "He's mad but...he's calmed down." She tucks her hair behind her ear. "He thinks you hate him."

My head snaps to look at her. "He hates *me*! And his dad!"

"He doesn't hate either of you. He's hurt. This was like...a very big bomb."

I nod in agreement. "Do you think he'll come around?"

"Yes...I think...maybe?"

"Rory..." I sit up, shooting her an annoyed look because there's no way she doesn't know anything.

"What! We don't really discuss it. It just puts him in a bad mood."

"Ugh." I scoff as I lay back down. "Pour me another."

Two hours and a few too many shots later, Rory has the brilliant idea to go to our favorite bar in town. While I don't necessarily think it's our best idea, I go along with it because it's better than sitting in the house sulking all night.

It's nearing midnight, so the bar is darker and has turned into more of a club scene. Rory and I are dancing amongst ourselves while drinking our vodka sodas when a very familiar and very bad idea comes over me. I look at Rory who's got her eyes closed as she shakes to the beat. "Should I text him?" I shout over the music.

"Who?" I give her a look as she takes a sip of her drink. "Oh yes! Obviously!" Her eyes widen. "I won't tell." She zips her lips and continues dancing.

I take a long sip of my drink. *Fuck it.*

Me: Hi

His response is almost immediate. *Okay, this is good.*

TG: Hi there. How was the move?

Okay, you can do this. Sound sober.

Me: Great!

TG: Good. Glad to hear it. It's a little late. Everything alright?

Me: Yep. I'm just with Rory

TG: I see. Well, you guys have fun!

Okay, that was anti-climactic. You sounded too sober. Say something risky!

"What should I say?" I ask Rory.

She taps her chin. "Can I come over and sit on your face?" She shakes her head. "No! Do you want to come over and break in my bed at my new place!" She looks at me with a smile. "I'll totally go stay at my parents'. Or Justin's." She shrugs as she raises her hands and begins dancing in a circle. *Lord, she's drunker than I am! I might need Theo just to come get us.*

"You're still sleeping with him!?"

"It's like...comfort dick. It's familiar, I know how everything works. No surprises. Ya know? Like my emotional support dick!"

I roll my eyes because for the life of me, I can't understand her and Justin. They've been doing this same song and dance for almost five years and I thought one or both of them would have been over it by now or they'd just decide to get married.

"Fuck it, I'm saying it."

Me: Do you want to come over and help me break in my bed?

I see the three dots indicating that he's typing before they disappear and they show up again and then disappear and I giggle at the memory of that first night we slept together. I look next to me, remembering Rory dancing then too, and this really is déjà vu.

TG: Where are you?

Me: Bar downtown...want to come?

TG: Did you Uber?

Me: Of course, we are a little tipsy.

TG: Both of you?

Me: I don't know let me ask Rory.

I take a picture of her and she snaps her head towards the flash. "Hey!" she squeals as I hit send.

Me: I think so.

"You should send him a picture of *you*!" Rory says. "Or a video!" she snaps. "A video of you dancing! You look hot."

I'm grateful she convinced me to wear a dress tonight because it might be just sexy enough to entice him to come out. I'm glad the song playing is on the sexier side as I shake my ass for the camera for a few minutes and then I blow a kiss towards it.

"Oh yeah, you look hot. Send it!" She hands the phone back to me and I bite my lower lip because she's right, I did. I send it and within seconds I get a reply

TG: Jesus Christ, Avery

Me: I think you should come downtown.

TG: I don't think I should.

Me: Why?

TG: You know why. Plus, you're drunk.

Me: So? I don't think that matters if I'm in love with you

TG: Avery...

Okay not sweet. Sexy! Divert the conversation!

Me: Don't you want to fuck me again?

TG: Obviously. We both know that.

Me: Then come. Besides, don't you want to make sure I get home safely?

TG: I know what you're doing.

Me: Okay, but do you know that I'm wet?

TG: Fuck me.

Me: Yes please. I've missed your dick so much. My vibrator really isn't the same. I actually took a video of me using it...do you want to see?

He doesn't respond right away and a part of me thinks I may have gone too far when my phone buzzes in my hand.

TG: Yes.

I go into my secret folder and pull up one of the videos that I actually took while we were together and just never sent it to him. I've been saving it for a night when I really needed it, and I'm glad I have it because I am fucking desperate to break him. The video is only about a minute long and surely enough sixty seconds later, my phone begins to ring in my hands.

"Hi." I giggle.

"Which bar are you at?"

Chapter
TWENTY-FOUR

THEO

THE BAR IS SO LOUD AND IT'S BEEN A WHILE SINCE I'VE been in a place like this. It's also huge and I have no idea where they are. I've watched that video she sent me at least ten times on my way over here and each time I get angrier for torturing myself by watching it. I should just delete it.

Don't you fucking dare.

The way she gasps my name the second she goes over the edge and shoots the sexiest wink to the camera, almost has me coming in my pants every time. There are two large bars both positioned in the center of the room and I walk around one and then the other before I see her in that sexy gold dress. I get closer and *fuck she looks gorgeous,* like she's been out in the sun since the week I've seen her making her even more bronzed than usual. Her lips are painted red and quirked up in a smile towards some fucking asshole standing next to her.

Fuck that.

He leans down to whisper something in her ear, his hand resting at the small of her back, and I instantly feel the aggression rushing back from when I played football. I want to hit something. *Hard.*

As soon as I'm within arm's reach, I grab her by the wrist and pull her hard against me, tilting her chin up to meet mine. I seal my lips over hers and kiss her with the two weeks' worth of passion it's been since I've kissed her. My tongue flicks against hers tasting tequila and lime and she reaches up to grab hold of my leather jacket as she rubs against me.

Fuck, I want her.

I pull away and I see the stars in her eyes as her eyes flutter dreamily.

"Is there a problem here?" I ask while staring down at Avery.

"You know this guy?" The asshole who is not getting the fucking picture spits out and I turn my head towards him.

"I'm her man. So again, I ask, do we have a problem?"

He nods at her. "She said she was single."

I look down at her, and she's still looking up at me drunkenly like I hung the fucking moon. I rub my nose against hers. "You told him you were single when you know you're mine?"

"Am I?" She sasses.

I glare at her. "Don't test me, Avery."

She narrows her eyes at me before turning back to the guy standing in front of us. "He's my Daddy." She giggles before she gives him an innocent smile and then turns back to me, looking pretty pleased with herself. I narrow my eyes and shake my head at her trying to ignore the spark in my dick that word causes.

"I'm taking you home. Where's Rory?" I ask her as the guy finally leaves. I look over my shoulder. "You really tell that guy you were single?" *While yes, I suppose she is single, I hate that she is going around broadcasting it.*

"Well, aren't I?" She cocks her head to the side and I push against her, forcing her back against the bar and rubbing my dick against her.

"Is that why you sent me a video of you fucking your tight little pussy? Because you're *single*?" I ask as I drag my finger over the tops of her breasts and between her cleavage.

She shivers and flashes me a mischievous grin. "No, I did that because I'm horny." She pushes against me. "And because I missed you." She wraps her arms around my neck. "I didn't say I was single." She blinks up at me. "I barely had a chance to say anything before you showed up but I did very much enjoy this display of jealousy, you caveman."

"Is your tab still open?" I ask ignoring the fact that she called me out because frankly I don't care, I was fucking jealous of any man that's breathed the same air as her the last two weeks.

"Yes, wait! Do you want a drink?"

"No, and we're leaving. Where is Rory?" I ask her again.

"Right here!" I turn and she's standing behind me with two shots in her hand. "For you!"

"You don't need anymore," I say looking at Avery as she takes the tiny glass of clear liquid from Rory.

"You'll be happy I took this when I'm sucking your dick on the ride home." She downs the shot and sets it on the counter. "Woo!"

I'm equal parts annoyed and turned on with how she's acting but I know I'll be way less irritated when I have her in the car.

"Rory, where do you want me to take you?"

"Justin is out of town. He did say I could still go over; I have a key, but can I just stay at your place since my car is there?" She asks Avery. "Can't you go to his house?" She points at me like I'm not the only coherent person between the three of us.

"That's fine with me!" She looks at me. "Can I sleep over?" I don't say anything and she looks up at me with those gorgeous eyes that can make me do whatever she wants. "Don't you want to kiss me again?" She shrugs. "Maybe somewhere else?" She drags her finger up my chest. "When we drop Rory off, I could grab my vibrator and I'll give you a live show."

Visions of her using that hot pink toy come flooding back and I'm hard as a rock. "Let's go, both of you."

⁓⤫⁓

After a very long forty-five minutes—*trying to wrangle two intoxicated girls alone is no easy feat*—I'm back at my house with Avery. As soon as we're in my room, she's already pulling off her clothes.

"Avery," I tell her just as she pulls her dress over her head.

"Do you want to shower with me?"

"I think…maybe we shouldn't…"

"Oh," she scoffs, "we *definitely* should."

"I just don't want things to get more complicated between us. I mean things are still unsettled with Lucas and—" I shake my head. "This puts us right back where we were two weeks ago. Sneaking around."

She stomps her foot. "You came to get me!"

"Because you are drunk."

"And? This is not new! I know how to get myself home when I've been drinking, Theo. You wanted to fuck me and now you're having second thoughts while I'm naked in your bedroom? You sure picked a fine time to stop thinking with your dick!" She unsnaps her bra and as her perfect tits spring free, I instantly crave the taste of them.

"Avery." I groan. "You're fucking killing me."

"I'm going to shower." She looks me up and down as she slides her panties down her legs. "If you don't want to join me, you can watch." She walks away without another glance in my direction.

I am very familiar with every inch of Avery Summers' body and something is different since the last time I saw her. I follow her and I make it to the bathroom just as she opens my glass shower door. "Turn around," I tell her and when she does, my eyes immediately drop to the space between her legs. "You..." I take a step towards her, my eyes staring at her smooth, bare cunt. "You're bare. You waxed?"

"Mmmhm, I told you, I like to switch it up."

"And I told *you* I liked the landing strip."

"Well," she sasses, "you aren't fucking me anymore. So, *you* don't get a vote." She taps my nose and turns around to turn on the water and I'm already pulling off my clothes to follow her into my walk-in shower. When she turns back around and sees me unbuckling my pants she backs up and lets her head fall back under the water allowing it to glide sexily down her body.

"I want a fucking vote," I tell her as I close the door behind me.

"You do, huh?" She grabs my dick, wrapping her hand around it and stroking it up and down. "Why?"

I push her hand away and get on my knees in front of her. "Because you're mine." I run my fingers through her slit, relishing in the smoothness of her for the first time. "Fuck this is sexy though." I lift her left leg to open her up and let it rest on my shoulder as I press my lips to her pussy.

"Yes, oh fuck." I hear her moan as I rub my tongue over her clit. She pushes her fingers through my hair and rocks her hips against my face and fuck I've missed this. I miss her being so desperate and needy to come that she literally fucks my face. "Oh God."

"Tell me who you belong to."

"You! Oh God, I'm going to come. Fuck." She cries out. "Oh my God, yes yes right there! Theo!" I grip her hips to keep her steady while she goes over the edge. "Oh my God, I love you so much." She moans and those words combined with the taste of her orgasm on my tongue have me ready to explode. I stand up in front of her and she grabs my jaw. "Tell me who you belong to."

"You know I'm yours. I've done nothing but think about you for two weeks." I press her wet hair out of her face and drop a kiss on her lush mouth. "I love you too." I whisper against her lips.

Tears form in her eyes and she reaches for my dick. "I need you inside me."

"I need to make love to you in my bed, not here. I just thought we both needed something to take the edge off." I wink at her.

I squirt some of her body wash into her loofah that I hadn't gotten rid of. In fact, I'd sometimes just sit in here and hold it under my nose just to get a whiff of her. I begin washing her all over and when we're both clean I help her out of the shower. I help her dry off and when she's done torturing me by rubbing that sinfully good-smelling lotion into her skin that also fucking makes my dick hard, I carry her to the bed and I'm on her instantly.

"Get your vibrator," I tell her and she grabs it from her bag and hands it to me before lying down on the bed.

I hold the phallic-shaped toy in my hand and turn it on, rubbing it over her perky nipples before dragging it down her body. "I want to fuck you here," I tell her as I reach under her to grab her ass.

"Okay." She wraps her hand around me and strokes me gently. "I want a taste first. I haven't sucked your dick in two weeks." She pushes me to my back and kneels between my legs.

"I don't want to come in your mouth so don't get cute." I point at her and she gives me a look of shock and feigns innocence.

"Hmmm." She straddles me, sitting directly on my cock as she leans down to kiss me. "I don't know what you're talking about." She moves, gliding her wet cunt over my shaft as she takes her place between my legs.

"Fuuuuck." I groan, trying my best to talk myself back from the edge. She circles the tip with her tongue before she slides slowly down my dick that's already leaking precum. "Baby." I let out a breath. "Okay, that's enough."

She pulls off of me, thankfully heeding my warning. "Really? I didn't even get comfortable."

"Well, I watched your little porno about ten times on the drive to the bar, so *you* did this."

She giggles as she turns on her stomach and I hand her the vibrator while I grab the lube that I'd gotten out. "Fuck yourself with it, while I fuck your ass."

I squirt a considerable amount of lube into my hand and then on my dick and then her ass as I prepare to push my way in. She's already pushed the vibrator in her pussy and I can hear her muffled giggles into the pillow as she fucks herself with it. "You ready?"

"Mmmhm. Fuck, I think I'm going to come already. This toy is a little dangerous." She sighs as I push a finger and then a second into her ass to do my best to prepare her. She lets out the sexiest little moan that makes my dick jerk in anticipation of being inside of her.

"You ready?" I ask her and she nods her head.

"Fuck yes, fuck me please." She cries just before I push into her ass.

Fuck I forgot how good this feels. We'd done this a handful of times and every time I swear, I forget how tight her little asshole is. "Jesus Christ, I've missed this. Missed you so fucking much." I continue fucking her slowly even as she pushes back onto me and I can feel the faint buzzing of her vibrator tingling through me. "Careful," I tell her, not wanting to hurt her and knowing it takes a minute for us to get going.

"Theo, I'm so close," she moans and the thought of her coming while I'm in her ass is pushing me closer to my orgasm as well.

I pull out of her slowly and slap her ass cheek. "Turn on your back, I want to see your pretty face when you come."

She turns on her back and I push her legs back towards her ears. I lean down and press a kiss to her lips. "I fucking love seeing you like this spread out beneath me. You're fucking incredible, Avery."

"You're incredible," she mumbles because I think she's on the brink of her orgasm.

I slip back into her, slowly fucking her as I press the vibrator to her clit. Her eyes flutter shut as I rub it in circles against her. I guide her hand to hold it, so I can hold her legs back for her. "When you come while I'm in your ass, you squeeze me so fucking hard." I can already feel my orgasm brewing just as she begins to shake beneath me.

"Oh my Godddd, please, Theo," she begs. "Please, baby make me…come, oh fuck!" I know the exact moment she goes over the edge because she clamps down on me, squeezing me so hard that I shoot my entire load into her ass.

"Fuck, Avery." I bottom out inside her completely as I press my lips to hers and fuck her through my climax.

She kisses me back with equal urgency as I soften and slowly pull out of her. I roll to my back and bring her on top of me, pressing my lips to hers. "I love you," I tell her. "I don't know where we go from here, but I don't know how I can be without you anymore."

Chapter
TWENTY-FIVE

Avery

A FEW DAYS LATER, I'M AT THE CAFÉ AT THE CRACK OF dawn to help my mom when Lucas walks in and my mouth drops open. He casually waves and I immediately run around the counter. I'm hoping that his being here means he's forgiven me or at the very least wants to talk, and that's something.

"Lucas." I stop myself before I hug him in case he isn't ready for that yet.

"Hey, Ave."

"You look good." I nod at him because he does. I haven't seen him in almost three weeks and he looks like he's lost a bit of weight but somehow also gained some muscle. He's typically clean-shaven but he's got more of a beard coming in and it's startling how much more he looks like Theo now.

"Been at the gym and running." I nod. "I heard you moved."

"I did. You should come by and see it." I hate how awkward things are between us when they've never been this way. *Is this the new normal between us?* "You want some coffee or breakfast?"

"Sure." He smiles. "Whatever. You know I like everything." I move around the counter and make his coffee with hazelnut creamer which he pretends he doesn't like but I know he secretly loves and put a bunch of different pastries on a plate for him to choose from. I sit down at a table in a corner and place everything in front of him.

He lets out a breath. "So, you and my dad, huh? How did that happen?"

"I've had a crush on him for a while, Luke. Since we were in high school... even before that. You remember, all the girls did," I explain.

"Yeah, but *you* always said you didn't. You said it would be weird because of how close we are."

"I know. I lied," I say weakly, "so things wouldn't be awkward between you and I." I sigh, as I prepare to tell him the truth. "I probably had it worse than all of those girls who just thought he was hot. I knew him better than most people so I developed feelings beyond how he looked."

I give him a weak smile and put my hand on top of his. "I hope you know, that is not how you were supposed to find out and I am so sorry for that. I was being emotional and your dad was trying to make it better and...I wish I did everything differently."

"Everything?" he asks with a laugh but I hear the underlying question. He picks up the chocolate chip muffin, which is what I knew he'd go for first, and pulls off a piece before putting it in his mouth. "God, I forgot how good these were." He takes a sip of his coffee and gives me a smile over it, knowing how I made it. "Do you love him?"

I contort my mouth into a sad smile. "Yeah."

"My Dad is probably my best friend in the world, even more so than you. Being angry at him the last two weeks..." He puts a hand over his eyes. "I felt like shit for the things I said to him. I've wanted my dad to meet someone and be happy for years. You remember, I used to try and get him on dating apps." He laughs and I do remember his failed attempts to get Theo on *Tinder* more than once. "But, it's so weird that it's you."

"I know."

"But you two are in love with each other and...how can I stand in the way of two of my favorite people being happy."

"Lucas..." I trail off, hearing where he's going with this train of thought.

"This is what you want, right? To be with him?"

I nod. "Yeah, Lucas I do. But I want us to be okay too." I bite my bottom lip to try and stop the tears from coming. "Is it selfish of me to want both?"

He shakes his head. "It doesn't make you selfish but it might always be weird for me on some level? Weird between us? I mean like, it's my *dad* and *you*." He leans back in his chair and puts his hands over his face. "I feel like I lost both of my best friends to each other." He laughs and I hadn't thought of it like that. I hadn't thought that maybe it wasn't all about his feelings for me but how much this changed the dynamic between the three of us and the eight years of history we had. How keeping a secret from him when he trusted us both altered our relationships. "But I want you to be happy, Avery."

Tears well in my eyes. "I want you to be happy too."

"I will be." He puts his hand over mine. "Gonna be kind of weird seeing you like a stepmom though." He cocks his head to the side.

"How about I'm just your best friend and also your Dad's girlfriend and we don't have to go further into detail on what that means."

He moves his head back and forth like he's thinking it over. "Maybe eventually."

"I'm really sorry that I hurt you," I whisper. "I'm sorry that I couldn't... be what you wanted."

"You don't need to apologize for that." He shrugs. "And I swear... I haven't had those feelings in years."

"Have you talked to your dad?" I ask.

"No, I'm going to go there next. I just took the train down this morning." He stands up and pulls me into a hug and presses a kiss to my forehead like he's done a million times before. He pulls back and makes his way to the door, with the muffin in one hand and the coffee in the other. "I'm going to be in town for the weekend. I think Rory is going to come down tomorrow, maybe we can all get a drink? Like old times?" He shrugs. "You can bring your new boyfriend." He smiles and I laugh even as emotion builds in my throat that maybe everything is going to be okay.

"You're the best, you know that?"

"Yeah, I know…it's kind of the worst," he jokes before he's out the door.

＊

That night, the three of us and Raegan and Wes are at Theo's house for dinner when Lucas speaks up. "So, how'd Camille and Shawn take it?" Lucas says as he takes a bite of the steak Theo had prepared.

Theo and I exchange a glance. "Well…"

Lucas' eyes widen. "Holy shit, they don't know?"

"My mom does!" I say and Lucas' mouth drops open.

"Oh, shiiiiit. Please. You both owe me. Just let me be there when you tell Shawn." He puts his hands together like he's praying.

Raegan giggles and shoots me a look. "You do kind of owe him."

"You're absolutely not helping," Theo interjects as he glares at her.

"I've helped a lot, thank you very much," she says with a snap of her fingers. "Besides, this is not why we're here. We're here to talk about wedding things." She points back and forth between her and Wes. "This is the whole reason you're home," she says to Lucas as she smacks his arm. "Tuxedos. Tomorrow. All three of you. Ten a.m."

"Yes, I know," Theo says like he's heard this a hundred times, and based on how Raegan has been in wedding planning mode, I don't doubt it.

"Do Avery and I need to come?" She says and Wes presses a kiss to her temple.

"Baby, we got it," he tells her and she puckers her lips for him to kiss her lips which he does instantly.

"But no seriously, when are you going to tell Avery's dad? And can I be there? For moral support of course," Lucas asks again.

Raegan laughs. "Yeah right, you just want to stir the pot."

"I mean, I think Shawn will love it. He doesn't have to worry about not having anything in common with his daughter's boyfriend. I mean you golf with him twice a month!" He claps. "I think it's great! You think he'll call you son?"

Raegan and Wes chuckle quietly and I roll my eyes at all three of them. "I am glad you're all so amused!"

Theo pours me a glass of wine and sits next to me. "Everything is going to be fine. Telling you was always going to be the hardest. Shawn will be," he swallows, "interesting."

"Oh God." Raegan chuckles. "Who's going to tell Mom?"

Theo and I are at my apartment because Lucas is definitely not ready to be in the house while his father and I share a bed. But we don't hate it because this allows us more privacy *and* also for us to be very loud. "I still think you should get out of your lease and move in with me." He pulls me to rest my head on his chest. "Lucas will get over us sharing a bed at some point."

"Okay, but I literally just moved in."

"All the more reason to get out of your lease now."

"It would be so expensive," I argue.

He tilts my chin up to look at him and raises an eyebrow. "We can afford it."

That we *makes me fucking melt.*

"Just let me keep it for six months. We just started dating. Let's crawl before we walk," I offer.

"Fine." He kisses me. "I'm not agreeing to sleeping away from you though."

"Works for me. You cook me breakfast in the mornings I don't go to the café," I tell him as I press my lips to his bare chest. He doesn't say anything for a minute and when I look up at him he's staring at the ceiling. "What are you thinking about?" He meets my gaze and gives me a heart stopping smile. "Tell me something good."

He picks my left hand up and runs his thumb over my ring finger. "You said we should crawl before we walk but...I've been walking for a while now." I gasp, hearing the implication and sit up. "I think this finger would look better with a ring on it. *My* ring." He drags his lips over the skin and gives me a smile. "What do you think?"

My heart thumps wildly in my chest thinking about marrying this man. I lean over and press my lips to his. "You want to marry me?"

His lips turn upwards and he gives me a sexy grin. "Yes."

I move so that I'm lying on top of him. "Well, then you should really think about telling my dad soon."

Epilogue

THEO

Ten Months Later

"**M**RS. GRAHAM," I WRAP MY ARMS AROUND MY wife—as of twenty minutes ago—and press a kiss to her neck.

She turns around and rubs her hands up my chest before she reaches up on her toes to kiss me. "Mr. Graham." She scrunches her nose. "You know? I think I'm just going to call you *husband* instead. Mr. Graham makes me feel like I'm thirteen again." She giggles.

"I don't care what you call me as long as you've got this ring on your finger." I rub the wedding band I'd just slid on her finger that joined the four-carat oval-cut engagement ring. We'd snuck off to the bridal suite for a moment before we have to join everyone at the reception and I am hoping that I can entice her to let me see what's under her dress again. "You look so beautiful," I tell her as I help her take her veil off. "I am the luckiest man in the world." I cup her face and press my lips to hers.

"Theo…we really can't." She giggles. "It's bad enough we started the ceremony twenty minutes late because *someone* needed to fuck me with their mouth one more time before we got married."

I run my gaze down her body, wanting my mouth between her legs again. "I did *not* hear you complaining."

"They probably thought one of us had cold feet!"

I snort as I pour us both a glass of champagne and hand her one. "No, they all knew what we were doing."

"I don't know which is worse." She groans as she taps her glass with mine.

"What will be worse is when I want to leave this party after twenty minutes to get our honeymoon started."

"Okay, seriously, the fact that you've been able to keep a whole trip a secret is wild. Can I know where we're going yet?"

"You'll know when you get there." I smile, thinking about how excited she'll be when she finds out we'll be honeymooning in the south of France. "Rory and Rae packed for you; you'll be fine. Not that you really need any clothes."

She raises an eyebrow at me and presses her body against mine. "Really? That sounds promising."

I go to press my lips to hers when there's a knock on the door. "Okay, come out or I'm coming in," I hear Lucas' voice. "Dad, can you keep your hands off of her for five minutes? Jesus."

"You can come in." Avery laughs as Lucas comes in holding a glass of wine, and I already know we're in for a long night especially since Raegan had her very adorable daughter two months ago and this is her first real outing since.

"We're waiting on *you* guys, you know. The party can't really start without you."

"Five minutes," Avery says and I'm surprised she's not suggesting we follow him now. He closes the door behind him and she turns around to look at me. "I love you and I'm so ready to start my life with you."

"Me too, baby. I'm going to make you so happy."

"You already do," she says, shooting me her gorgeous smile.

"Shall we?" I guide her towards the door and open it for her.

"Yeah, I guess before they send another search party." She giggles and when we make it into the hallway, we see Rory and Lucas... *kissing?* They stop, not having realized that we are in the hallway before they make their way outside towards the tent, where we're having the reception.

"No freaking way!" Avery looks at me with wide eyes. "Did you know?"

"Absolutely not. If I did, you'd know."

"Wowwww," she says as we start walking towards the tent. "Those jerks are keeping a secret from me?" I shoot her a look thinking about a very big secret she kept from them both once upon a time about her relationship. "That is..." she starts. "Okay, fair."

I hear someone in the distance preparing to announce our entrance and I lace our fingers together. "Let's just enjoy tonight. We'll have the rest of our lives to bug Lucas about his love life."

The End

Want to know what to read next?
Check out *What Was Meant to Be*:
a steamy dad's best friend romance!

Acknowledgments

This book was born out of the many times I've been asked to write an ex boyfriend's dad book. *(I may still do that someday.)* But, the idea of a messy best friend's dad romance had been on my mind for over a year and it was finally time to share it! I hope you loved Avery and Theo's story—you'll see them again!

Anna, Alexandra and Logan: Thank you for Beta reading and all of your early feedback and ideas! Some of my favorite parts of this book were inspired by your dirty thoughts. Thank you for loving hot dads as much as I do!

Tanya and Rachel, thank you for always being in my corner. Thank you for stepping up and helping me with so many things. For your advice and your support. I love you guys so much.

Kristen Portillo, thank you for helping make this book perfect! One day I'll get my tenses and my timelines right the first time around. Until then, I'm grateful I have you to catch them. I appreciate you immensely!

Stacey Blake, thank you for always making the interiors so gorgeous and exactly what I want! Thank you for making my books so pretty!

Shaye and Lindsey: Thank you for all the things and keeping me so organized. What would I do without you? You guys are rockstars and I love you!

Ari Basulto, I would be lost without you. Thank you for all that you do to keep me organized! Thank you for running all of my teams and overall Q.B.'s life better than I could. A million thank yous.

Emily Wittig, These are easily my favorite covers you've done! I'm obsessed. They are so perfect and I love them. Thank you for always understanding my vision.

Pang Thao, thank you for all of my gorgeous teasers and all of my last minute promo things and all the things I ask you to make me all the time. You're so good to me and I appreciate everything you do!

Becca Mysoor, Thank you for all of your help with this book and always being available when I'm on the ledge. You're the best.

To the babes on my street team and ARC team, thank you for your excitement! Thank you for your love for me and my books and that you're always willing to let me take you over a cliff. The reason I can do what I do is because of you guys in my corner. Thank you for always clapping the loudest. I love you guys so big.

To all of the bloggers and bookstagrammers and TikTokers, thank you for your edits and your reels and your videos and always sharing my books! For still talking about books I wrote two and three years ago and loving them so much. For sharing with your friends (and sometimes your family? Ha) Thank you for everything you do. (Because seriously? Videos are so hard.)

And finally, and most importantly to YOU, to the readers, thank you for letting me into your minds and your hearts again with another book. I hope you enjoyed it! I love you all. Let's do this again soon—like... really soon.

Also by
Q.B. TYLER

STANDALONES

My Best Friend's Sister
Unconditional
Forget Me Not
Love Unexpected
Always Been You
What Was Meant to Be
Keep Her Safe

BITTERSWEET UNIVERSE

Bittersweet Surrender
Bittersweet Addiction
Bittersweet Love

CAMPUS TALES SERIES

First Semester
Second Semester
Spring Semester

Available through the Read Me Romance Audio Podcast

Fantasy with a Felon

About
THE AUTHOR

Bestselling author and lover of forbidden romances, tacos, coffee, and wine. Q.B. Tyler gives readers sometimes angsty, sometimes emotional but always deliciously steamy romances featuring sassy heroines and the heroes that worship them. She's known for writing forbidden (and sometimes taboo) romances, so if that's your thing, you've come to the right place. When she's not writing, you can usually find her on Instagram (definitely procrastinating), shopping or at brunch.

Sign up for her newsletter to stay in touch!
https://view.flodesk.com/pages/6195b59a839edddd7aa02f8f

Qbtyler03@gmail.com

Facebook: Q.B. Tyler
Reader Group: Q.B.'s Hive
Instagram @qbtyler.author
Bookbub: Q.B. Tyler
Twitter: @qbtyler
Goodreads: Q.B. Tyler
Tik Tok: author.qbtyler

Printed in Great Britain
by Amazon